GW01336577

NIGHT IS FOR HUNTING

By the same author
THE QUEEN BEE

Night Is for Hunting

Phyllida Barstow

To Rupert and June with much love from the author
1 · XI · 1982

CENTURY PUBLISHING CO.
LONDON

Copyright © Phyllida Barstow 1982

All rights reserved

First published in Great Britain by Century Publishing Co. Ltd.,
76 Old Compton Street, London W1

British Library Cataloguing in Publication Data

Barstow, Phyllida
　Night is for hunting.
　I. Title
　823'.914[F]　　PR6052.A/

ISBN 0 7126 0002 7

Photoset by Rowland Phototypesetting Ltd
Bury St Edmunds, Suffolk
Printed in Great Britain by Redwood Burn Ltd
Trowbridge, Wiltshire

PROLOGUE

1954

BEYOND THE CIRCLE of light cast by leaping flames, the jungle shadow lay like a black velvet curtain, muffling and impenetrable, unnaturally silent, as if all the normal small squeaks and rustles of the equatorial night had been shocked into stillness.

Nolan Matthews eased sideways another foot to gain a clear field of fire and settled himself solidly in a triangle, legs spread and elbows firm, before thumbing forward the safety-catch with a barely audible snick. He waited until his ragged breathing was even, then took aim at the grotesque figure draped in monkey-skins over a tattered khaki greatcoat, hair a halo of frizzed pigtails, features daubed with mud, standing beneath an arch of thorn saplings on which was impaled a round dark object. For a moment Matthews held the sight's pillar steady on the oath-giver's heart, then lowered it as a warning hand gripped his ankle.

'Steady, sir,' breathed Sergeant Timbers. 'Don't jump the gun. Wait till my boys are in position.'

Matthews grunted assent and in an instant Timbers was gone, wriggling back along the game-trail with no more noise than a snake.

Matthews waited, taking in the scene before him, feeling the anger mount and burn within him until all sensation of cold and fatigue, uncertainty and fear melted into a single white-hot bloodlust, a concentrated desire to kill that would sustain him through the uncomfortable hours until the time came to squeeze the trigger.

Between his hiding-place and the central arch of thorns

lay the mutilated hulks of a dozen cows, his own purebred Hereford heifers, legs hacked off at hock and knee, bellies gaping open, still feebly stirring and grunting as long knives wielded by stringy black arms flayed the skin from them. Matthews was a hard-headed farmer – no one struggling to breed pedigree cattle in Kenya could afford to be sentimental about animals – and he had seen too much of the African stockman's callousness towards his charges to be surprised by any brutality, but the wanton cruelty inflicted on these beasts made his stomach heave and had it not been for Sergeant Timbers' warning he would have opened fire there and then on their murderers.

With an effort he averted his eyes from the pathetically twitching carcases and forced himself to go over the day's events in his mind. Of course he had known it could happen: they'd all known ever since the Emergency was declared that sooner or later terror might strike even the remotest farm. Since early morning that day he had been conscious of trouble brewing. Small things went wrong from the very moment he shouted for Karanja to bring his shaving water and was answered by Juma with the news that the old houseboy was missing. There might have been a dozen reasons for Karanja's absence. Matthews was no more psychic than he was sentimental, but cold fear gripped his stomach as he listened to Juma's stumbling explanations. Juma was scared. His shaking hands and grey-tinged skin proclaimed it in every word he spoke; as the day wore on Matthews was to see the same fear reflected in his entire work-force.

An atmosphere of brooding menace lay over Redstone Farm. Machines broke and animals sickened for no reason. Half the staff seemed to be absent and those who appeared obeyed his orders sullenly. At first Matthews had tried to ignore the warning signs, keeping a cheerful face in front of Janet and the children, but when Joshua the fat herdsman reported that the fence in the Upper Pasture had been breached and a dozen of his best heifers were missing, he could no longer keep up the pretence of normality.

Copper-haired Janet, nine years his junior and as reckless as he was cautious, had wanted to stay. 'I'm not going to run away!' she exclaimed incredulously when he told her to pack. 'You can't make me. We're in this together, darling. I'm staying here until you come home.' She was a good shot and brave as a lioness; she refused to believe that their own 'boys' would ever lift a finger to harm them.

Matthews shook his head. 'Sorry, darling, but you've got to think of the children – and me. I shan't have a moment's peace if I leave you here on your own.' He hesitated a moment then added quietly, 'Karanja's disappeared.'

'Disappeared? Oh God! Why didn't you tell me?' He could see she was shaken. Karanja was their protector, a tribal elder whose influence was widely respected. Without his benign presence Redstone Farm was far more vulnerable to the creeping spread of terrorist subversion.

Matthews pressed his advantage. 'It'll only be for a couple of nights. I've asked Dick and Emily to put you up. The twins always like staying there. Pack them into the car as quick as you can and get going, darling. The police will be here any minute and I'll have to show them the way. I want you all off the place before I leave.'

The eight-year-old twins, George and Alison, were as reluctant as their mother to leave home. They had lost their curly-coated spaniel, Cindy, and refused to budge until she was found. Losing patience, Matthews bundled them bodily into the big Ford van, ignoring their wails of protest.

'I'll tell Juma to feed Cindy and look after her,' he promised. 'She's bound to turn up the minute you've gone – you know what she's like. Anyway, she hates the car. Be good and give my love to Uncle Dick.'

He leaned in through the window to kiss Janet on the lips. ''Bye, sweetheart. Take care of your darling self,' he whispered; and her amber eyes crinkled in the teasing smile he loved.

'Of course I will. Don't be such an old *worrier*!' She let in the clutch. With relief he watched the red dust-cloud follow them down the hill and over the cattle-grid. Five minutes later a truckload of police under the command of Sergeant Timbers roared up to the farm.

For eight hours they had followed the cows' trail up the mountain, crossing the mist-shrouded ridges and vine-tangled valleys of the Aberdare range until they had climbed to the dense bamboo thicket surrounding the high plateau; going ever more warily, the police trackers ranging ahead, until this final nerve-tingling crawl in the dark brought them within sight of their quarry.

Too late to save the heifers. Too late to save the head of old Karanja, which was roughly impaled on the arch of thorns in the middle of the clearing. Matthews swallowed the lump in his throat. Karanja was a proud man. He would have scorned the Mau Mau oath and met death with dignity; but it was clear that any resistance among the rest of the Redstone Farm workers had vanished when Karanja was murdered.

One by one Matthews watched his cowmen and pigboys, his syces, mechanics and fieldhands, pushed forward to stand with head bowed before the skin-clad oath-giver, grimacing as they swallowed the bitter brew of blood, earth and semen which would bind them irrevocably to the cause of destroying the white man.

'If I am ordered to bring in the head of a white man, I will do so or this oath will kill me. If I see anyone stealing from a white man, I will say nothing or this oath will kill me . . .'

Although he could not hear the words, Matthew knew all too well what his boys were saying; knew, too, from their rolling, white-rimmed eyes and jerky movements how seriously they took the oath.

Filthy mumbo-jumbo, he thought with angry disgust. They needn't think they can scare me away with their revolting rites. Every week white families were giving up their farms and returning home, but he and Janet were determined to stick it out. I'm not giving up a hunk of the best land God ever created just because a mob of Kikuyu scum want to lay their filthy hands on what isn't theirs and never was. This land was *empty* before the white settlers took it in hand. The Kikuyu skulked in the forests and never came out in the open for fear of Masai spearmen. How can they lay claim to it now? But he knew the time was long past for such rhetorical questions to carry any weight. Reason was no protection against the Mau Mau terrorists.

Force is the only argument they understand, and by God! they'll get it, he thought, if I have any say in the matter. If it wasn't for Janet and the kids I'd join the *Shenzis* and teach those black bastards a lesson they wouldn't forget. My cattle . . .

At least their agony was over now, the carcases skinned and dismembered. Already the women were packing up as much meat as they could carry and staggering away out of the light of the dying fire to their mountain lairs where they would dry and store their booty. The men were eating; the skin-clad oath-giver, flanked by his lieutenants, tore at a half-cooked joint with the ravenous ferocity of a starved hyena.

Matthews felt a touch on his ankle and turned as Timbers slithered alongside. The sergeant jerked his head, indicating the oath-giver. 'It's Tembo himself – General Tembo. One of my boys recognised him. We've orders to take him alive.'

Tembo, the Elephant, one of Dedan Kimathi's most trusted lieutenants. Matthews had no wish to preserve him alive. He was cold and stiff and the prospect of lying watching the gangsters gorge themselves on his cattle had no appeal.

'How can you tell? It could be anyone.'

Timbers shook his head. 'It's Tembo all right. My boy knows his style – with or without a mask. He ought to: he belonged to the same gang himself a month ago. We'll wait till they're asleep and then clobber the sentries. That way we should get him alive.'

There was now enough noise and movement in the clearing for Matthews to speak normally. He said, 'Murdering swine. Wasn't that the gang which did for the old chief in Nanyuki last week? Calls himself Tembo because he's protected by the elephants or some such crap?'

'That's him. Odd for a Kikuyu,' said the sergeant reflectively. 'They don't often identify with animals.' He paused, then added, 'There's elephants not far off now – can you hear them? Let's hope they keep their distance from the fire. The bombing of the forest has played merry hell with their nerves. They're all on edge and the least thing's enough to panic them nowadays.'

Matthews raised his head and listened but could hear nothing to suggest the presence of elephant. Nevertheless he scanned the clearing with new interest, noting the trampled mud and deep holes gouged in the side of a bank. He rubbed a finger in the earth and licked it cautiously. He said, 'It looks like a saltpan over there, beyond the stream. So General Tembo chooses a hideout where his pals the elephants will warn him of any disturbance. I don't like it. The longer we wait the less healthy this clearing's going to be. Why don't we grab Tembo while the going's good and get the hell out?'

His fingers itched on the trigger. He was sick of waiting in suspense. He had a sudden urge to finish the whole business, even if it meant losing half the gang. To hell with Timbers and his orders. A bullet in the head would put paid to General Tembo and good riddance. Again he raised his rifle.

'Wait!' said Timbers sharply.

Behind them a branch snapped and the earth trembled. Both men froze into utter stillness. On the light wind the smell of elephant was borne to them, suffocatingly strong; musty, ammoniac, unmistakable. Very slowly Matthews turned his head. His eyes were well accustomed to the darkness and with a sudden jolt to the heart he recognised the looming, towering black shapes approaching swiftly to their right, trunks and ears outlined against the lighter grey of the trees like the peaks and crests of a gigantic tidal wave. They were making for the stream. The great bodies, hunched close together, moved with nervous haste, heads swinging, tails stuck out at an acute angle to the rump. He heard the leathery flap of ears and a click of ivory as two tuskers jostled for position. It was one of the largest herds he had ever seen in the forest, and they looked wary, agitated, and extremely dangerous.

He heard a stifled exclamation from Timbers. More elephants were coming up on their left, swaying and pushing, an army of immense black shadows. They were surrounded, their weapons useless against such a wall of flesh. Matthews had never been so scared in his life. There was nowhere to run, nothing to shelter against. He could only pray that the elephants would not catch their wind and panic. He pressed himself against the roots of the nearest tree, knowing as he did so that it would be no protection at all if the great monsters were to stampede. One blow from tusk or trunk and his slender refuge would be smashed to matchwood.

Hardly daring to breathe, he waited. The solid bulk of the herd was past him now; patches of light and shade showed as the stragglers hurried towards the stream. As if released from tension by the feel of water in their trunks, the younger elephants began to splash and squeal like bathing children, milling about knee-deep in the water, while their elders scraped industriously at the saltpan, plunging their trunks deep into the holes and sucking up the minerals they craved. Bellies rumbled cavernously, tusks clashed, trunks slapped as if the need for silence was mysteriously over.

Timbers jerked a thumb over his shoulder. 'Let's get out of here.'

They began to crawl back down the game-trail with what seemed agonising slowness, suppressing the instinct to jump up and run as fast as their legs could carry them. Vines tangled round their thighs and thorns plucked their hair. If they could reach the shelter of the rocky outcrop where Timbers had briefed his men, they could lie up in safety until the elephants retreated. Keeping their heads down to protect their eyes from thorns, they made the best speed they could down the winding tunnel of vines. They were no more than twenty yards from their objective when a human scream cut like a knife through the confused splashing and grunting of the elephants.

A man's scream, shrill with pain. It was followed an instant later by the crack of a rifle and for a tense moment, as the echoes died away, there was utter silence. Then a furious blast of trumpeting ripped the night apart.

'Get under the rocks!' yelled Timbers above the din. 'They're coming!'

He leapt up and began to slash with his panga like a madman at the wall of vines lining the trail, trying desperately to cut through to the overhanging cliff. Matthews heard his sobbing breath as he fought the tangling mesh like a fly struggling to break through a spider's web; but he did not follow. A sense of resignation, of utter futility, kept him pinned where he was, pressed against the hard-packed earth. It was too late. There could be no escape from the pounding, pulverising feet that were crashing towards them, as unstoppable as tanks, flattening the thick underbrush as effectively as steamrollers. How could Timbers hope to run away from them?

The ground was shaking, sending shockwaves through his whole body, and the noise was deafening. He clung to the ground as the great black wave crashed over him. From the corner of his eye he saw the dark shape of Timbers tossed skywards like a broken doll, his glinting panga cartwheeling against the stars. Flashes of light alternated with inky black as the monstrous bellies stampeded over him. Something caught him a blow on the side of the head and he knew no more.

'Bwana?' said a voice through the foggy mists. Matthews opened his eyes and flinched at the dazzle of sunlight on wet leaves. I'm dead, he thought. I *know* I must be dead. How come I'm still alive?

Turning his head painfully he recognised the anxious black face of James Koinange, one of Timbers' young constables.

'Water, bwana?'

He took the flask and gulped thirstily, then sat up, amazed to find his limbs in working order. The elephants had gone right over him, but apart from an aching head he was undamaged. He could not understand it.

'Sergeant Timbers?' he croaked, although he knew what the answer must be.

Koinange shook his head. 'Dead, bwana.'

'And General Tembo?'

'Gone.'

Of course he had gone. Matthews felt a surge of anger. If only those fools at HQ hadn't insisted on taking him alive, we could have wiped out the blighter and his whole stinking mob before the elephants came near us, he thought bitterly. Now it's too late. A good man killed and we'll never get a chance like that again.

A sense of urgency gripped him. He must get back to the farm. He had been away too long. God alone knew what might be happening there with half his work-force up in the hills vowing death and destruction to the white man and only the lily-livered Juma in charge of the place. He hadn't reckoned on the operation taking more than a few hours. Thank heaven he had sent Janet and the children off to Nairobi, out of harm's way. They would be worried sick, wondering why he hadn't telephoned.

The police and trackers were standing around, eyeing him uncertainly. They seemed all at sea without Timbers and weak as he was, Matthews knew he must take command.

'Help me up,' he said brusquely, stretching out a hand to Koinange. 'We've no time to lose.' He ordered the two fastest runners to go ahead and warn divisional headquarters, while others cut a stretcher on which to carry Sergeant Timbers' body to the nearest track accessible by Land Rover. After a brief consultation with the trackers, he set off downhill.

Matthews remembered little of the gruelling four-hour slog from the clearing to the track where a police Land Rover picked them up. Expanding gas trapped in the bamboo sections exploded like pistol shots as the temperature rose, and the trackers, forging ahead through the tangled brush, kept a wary eye out for snakes and ears alert for the snort of a resentful buffalo or rhino. Colobus monkeys leaped chattering aloft, their splendid pied tails streaming behind them; and duiker and shy gazelle bounded away from the human intruders, dappled coats perfectly blended with the shifting shadows.

Matthews scarcely saw them. His whole concentration was centred on the problem of keeping himself upright. A stabbing pain pierced his temples whenever he stumbled, and his eyes refused to focus properly. Tree-trunks swam to and fro with confusing double images, and rocks seemed to move away when he put out a hand to touch them. Worse than his physical discomfort, though, was the gnawing anxiety that nagged his mind. There was something he had forgotten to do before leaving the farm. Something he should have said before rushing off in pursuit of his heifers. For the life of him he couldn't remember what it was. The memory floated tantalisingly before him, but each time he tried to pin it down it drifted away. It was still bothering him when the Land Rover drew up before the police post.

Mervyn Junter, assistant superintendent of the Special Branch stationed there, was a stocky, freckled, sandy-haired young man with the nails of his square, capable hands bitten down to the quick. He listened in frowning silence to Matthews' account of the abortive raid, then shook his head.

'That's bad. A bad business. We'll hunt down that bastard Tembo sooner or later – probably sooner – but we can't afford to lose men like Paul in the process.' He blinked and stared at Matthews as if seeing him for the first time, taking in his torn, filthy clothing and glazed eyes.

'You look all in,' he said abruptly. 'I'll get the M.O. to check you over before taking you home. You've sent the family into town? Hang on just a mo while I get this lot clear . . .'

Matthews nodded. An immense lethargy descended on him and he sat passively, slumped against the verandah wall while Junter dictated some brief reports and ordered a driver to bring round a car. While he was still busy the telephone rang in his office. Junter went inside to answer it. Through the open door Matthews heard his voice.

'Speaking . . . Yes, sir. On the gate-post? Yes, that's his signature, all right. We'll get someone up there at once. You have? Oh. Oh, God! But he sent them away. He told me he saw them go. Just a minute, sir . . .'

The door slammed shut. Matthews shifted in his seat. Junter's voice was lower now, but still plainly audible. 'Yes, he's here now. I was just going to . . . What? But I can't understand *why* they came back. The dog? Oh, I see. Yes, of course. All right, sir. I'll keep him here till you come.'

He put down the receiver, then immediately cranked up the operator again and asked for the police doctor. Matthews stood up quietly, putting his hand on the verandah rail to stop himself swaying. He had just remembered what had been bothering him all the way down the mountain. Junter's mention of a dog had brought it back to him. Of course, he had promised the twins that Juma would feed that tiresome black spaniel they were so crazy about; in the rush of departure it had quite slipped his mind. He must go and tell him now. No need to wait for young Junter. He was busy, and there was the police car ready, the driver dozing at the wheel . . .

Matthews crossed the square of hard-packed red earth. Seeing him approach, the driver sprang out to open the door.

'Redstone Farm, *pese-pese*.'

'*Ndio*, bwana.' He started the engine. As the car rolled out of the compound gate, Matthews glanced back to see if Junter had noticed his departure, but the door to the office remained closed. Matthews leaned back in his seat and let his thoughts drift as the car bucked and plunged over the murram road in a cloud of red dust.

There were some large white objects propped against the gate-post where the sign pointed to Redstone Farm.

'*Pole-pole*,' ordered Matthews, and the driver slowed. An elephant's skull flanked by two smaller skulls, probably wildebeest: Matthews glanced at the bleached bones in disgust, wondering who had dumped them there. He'd have to tell Juma to get rid of them before the twins came back and started asking questions.

As the car wound up the hill in low gear he looked about him with the pride and pleasure that re-entering his own little kingdom always evoked, noting the glossy coats and bulging udders of the dairy herd in its cedar-railed paddocks; casting an anxious eye at the flourishing coffee plantations. The pundits had predicted ruin for anyone trying to grow coffee at nearly 7,000 feet, but he had proved them wrong. The neat rows of multi-stemmed bushes astride the deep-soiled ridges gave him a glow of satisfaction. It had been worth all the early struggle, the back-breaking toil, the anxious years of nursing the young bushes, protecting them from sun and storm alike.

The car rounded the final bend and drew up in front of the long low single storey bungalow, with its welcoming pink-washed wings. So Janet's beaten me to it, he thought, seeing the Ford van parked carelessly, characteristically, at an untidy angle to the flowerbed, all four doors hanging open just as the occupants had left them. He spent his time telling Janet and the children to shut doors. Automatically he pushed one closed as he walked past. His hand came away tacky and he rubbed it against his shorts. Needs a good wash, he thought. I need a good wash, too.

He noticed with surprise that there were more cars parked in the shadow of the baobab tree. Perhaps Janet had invited guests to lunch; she often did. She would be wondering where he was and whether she'd have to entertain them on her own.

Cindy the spaniel lay stretched out on the gravel to one side of the porch. He smiled. So she'd turned up the moment the twins left, just as he'd predicted. She was the most provoking animal. She was also a rotten watchdog. Any minute now she'd hear him coming and race up wagging her absurd tail and barking her head off. He always said she couldn't distinguish between friend or foe.

'Cindy!' he called. 'Here, girl!'

The dog didn't move. Instead the front door banged open and a black man whom Matthews had never seen before backed down the steps. He wore the stripes of a corporal in the Kenya Regiment and dragged one end of a long, blanket-wrapped bundle. Matthews had a fleeting impression of intense activity within the house.

'Who are you?' he exclaimed sharply. 'What are you doing here?'

The corporal twisted to face him and his mouth opened, but he said nothing. He stood stockstill, clutching his awkward burden, halfway down the porch steps. Matthews tried to push past, but he blocked the doorway solidly, deliberately.

'Get out of my way,' snarled Matthews. 'This is my house, damn you. What the hell's going on?'

Burly, immobile, the corporal continued to bar the entrance. His voice was deep and slow, tinged with pity.

'Do not go in, bwana. Wait here.'

'Who the hell are you to tell me what do do? Out of the way!' In sudden fury, Matthews caught the man roughly by the shoulder, spinning him off balance so that he stumbled backwards down the steps. He lost his grip on the long bundle and the blanket fell away.

For a frozen moment, Matthews stared in shocked disbelief at the bloody contorted features of old Juma, taking in the missing ears, the broken teeth, the dark holes where eyes should have been. Something seemed to snap in his mind, and he gave a choking cry.

'Janet!'

'Stop, bwana . . .'

With a quick lunge, Matthews fended off the corporal's attempt to stop him, bounded up the steps and rushed into the house.

Dick van Ryn and Nolan Matthews had been rivals in love and the antagonism lingered; nevertheless they were neighbours, and while Matthews was recovering from the effects of shock and grief and concussion, van Ryn visited the hospital in Nairobi several times. His motive was not entirely altruistic. He wanted to be the first to know when Matthews decided to sell up. He had long coveted Redstone Farm's fertile acres, and was determined to join them to his own property. While Matthews was too heavily sedated to protest, his neighbour took in hand the day-to-day running of Redstone Farm, and called at the hospital once a week to report on the state of its animals and crops.

Matthews listened with increasing restlessness, disliking his former rival's assumption of authority, but powerless to prevent it. Van Ryn, for his part, was surprised that Matthews made no mention of selling the farm; on his fourth visit he judged that it was time to discuss the future.

'May I come in?' he asked, putting his long dark face round the door.

'Well, Dick. Good of you to call,' said Matthews stiffly. The hospital room was a square white box, clean, stark, and antiseptic. There were no flowers or cluttered possessions to soften its severity; nevertheless van Ryn thought he smelt whisky. The suspicion was confirmed when Matthews fumbled in the bedside locker and produced tumblers and a bottle. 'Join me?' he said in his abrupt way.

'Thanks.'

'What's the news?'

'You've got a couple of nice heifer calves . . .' Van Ryn catalogued the week's farming events: the coffee prospects, the outbreak of footrot among the breeding ewes, a few minor administrative problems. Finally he broached the subject that was uppermost in his mind. 'Henry McIntyre was talking to me down at the club. He's interested in your Hereford bull. Wondered if you'd consider selling. I said I'd mention it when I next saw you.'

Matthews' tight mouth twisted a little. He knew exactly what van Ryn had in mind. 'So the vultures are gathering, eh, Dick? Taking a look at what they can scavenge. I suppose *you* wouldn't be averse to buying my land, and Delacroix would snap up the sheep, while good old Henry takes his pick of my cattle. You want to carve it up among you so everyone gets what he's been coveting for years. That's what you're after, isn't it? Why don't you say so straight out and be done with it?'

The expression on van Ryn's dark, high-nosed face showed clearly that he found such bluntness distasteful. He said, 'I only mentioned it because I see no sense in letting good land go to rack and ruin under native management while the owner's away . . .'

'Who says the owner's going away?'

Van Ryn coughed, embarrassed. 'Well, I suppose we all assumed . . .'

'Assumed! You mean you and your gin-swilling friends in Muthaiga Club have been planning my future for me,' said Matthews cuttingly. 'How kind. How considerate. Tell me, where do you suggest I remove myself to? I have no other home, you know. I suppose details like that hardly concern you so long as you get your grasping hands on Redstone.'

Van Ryn bit his lip, concealing his annoyance. Matthews wasn't himself yet. One had to make allowances. A man who had lost his wife and children so horrifically might be excused ordinary standards of politeness for a while. All the same, it was a blow to hear he had no intention of leaving the country. He said quietly, 'Don't try to pick a quarrel with me, Matt. I don't believe in bad blood between neighbours. We've all got to help one another these days. Listen, old boy: I'm perfectly happy to go on looking after your farm as long as you like, no strings attached; but I would like your assurance that if you ever decide to sell, you'll give me first refusal.'

'No strings? What's that if it's not a bloody great hawser?' snapped Matthews. He set down his whisky glass so violently that it cracked and a stream of liquid ran across the linoleum.

Matron put her plump, scrubbed face round the door. 'Time's up, Mr van Ryn. We don't want to tire our patient.' She clicked a disapproving tongue at the dripping whisky and summoned a nurse to mop up the mess.

Van Ryn picked up his hat. 'Any idea how long they'll keep you here?' he asked casually.

'Of course. I forgot. You want to go and spread the news. All right, Dick. I'll give you a date for my departure.' His mouth twisted in a smile that was more like a grimace. 'Go and tell McIntyre and Delacroix and the rest of the hyena pack that I'm not selling up just yet. I've got a score to settle first.'

'A score?' said van Ryn uneasily.

'With General Tembo and his four-footed friends. I shan't be leaving Redstone until I've wiped out every elephant in the Aberdares. Go on, you tell them that.' His voice cracked distressingly and he turned his face away.

Van Ryn raised his eyebrows at Matron, who gave a tiny shrug. 'Time for your tablets, Mr Matthews,' she said brightly. 'I'm sorry, Mr van Ryn, but if you'll excuse us . . .'

'I'll look in again next week,' van Ryn muttered, glad to escape. Outside in the corridor he and the Matron exchanged glances.

'I'm sorry – he's not usually like that,' she murmured. 'You caught him at a bad moment. It's the shock. He doesn't know what he's saying. He doesn't mean it.'

Van Ryn nodded. 'Of course. It's the shock. I shouldn't have encouraged him to talk about the future.' He cursed himself for rushing things as he strolled away past the bougainvillaea's brilliant explosion of colour on his way to the car. Matthews had always been a stubborn bastard. He'd never known how a sweet kid like Janet could put up with him. A typical handsome, stubborn, pigheaded Englishman. Now he'd hang on to Redstone Farm like a dog in the manger, whether he wanted it or not, just to prevent van Ryn buying him out. Matron was bound to excuse her patient, but Dick van Ryn himself had a strong feeling that not only did Nolan Matthews know exactly what he was saying, but he meant every word of it.

CHAPTER ONE

WHEN THE TELEPHONE bell fixed to the cowshed wall sent its shrill clamour across the farmyard, Sally Tregaron's first instinct was to ignore it. She had just succeeded in manoeuvring the weaker of the twin calves into a suckling position, and if she left them now to answer the phone she would have to start the whole delicate operation over again on her return.

Automatically she counted the rings. Eight . . . nine . . . ten . . . The trouble with having an outside bell on your telephone was that although you could hear it all over the little Oxfordshire farm, frequently it was impossible to run back to the house and answer it before the caller despaired and rang off.

Fifteen . . . sixteen . . . seventeen . . .

'Come on, poppet,' she urged the calf. 'Try a bit. You've got to help yourself.' She pushed the pink rubbery nose against the cow's tight udder, but the calf wouldn't suck. I'll have to get the vet, she thought.

Still the bell rang maddeningly. Whoever it was didn't give up easily. The Jersey cow shuffled and stamped impatiently. She was chained and couldn't move far, but with deadly precision she raised a sharp cloven hoof and placed it on Sally's rubber-booted instep. It hurt. Sally wrenched her foot free and the calf, deprived of support, slid weakly back into the straw.

The telephone went on ringing.

I'll have to go, she thought. She shut the cowshed door and ran across the yard, smashing thin ice on the puddles, aware of the ache in her foot where Duchess had trodden on it.

'Darkwood Farm. Hello!' she gasped, snatching up the receiver.

'Is that 049.17.205? Switzerland calling,' said a clipped foreign voice. 'Will you accept a call from Geneva?'

Geneva? She was on the point of refusing the call when she remembered Mark saying he might break his journey in Switzerland if he had time. But it couldn't be Mark yet, surely? Sally found that days tended to run into one another when Mark was abroad and the boys at school. Unless she had to write a cheque or a letter she was often unsure of the date. All the same, she hadn't expected Mark back so soon.

'Yes,' she said. 'Yes, I'll accept the call.' With her free hand she scrabbled under a heap of papers beside the telephone, searching for Mark's itinerary. The line whirred and clicked, then Mark's voice came through as loud and clear as if he was in the same room.

'Sally? I thought you were never going to answer. I've been ringing for hours. Another minute and I'd have hung up.'

'Sorry, darling,' she said guiltily. 'I was out in the cowshed.'

'Can't you hear the telephone from there? I thought with the outside bell . . .'

'Yes, I can, but it was a bit tricky. One of the calves doesn't look up to much.'

'Oh, God! Not again.' She could picture all too clearly his expression of bored distaste. She said quickly, before he could tell her the cattle were more trouble than they were worth, 'How was the trip, darling? Did you manage to fit everything in?'

She had found the itinerary now and saw with slightly ashamed relief that she was right; he wasn't due back until the following day. She would have time to shop, clean the house, wash her hair . . .

'Curate's egg,' Mark was saying. 'Not much joy on the business front because there'd been another Government reshuffle and the man I wanted to see had been kicked out of his job. Occupational hazard in Kenya. Still, it wasn't a dead loss because I had time to poke around a bit on my own account. Research into East Anglian activities, you know what I mean. When Fuzz hears what I have to tell him the shit will hit the fan.'

'East Anglian . . ? Oh – I see.' With an effort she adjusted her mind to a different wavelength. It was difficult to keep pace with the power struggle inside Ferguson Construction unless you were in daily contact with the protagonists, but even she knew that there was no love lost between her husband and Martin Essex. If Mark had spent his free time investigating Essex's activities in Kenya it would have been for no friendly purpose.

'Of course, it wasn't *all* hard graft.' She could hear from his voice that he was grinning. 'There was time to fish and swim and sunbathe down at Malindi. Some talent about there, I can tell you. Mostly topless, of course. Jealous, darling?'

Why did he need constant reassurance that women found him irresistible? 'Green!' she said dutifully, because that was what he wanted to hear, but in spite of the topless beauties it wasn't true. She didn't want to go to Kenya. Not after what happened to Aunt Janet.

Memory whisked her back to childhood: to the morning when the grown-ups fell oddly silent when she ran into the dining-room calling her mother to come and see the tabby's new kittens. Her mother had looked up from the paper she held, her usually-laughing mouth a scarlet gash against chalky skin. Her eyelids were puffed and pink. The ripped envelope of a telegram lay vividly yellow against the dark carpet.

'Mummy's not feeling very well,' her father had said, and his voice sounded husky, almost rusty. 'She'll come and see the kittens later.'

From Gerda, the draconian Swedish au pair who ruled the nursery by fear, she learnt the gruesome details. Aunt

Janet, her mother's youngest sister, who had sherry-brown eyes and copper curls like Sally's own, had been killed. Her head had been chopped off by cruel black men at her home in Kenya. Her cousins the twins, who had made her laugh so much last summer by pouring water over Gerda's head when she was hanging out the washing, and hadn't even cried when they were spanked for it, had been cut into little pieces and carried away to be eaten in the jungle.

'Such is what befalls naughty girls and boys,' declared Gerda gloatingly. 'To you also, if you do not obey.'

Sally had nightmares about it for years after Gerda's abrupt departure a few weeks later. Out of a sense of family duty, now that her parents were dead, she still sent an annual Christmas card to 'poor Uncle Matt', as Janet's husband was always referred to thereafter, but she had no wish to visit Kenya herself.

As if aware of her thoughts, Mark's voice said, 'I wished you'd been with me, you'd have been useful.'

'Me?' She could think of no circumstances in which that would apply.

'Yes. I tried to see your Uncle Matt. He could have saved me a lot of legwork, but the old devil chased me off. Set his dogs on me.'

'But you saw Redstone Farm?'

'Not much of it.' She imagined his grimace. 'He's paranoid: greets visitors with a ravening pack and a shot-gun. But it's a peach of a place, all right, and he's clinging on to it like grim death in spite of several – er – polite suggestions that he might like to hand it back to the original owners. That's what I heard at Muthaiga Club.'

'That's absurd. The original owners were buffalo and elephants,' said Sally indignantly. 'Poor Uncle Matt's place was nothing but bush before he cleared it – I remember my parents saying he was mad even to try to farm there. How can anyone say it doesn't belong to him?'

His laugh came clear along the line. 'Simmer down, darling. Don't fly off the handle at this distance. Wait till I get within throwing range. What's wrong with your voice? You sound very odd.'

'I think I'm getting a cold,' she admitted. 'Awful sore throat.'

'You and your colds!'

'I seem to get them from the boys . . .'

'Well, keep this one to yourself,' said Mark crisply. 'Fresh air and exercise is all you need . . . Ah they're calling my flight.'

'You're coming back *now*?'

'Of course. That's why I rang. Aren't you pleased?'

'Well – yes. I mean, how marvellous! I wasn't expecting you until tomorrow night.'

'I told you, I finished early. I want to see Fuzz Ferguson the minute he steps off the plane from Hong Kong. Look, meet me at the office at half past six, and we'll celebrate. I've got some good news.'

'Darling, I can't. I'll have to stay with this poor calf . . .'

'Damn the calf. Get someone else to look after it.'

'It's too bad for that. I'm sorry, darling. Why don't you come straight home and we'll have a quiet evening, just the two of us?'

'God, that sounds dull! The last thing I want is a quiet evening, thanks very much.' His voice was irritable. 'I've been working my guts out for the last week and now I feel I deserve a bit of fun. I want to see *you*! Damn it, you can't stand me up because of a miserable calf. What's one calf more or less? I've got so much to tell you. Exciting news. Can't you make an effort?'

'I'd love to – but it's just not on,' she said doggedly. 'You must be exhausted after all that flying. Do come home and forget about the office. I'll ask James and Juliet over if you want company.'

He didn't respond at once, and across the line she could hear jumbled airport noises, a staccato voice calling flights. Then Mark said curtly, 'Look, I've got to go now or I'll miss the plane. Be at the office at half-past six and I'll tell you how your uncle and Essex together have worked out a nice little racket in poached ivory. I haven't got all the links in the chain, but I've found out enough to put the skids under that bastard Essex, all right. Surely you'd rather spend the evening with me than in a stinking cowshed?'

He rang off before she could reply.

Sally stared at the telephone, conscious of her heart thumping heavily. Didn't Mark care if the calf lived or died? Silly question: she was well aware that the answer was No. Mark looked on her farm as a plaything – a toy that kept her occupied while the boys were at school but which, like a toy, must be put aside when important matters called.

Important matters, in Mark's terms, meant his career. Thirty was the make-or-break age when a rising young executive either burst his way out of the middle-management cocoon and headed for the top, or settled for a lifetime of taking orders. Mark was ambitious and he would be thirty next month.

Slowly replacing the receiver, Sally looked across the hall and met her husband's assertive gaze in the framed photograph on her writing table. It had been taken when they were engaged, and even then his level grey eyes under slightly hooded lids, full, well-shaped mouth and arrogantly tilted head seemed to say, 'I know what I want. Give it to me or I'll take it from you anyway.'

Her eyes shifted to the girl in the picture: *was that really me*? A younger, plumper, softer version of herself with the same elongated eyes – 'tiger eyes', Mark called them – and wide jaw tapering to a pointed chin, pale skin, copper hair, every feature the same and yet subtly different. The girl in the photograph smiled at the camera with the trust of an adored, indulged only daughter who'd never known a disappointment or heard a harsh word from anyone she loved. The woman she now turned to face in the mirror had a different expression: reserved, even wary. The long eyes kept their secrets, the mouth had a firmer set.

After ten years of marriage she had built her defences, but though Mark himself had made them necessary she still loved him, even without the rose-tinted spectacles of earlier days.

'I'm sure he'll go far, darling, but are you sure it's where *you* want to go?' her father had asked rather helplessly, when she told him she and Mark were engaged.

'Quite sure,' she'd said with nineteen-year-old certainty, and he had nodded. He gave them Darkwood Farm as a wedding present, and she knew that Mark's dislike of the place stemmed partly from the fact that it wasn't something he'd earned himself.

Deep down, Sally knew he was right to look on Darkwood as a toy. Forty flint-strewn acres of marginal grazing hardly justified the title of farm, nor could the land support a family without large injections of Mark's salary to mend roofs and renew guttering, rebuild tumbledown barns and repair sagging fences. All the same, she loved it.

The handsome brick-and-flint farmhouse stood sturdy and four-square on the south slope of its narrow wooded valley, and the track that led to it had no other destination. The house belonged to no particular period, having been enlarged and contracted to fit the needs of its inhabitants for many years before planning permission was needed to alter the shape of a dwelling. Large light rooms of late Georgian vintage backed on to a sprawling rabbit-warren of smaller, older corridors and domestic offices haphazardly joined by roofs of varying pitches. It was an excellent place to play hide-and-seek: a peaceful, timeless house. Within a mile on either side of the valley, London-bound motorways carried their roaring, fume-laden traffic in an endless stream, but Darkwood's isolation was complete. Progress had gone past without stopping, unaware that the relic of another age lay hidden in the trees.

Electricity had found its way to Darkwood, and for this Sally was profoundly grateful. Wood-burning stoves took a lot of feeding even if you lived surrounded by trees, and to depend on a woodburning cooker would, she felt, be carrying fundamentalism altogether too far. The telephone wire wriggled, almost apologetically, between the beech trees which frequently reduced it to impotence by dropping branches across it in the wake of spring and autumn gales.

The tall proud beeches were the real masters of Darkwood. They could be aloof, protective, threatening: friend or foe according to mood. For Sally they were the true barometer of the seasons. In April the solemn grey trunks would suddenly sprout tiny delicate leaves, as if the pillars of a cathedral had adorned themselves with a frivolous green veil or an elephant attempted to hide beneath a green gauze canopy. By degrees the gauze would expand into a heavy rippling drapery that hid all but the smallest glimpse of trunk or branch; and almost before she realised that midsummer was past they would start to flaunt unexpected touches of colour, like bright badges of rank on a hunter's livery which summer's heat had dulled from glossy emerald to matt jade. As the year rolled on, yellow, red and ginger would submerge the last remnants of green, and for a space the handsome brick-and-flint house would seem to stand at the centre of an immense bonfire, the flame-leaved trees glowing in low-slanting sunlight like pillars of molten copper. Then the first frost and the first wild winter wind whirled them to earth in a thick, crunchy carpet of bronze.

There were drawbacks, of course, to this splendid isolation. Sally would have liked her sons to live at home during their schooldays, but after the first winter of missed buses, streaming colds, and punctures in the freezing dawns and dusks, she had to agree with Mark that the boys would be better off at boarding-school. To fill the gap left by their departure she flung herself into the business of turning Darkwood into a real farm, forgetting that animals were even more of a tie than children. You could hardly give a calf a fiver and tell it to amuse itself at the cinema; nor could you park it in your host's spare bedroom while you wined and dined. There wasn't enough work on the farm to justify the expense of hired labour; she could manage on her own except at moments like this, when Mark suddenly required her presence – *soignée*, sparkling, and sophisticated – to complete his image as the man most likely to succeed.

Sally stood irresolute, one finger tracing patterns in the dust of the telephone table, feeling the pressure build up. What should she do first? Wash hair; clean the house; cook, shop . . . ? A whole day's work to be compressed into two hours. She visualised Mark following the other passengers down the long shiny walkways, smiling at the stewardess, boarding the plane. In a couple of hours he would be back in the office, expecting her to join him in an evening's expense-account fun. She would have to be there, no question. *Surely you'd rather spend an evening with me than in a stinking cowshed*? She'd caught the ominous note of irritation in his voice: irritation that could herald a major fit of sulks. She didn't want a row the moment he got home: it wasn't worth it.

Already the hall was darkening as the short November afternoon drew in. The precious minutes were ticking past: she forced herself into action. First, the calf. She rang the vet's surgery and was lucky to catch Mr Foster, the junior partner, about to set off on his evening round. He promised an immediate visit.

Next, the house. She knew from long experience exactly which aspects of skimped housekeeping Mark would notice and which he'd never see. She disliked the routine chores of sweeping and dusting as much as the next woman, but when it had to be done she preferred a real blitz to the little-and-often technique.

This evening the need for speed gave a dramatic urgency to essentially dull tasks. Rapidly she polished the furniture in Mark's study and dressing-room, emptied waste baskets and filled big vases with glowing autumn leaves. She fished a loaf and a joint from the freezer; eggs, cheese and butter from the dairy, and constructed handsome wigwams of dry logs in the open fireplaces.

In less than an hour the house looked fresh and welcoming and she could turn her attention to the other thing Mark always noticed and commented on: her own appearance. Here, too, she had a technique for instant glamour. Twenty minutes with shampoo, hot air blower and heated rollers transformed her copper head into a swirl of curls any hairdresser would have been proud of.

She bathed, discarded jeans and sweater in favour of a sleek black dress with a plunging neckline, and embarked on a glitter-based make-up using swift strokes of eye crayon and mascara to dramatise her eyes and darken their curly lashes.

Another five minutes and she was finished, all dressed up and ready to go – but of the vet there was still no sign. Quarter of an hour crawled by, half an hour. Sally fretted restlessly round the kitchen, unable to do anything constructive for fear of spoiling her careful finery. She dialled the surgery again and this time her call was put through to the night operator.

'Yes, Mrs Tregaron, Mr Foster's on his way to you,' said the girl patiently. 'He was delayed by an emergency call, but he'll be with you any minute now.'

This is an emergency, thought Sally. If I don't leave in ten minutes I shall be late and Mark will be furious. Aloud she just said, 'Thanks,' and replaced the receiver.

She stared out of the window at the shadowy trees, willing Mr Foster to hurry. There was going to be a frost. The branches looked sharp and black against the fading orange of the sunset, and she could smell the nip in the air. Mark would be leaving Heathrow now, collecting his car from the multi-storey, easing into the rush-hour traffic.

The growl of an engine in low gear reached her ears, and a moment later headlights scythed across the yard, gilding the gables of the barns. The vet, at last! Putting an outsize anorak over her slinky dress, she thrust her stockinged feet into gumboots and hurried out to meet him.

Mark Tregaron slung his briefcase into the overhead locker, slid into the aisle seat and smiled into the eyes of the attractive dark-haired woman next to him. He had a special smile which he reserved for attractive female strangers, carefully practised and kept in good repair it rarely failed to provoke a warm response.

'What a rush! I thought I'd miss the flight,' he said. The dark-haired woman smiled back but raised her shoulders slightly, turning her palms outward to signal her lack of English.

Waste of effort, thought Mark. Pity. He enjoyed chatting up pretty women on planes and felt in need of a little gentle flirtation, a few compliments, perhaps an exchange of addresses.

Excitement bubbled inside him. He couldn't wait to tell Sally that Martin Essex had cooked his own goose; the job of Deputy Chairman was as good as his.

Mark had been deeply chagrined when Essex was brought into Ferguson Construction over his head as a result of a merger, and the promotion he'd confidently expected receded into the future. It had taken a good deal of Fuzz Ferguson's renowned tact together with a substantial increase in salary to placate him.

'Believe me, your chance will come,' rumbled Ferguson from behind the polished acre of desk. The halo of crinkly white hair that gave him his nickname stuck up wildly as he ran a hand through it. 'I don't like putting you on ice like this, but we do need Essex's experience of the Far East if we're to succeed in the Chinese market, and I can't risk having him join the opposition.'

He'd held up stubby, capable fingers, ticking off his points. 'He knows China, speaks the language; he's lived half his life in the East and knows their ways of doing business. No one seems to know why *he* gets the contracts signed when others can't, but frankly I'd be a fool to pass up the chance of collaring him. Now that Mao's gone the Chinese are beginning to realise that they need our technology, and half the construction firms in the Western world are queuing in Canton, trying to pin the big contracts. You don't sell to the Chinese: they buy from you. Martin Essex is currently top scorer in that department.'

He smiled and leaned forward to pat Mark on the shoulder. 'You watch him like a hawk, and maybe you'll learn a few of his secrets, Mark. Then in a couple of years' time we'll review the situation. You might be able to replace Gerry Maitland at the Hong Kong office. How about that? I can't say fairer than that, eh?' It was a plum job and Mark's sullen expression lightened. Ferguson ran his hand through his hair again and said, 'Meantime, you stick to the warehouses. You've got a free hand to run Ferguson Storage. Once we've dug ourselves a toehold on the Chinese mainland, we may find we can do without Essex after all.'

After suitable haggling Mark had agreed to put his pride in his pocket and temporarily accept Essex's superiority. As one of the most favoured of Fuzz Ferguson's bright young men his career prospects were still excellent, despite this setback, but it didn't make him like Essex any better.

Slight and balding, with a smooth pale face and soft pale hands, Essex looked older than his thirty-three years. His full mouth with its deeply indented upper lip stretched often in a smile which never reached his level grey eyes, and he walked with head thrust forward between his narrow shoulders, like a contemplative tortoise. Like a tortoise, too, his sexual reputation was formidable. Mark's chagrin at his appointment turned to outrage when he learned that his own secretary, the beautiful almond-eyed Elaine Chan, whose face had haunted his dreams for the past two months, was leaving to become Essex's personal assistant.

'You can't do it,' he protested, when she came to tell him of her decision. 'It's – it's unethical.'

Dimples appeared on either side of Elaine's soft red mouth. She wore a slender pale green sheath dress with a stand-up collar; the clinging material outlined her small pointed breasts and stretched tight across her neatly rounded buttocks. She looked as enticing as a pistachio water-ice on a sultry day. 'Are you accusing me of immorality?' she asked softly, smoothing the silk dress over her thighs.

'Not you, him!' Mark exploded. 'It's totally unethical to suborn another employee's secretary to suit your own convenience. I shall speak to the boss about it. If that bastard thinks he can march in here and start re-shuffling the whole department as he pleases, he's got another think coming.'

Elaine's long eyes laughed at his expression of disgust. 'Mr Ferguson has already agreed to my new appointment,' she said demurely. 'He thinks that Mr Essex will need my services even more than you do, Mark.'

Mark had glowered, disliking her choice of words. *Services* hinted at a relationship not confined to office hours. The kind of relationship he had wanted for himself. 'Then don't expect a glowing reference from me,' he said curtly. 'There are half a dozen girls in the typing pool who'd make better secretaries than you, Elaine.'

Now she was laughing at him openly. 'I don't think my – er – clerical skills, or lack of them, matter very much in this new position,' she said. 'I'm going to have a secretary of my own for that side of things. I shall be travelling a good deal with Mr Essex . . .'

'Make sure you lock your hotel door,' snapped Mark, knowing that he was out-gunned. 'All right. I can't stop you. I suppose I'll have to start looking around for a new secretary, though it's damned inconvenient just when I'm off on my travels.' He paused, playing for sympathy. 'It's a pity it had to end like this.'

Her pointed fingers brushed the back of his neck in a fleeting caress. 'Nothing is ended, Mark. Nothing is even begun. Don't be angry. We've had some good times. Who knows, we may have more.'

With that crumb of comfort he had to be content. Over the next eighteen months he schooled himself to conceal his gnawing rage against the man who had so cavalierly snapped up his job and his secretary, and watched Essex as closely as he could. There was no doubt about it, the man had a way with the dilatory, vaccillating Chinese trade delegations whose changes of mind were anathema to so many western firms. With Essex in charge of negotiations, Ferguson Construction landed two big plant-building contracts in Shanghai, with the promise of more to follow. Essex believed in getting out and chasing business where it originated, and seldom spent more than a couple of days together in his spacious office at the Ferguson headquarters. Now and again, when Mark visited the warehouses on Dean's Wharf where the container ships from Kenya landed coffee, tea, and sisal for storage on its way to the British market, he would catch a tantalising glimpse of Elaine's smooth black hair and clinging sheath dress as she flashed about the premises like a busy exotic bird. Having worked there herself, she knew the staff well and ordered them here and there with pretty, peremptory gestures and shrill orders which none of them appeared to resent, earning herself the affectionate nickname of 'Madam Butterfly'.

From time to time chests of tea addressed personally to Martin Essex would arrive at the warehouse, and these were always collected by Elaine in her smart little silver-blue Mini-Metro. Mark fell into the habit of checking the tea-consignments for these chests in order to snatch a few minutes' conversation with Elaine when she came to fetch them. Idly he wondered what on earth Essex did with so much tea.

Most of the Kenyan estates now used strong paper sacks lined with foil to transport their leaf, but a few still clung to traditional plywood chests, despite spiralling costs, and Mark noticed that tea addressed to Martin Essex was always in a chest.

One day, out of sheer devilment, he switched the labels on two chests, and watched from his upstairs window as Elaine drove away with the substitute.

Next morning the warehouse foreman entered his office, grinning broadly. 'Trouble, sir. Seems like Mr Essex got the wrong cuppa char yesterday and Madam Butterfly's out there raising merry hell over it. She wants to speak to you, sir, if you can spare the time.'

'Send her up, Johnny.'

Almost before he had spoken, Elaine whirled into his office like a small tornado. There was no doubt that she had gained status since her days as his secretary. He noted the expensive shoes and shoulderbag, the sleek tailored suit which proclaimed the successful career woman. Slender and petite as ever, there was new authority in her stance. She looked very expensive.

Yet he seemed to detect a hint of uncertainty, even fear, in her voice as she said, 'Mark, I can't understand it. When I came here yesterday to collect Mr Essex's special tea, your people gave me the wrong chest. He was expecting the first crop from a new clone which the manager of the Dante Estate has bred, and instead the chest was full of some awful rubbish fit only for teabags. He's very annoyed.'

'All right, leave it to me; I'll check through the stuff we sent out yesterday and see where it's gone,' said Mark easily, and watched her natural colour recede until the blusher stood out in harsh contrast on her cheeks.

'You – you mean that chest has gone to somebody else?'

'I don't say it has, but it may have,' said Mark. 'Don't worry. Nothing goes astray for long from this warehouse. I'll give you a ring when we've tracked it down.'

'I can't go back without it.' Her agitation was becoming more obvious every minute, and one small foot tapped nervously as she said, 'Please ask Mr Willis to look for it now. Mr Essex will be so angry.'

'What a tyrant the man is. Surely he won't blame you? A

simple handling slip-up? It happens all the time.'

'No. Yes. Yes, he will. He has promised to give a sample of this new leaf to some Chinese officials he is meeting. A trade delegation. He will lose face if he cannot produce it.'

Mark had a strong impression that she was inventing the story as she went along, but there was no doubt that she was rattled. He thought he would press her a little.

'Tea? For Chinese officials? Is that how he gets his contracts signed? I must tell the Chairman.'

Elaine said unhappily, 'It is the custom to give small presents when you do business in the East. Please, Mark, ask Mr Willis to look now. I really will get into trouble if I go back without it.'

Mark said softly, 'And if I do, will you dine with me tonight? One good turn deserves another — or isn't that the custom when you do business in the East?'

She hesitated. 'I wish I could, but tonight I'm tied up.'

'The Chinese delegation?'

'Yes. Perhaps next week? Now, please will you search for that chest?'

'Of course,' Mark had said briskly. He knew exactly where the chest was. 'Johnny, can you give us a hand here?'

Ten minutes later Elaine sailed out of the warehouse forecourt, at the wheel of her Metro, and Mark grinned as he watched her go.

Now, at least, he had an inkling of how Martin Essex won friends and influenced people in Red China. Not by his fluency in the language or because he promised a better deal than his rivals. Not by patient negotiation or convincing the bamboo bigwigs of his ability to produce the goods.

Oh no, simpler than any of that crap, thought Mark. What you need to succeed in the People's Republic of China is the power to dangle something no Chink can resist in front of those inscrutable Oriental noses. Fuzz will *not* be pleased when I tell him just how his expert on the Far East gets contracts signed for Fergcon.

It wouldn't be easy to convince him. Fierce loyalty to his

employees was one of the aggressive little Chairman's most likable characteristics. He would have to have proof.

Essex. Elaine. Who else was involved?

Mark rummaged in his briefcase for pen and paper and began to draw animals. His nib moved busily across the white surface. Tim, his elder son, had inherited his talent for sketching and he was crazy about animals. He would like a letter decorated with *Loxodonta africana* in characteristic poses.

'You draw good!' said the dark woman, looking over his shoulder. 'Is for bambino?'

Bambino – hell! Embarrassed, he hid the little sketches under his hand and embarked on a short letter to Tim. Nearly there, he thought, as he finished. I'll drop it in the airport box. With a glow of conscious virtue he leaned back and lit a cigarette, letting his thoughts drift. Tonight he would see Sally. He was suddenly eager to be with her again. After a series of one-night stands with women of varying colour and allure, the thought of going to bed with his wife was unexpectedly attractive.

He became aware that his dark-haired neighbour was stirring uneasily and pointing to the NO SMOKING signs. Bossy bitch, he thought, turning his shoulder. He began to plan the evening: drinks at the office and on to Keables' for dinner. Dancing at Abella's or perhaps The Chocolate Mouse. They might look in at the Quod, to see if there was any action, then back to the flat. Sally could drive home in the morning to see to that calf or whatever it was bothering her. It wasn't as if he was against her farm: on the contrary – it kept her happy and he'd never heard the least whisper that she amused herself with other men during his business trips as the bored wives of so many jet-setting executives did. In that way, the farm was a definite asset, so long as she didn't take it too seriously.

In response to his neighbour's urgent signals, Mark at last stubbed out his cigarette and fastened his seat-belt as the Jumbo prepared to land.

CHAPTER TWO

HIS WIFE WAS not the only person to find Mark Tregaron's return ahead of schedule extremely inconvenient. Elaine Chan got the news from the drivers' pool and rang through to her boss immediately. She had to wait several seconds before his curses gave way to intelligible speech.

'We'll have to get those chests moved tonight,' he said at last.

She heard the gulp as he downed a steadying sip of the malt whisky she had just poured for him. In imagination she saw him switching on again, tilting the swivel chair forward, the bald, domed forehead wrinkled as he grappled with this unexpected hitch. 'Get on to the warehouse at once, Elaine. Tell the foreman a lorry is on its way to collect the Dante chests tonight. Tregaron's been blundering round Kenya like a bull in a china shop, stirring up the mud. Whatever happens, he mustn't get a look at those chests. Go on, hurry.'

She had never heard him so ruffled. 'It's no good, Martin,' she said. 'Mr Willis leaves at five o'clock and it's nearly half past now. There'll be no one at the warehouse except the night watchman.'

'Then ring Willis at home,' snapped Essex. 'Tell him it's urgent. I want those chests shifted tonight.'

'He'll think it very odd.'

'I don't care what he damned well thinks. Get on with it and tell him we're on our way.'

The internal line clicked dead. Elaine shrugged and tried Willis's home number without success. Even as one part of her mind registered how futile it was to try and bring him back to the warehouse after hours, another was evolving a plan of her own. Mark was always asking her out: always trying a pass. If she invited him to her flat tonight she was sure he'd jump at the bait. She could delay him, making him late for work. Too much wine, a sleeping tablet, an unreliable clock . . . Her brain buzzed with possibilities. In the morning Essex could spirit away the Dante chests, leaving neither Mark nor Mr Willis any the wiser.

'Well?' said Essex, as she came through the communicating door. His handsome top-floor office reflected his taste for the East with red-lacquered tables and silk scrolls adorning the walls. Silently he held out his glass for a refill. His hand, touching hers, shook a little.

'I couldn't get him, Martin. He goes for a beer with his mates. We'll never find him: there are dozens of pubs around there. I've got a better idea.'

As she explained, Essex began to smile and he waved her to a chair. 'It might work. He's a randy devil.' He took a couple of turns across the room, head out-thrust, hands clasped behind him. 'Look, this is where I'll be,' he said, handing her a square of pasteboard. 'If you run into any trouble, ring me on that number. It's the private phone of the restaurant where I'm meeting our friends. Oh,' he added as she got up to go, 'remind me to review your salary next week. I think you're due for an increase.'

'Thank you, Martin,' said Elaine demurely, and whisked out of the office in a whirl of skirts and laughing almond eyes.

'One of your Jersey crosses, is it?' asked the young vet, as he held open the door for Sally to precede him into the calving-box.

She gave him a brief run-down on the calf's history and watched while he examined the limp yellow body. Duchess and the other calf paid no attention.

'She did try to lick it at first, but then she lost interest.'

'Can't blame her, can you? Probably thinks one baby's enough to worry about. I know my wife does,' he said absently. 'Hm . . . Well. I think we can save it, but it'll be an all-night job for you, I'm afraid.'

Bang goes my evening with Mark, thought Sally. I should have known. 'What are you going to do?' she asked.

'First we've got to get some life into her. I'll give her a shot to boost her vitality, but she'll keep sliding back unless you keep up the stimulation. The main difficulty's going to be to make her take a grip on life.' He stared at her, assessing the flamboyant make-up, the black dress only partially concealed by the parka. 'Were you off to a party?' She detected disapproval.

'I'll say I can't make it. It doesn't matter.' Mark wouldn't agree, but that was just too bad.

Barry Foster smiled and his thin, rather drawn face was suddenly friendly. 'That's the way I'd see it,' he said. 'I'll need hot water, soap and towels. Can you fetch them? I'll want your help to hold her.' He gave the party finery another doubtful glance. 'It's a pity to spoil your dress . . .'

'I'll change it. Won't be a minute.' She ran back to the darkened house, glad to warm up in her comfortable sweater and jeans. She'd felt chilly and helpless in evening clothes and there was no point in ruining them to add to the evening's troubles.

The vitamin boost had a dramatic effect. When she returned to the byre, the calf had opened its beautiful long-lashed eyes and was making an effort to raise its head from the straw. With the reluctant co-operation of Duchess they managed to get a small quantity of milk down its throat, and half an hour later their efforts were rewarded when the calf managed to suckle unaided.

'Marvellous,' said Sally.

They lowered the patient back into the straw. It was surprising how heavy even a new-born calf could be, and how many sharp knobbly protrusions it possessed.

'Come in and have a drink,' she suggested as he packed

up his bag and prepared to leave.

The young vet grinned. 'Thanks, but I'll just wash off the worst of this and be on my way. I've still got a couple of calls to make. Think you can manage now?'

He roared off up the hill, scattering loose flints, and she went in to telephone Mark. To her relief she was answered by Georgina, the stocky capable secretary who had replaced Elaine Chan.

'I'm sorry, Mrs Tregaron, but he's not in the office yet,' she said. 'I'm expecting him any minute. He asked me to stay on until he arrived. Can I give him a message?'

Sally explained about the calf.

'Oh, the poor thing!' exclaimed Georgina, who cherished a romantic dream that one day she would exchange the city's rush for a cottage with honeysuckle round the door and live on familiar terms with cows and sheep and chickens. 'No, of course you can't abandon it. Don't worry, I'll tell Mr Tregaron. I do hope the poor little pet is better by the morning. What a worry for you!'

Nice girl, sensible girl, thought Sally. She knew she could rely on Georgina to present her defection in a diplomatic light. She must hurry now and get supper ready, and open a bottle of wine. But in case Mark didn't react as she hoped, Sally removed the telephone receiver from its cradle. If he couldn't get her any other way, he'd *have* to come home.

'Not coming up? What d'you mean?' demanded Mark. He stared at his secretary and a pulse began to beat in his temple. He had hit the worst of the rush-hour as he drove across London, and a pile-up on the Chiswick flyover which reduced traffic to a single-lane crawl had done nothing to improve his temper. 'I told her to be here by six thirty.'

'Your wife rang to say she was sorry, but one of her calves is ill and she's got to stay and look after it,' repeated Georgina placidly. He looks just like a sulky little boy, she thought, observing her boss's jutting underlip and lowered eyebrows. 'She thought you'd be tired after the flight and she's going to have supper ready.'

'Why the hell should I be tired?' snapped Mark. 'I've done nothing but sit in planes all day long. I'm not tired.' His voice shook with suppressed anger.

He snatched up the telephone and dialled with angry, jerky movements. Engaged.

He tried twice more at two-minute intervals. Taken it off the hook, he thought savagely. How bloody typical! His fury mounted into a physical pain. His chest was tight and for a moment he struggled for breath, then with an effort he calmed himself. Change of altitude: better be careful. To hell with Sally. He would take some other woman out to dance and dine.

'Book me a table for two at Keable's. Eight o'clock,' he said curtly to Georgina, who was standing by with a bunch of papers for him to sign. He hesitated, wondering if he should ask her to join him. Though too heavy for his taste, she wasn't unattractive, but there was something self-consciously righteous in her manner which he found off-putting. She didn't look the type to respond to light-hearted flirtation. He thumbed through his address book, wondering whom to ask. Clarissa? No: she was in France until the end of the month. Jessica? Perhaps.

'Oh, Mr Tregaron –'

'What is it?' he asked impatiently, wishing she'd go away.

'There was a message just before you came in from Mr Essex's assistant. She asked if you could spare her a few minutes. I said surely it could wait until morning, but she insisted it was urgent.'

Good for Elaine, thought Mark. It would take more than a supercilious cow like Georgina to choke off the fair Miss Chan.

'What does she want?'

'She wouldn't say – just that it was urgent.' Georgina sounded apologetic. 'In the end I said she could come. I hope you don't mind. She was very – pressing.'

No one I'd rather be pressed by, thought Mark. Observing his smile, Georgina wondered if there were any truth in the rumours she'd heard about goings-on between Mark and his former secretary.

He said, 'It's quite all right. I'm always glad of a chat with Elaine. Give me the letters to sign now and then you can go. Thanks for holding the fort,' he added with a conscious attempt to charm. 'I'm sorry to have kept you so late. Don't worry about locking up: I'll do it myself after seeing Elaine out. Ah, this sounds like her now.'

He smoothed his thick brown hair, straightened his tie, and moved towards the door with a new spring in his step.

After a broken night attending to the calf, Sally slept later than usual, and woke to a perfect blue-and-silver winter's morning with a fresh skim of ice riming the puddles in the yard. Hurriedly she dressed and went to the byre. Frosted cobwebs were strung like diamond necklaces on everything she touched. They trembled across the handles of the wheelbarrow and stretched from rim to rim of the feed-buckets. They brushed her face, a ghostly gossamer touch, as she opened the cowshed door and looked anxiously into the calving-box.

Knee-deep in yellow straw, Duchess turned a complacent muzzle towards the light and lowed impatiently for her ration. Then she put down her head and shoved impartially at the two small apricot bodies entwined beside her. To Sally's delight both calves scrambled to gangly legs. Both of them! She could hardly believe it.

'Good old lady. Clever girl,' she praised, and emptied the cake into the manger with a satisfying rattle. For several minutes she stood watching the little family, feeling a glow of achievement as warm as the sun on her back. So it had been worthwhile. The vet's fee, the missed sleep, the risk of a row with Mark. For once her determined interference with Nature's arrangements had worked. So often one struggled to save an animal which Nature had already condemned.

Half-drowned chicks, half-frozen lambs, orphaned kittens and fox-cubs: at times Sally had wrestled with them all, forcing open mouths reluctant to accept nourishment, attempting cross-species fostering arrangements, waking at hourly intervals to feed and tend. Nine times out of ten the patient died. She would find a stiff, reproachful little corpse in a cardboard box, surrounded by hot water bottles, saucers of baby-food, all the pathetic paraphernalia of amateur nursing.

But this time her efforts had been rewarded. Surely even Mark would be pleased?

Through mists of sleep and aspirin she had heard him return in the early hours, and listened for a while to his footsteps moving about the house, but he hadn't slipped into bed beside her. Either he was avoiding her cold or the memory of the broken date still rankled. Let him sleep it off, she thought, and tiptoed past the closed dressing-room door. He'd probably wake at noon with his temper restored, if she could keep the boys quiet that long.

They would soon be here, bursting with school news and hearty appetites; she must get on with lunch. Nevertheless, she lingered, reluctant to leave the friendly byre with its contented munchings and stampings. Half a dozen bantams preened in the hayrack above the calf-pen, and three red hens, sole survivors of a vixen's raid, scuffled luxuriously in the thick dust near the door. A tortoiseshell cat, topaz eyes slitted, watched them from a respectful distance.

Sally scattered corn to the hens, but left the eggs for the boys to collect later. They enjoyed hunting through the sweet-smelling haybales in search of nests. She was indoors, heating coffee, when her ears caught the low snarl of an engine descending the hill. Worried that the noise would disturb Mark, she hurried out to intercept it, and reached the cattle-grid just as a police car scrunched to a halt.

Two officers got out, stretching, as if they'd been sitting still too long. She recognised the square pale face and rolling gait of Sergeant Bernardson.

'Hello,' she said, smiling. 'Isn't it a lovely morning? Have you come about the licence? I'm afraid my husband's not up yet. He got back very late so I'm letting him sleep on.'

Her voice died away as the officers exchanged glances.

'What is it?' she said. 'Is something wrong?'

The sergeant cleared his throat. 'You say your husband's at home, madam?'

She laughed nervously. 'Well, I heard him come back but I haven't actually seen him. Why? Isn't it about the licence?'

'I'm afraid not. D'you mind if we come in for a minute?' The sergeant moved purposefully towards the door.

Sally's mind raced. Not the licence? Oh God, what now? Speeding? She seized on the idea of speeding and clung to it, not wanting to face the possibility of something worse: drunken driving, hit-and-run . . . It had been *very* late when she heard Mark come in – three or four in the morning. And *why hadn't he come to her room*? Hadn't he wanted her to see him, covered in blood perhaps?

Panic threatened. The officers were staring about the kitchen as if they expected to see something. The silence was growing oppressive. She said in a high, forced voice, 'Aren't you going to tell me what it's all about? Shall I wake my husband?'

Another covertly-exchanged glance. The younger policeman moved to the telephone. Without asking her permission he picked up the receiver, held it to his ear, and quickly replaced it.

'Phone out of order, then?' he asked.

'Out of order? Oh!' she said, remembering. 'No, it's all right really. I left the extension off the hook last night. I – I didn't want to be disturbed.'

'We've been trying to ring you,' said Bernardson heavily. 'We thought you must be away, but old Jim Froud at the cottage said he hadn't seen your car go out. So we came down to check.'

Sally grasped at the edge of the table to steady herself. Her legs felt suddenly weak. 'Is it . . . is it one of the boys?' she whispered, her face deadly white. 'Has something happened?'

With cold dread she recognised their expressions of pity.

'Please tell me,' she said.

'Better sit down, Mrs Tregaron.' Bernardson's square capable hands guided her to the kitchen chair. The ticking of the clock was unbearably loud in the silence, or was it her heart?

'I'm sorry to say we've got some distressing news for you. There's no way of wrapping it up or pretending it isn't. Your husband had an accident in the early hours, and we've been trying to get in touch with you ever since.'

'An accident? Mark?' Her lips seemed stiff. She could hardly frame the words. 'But he's here. I heard him come in.'

She turned away from their steady gaze and ran out of the kitchen, pounding up the stairs and along the landing.

'Mark!' She flung open the dressing-room door. The bed was empty, undisturbed.

The young policeman had followed her upstairs. She turned to him. 'I heard him. I did!'

He coughed, embarrassed. 'Could have been a dream, ma'am. You know, you heard what you were expecting to hear.'

Gently he guided her back to the kitchen and pulled out a chair for her. She said dazedly, 'An accident? A car accident? You mean he's *dead*?'

'Looks as if he went to sleep at the wheel,' said the sergeant. 'He'd been to a bit of a party, it seems; had a few drinks. It looks as if he just blacked out and the car ran out of control.' He paused, then said again, 'I'm sorry.'

Sally bowed her head on her arms. Her mind felt numb, unable to grasp what they were telling her. Mark dead? It wasn't possible.

The sergeant regarded her with weary compassion, searching for something to say that would soften the blow. Poor soul, he thought, she hasn't heard the half of it yet. Drunk, drugged, having it off with a fancy Chinese piece. No need to add to her troubles by telling her that now, but she'll hear it in the end, poor lady. Bound to.

Baffled, he fell back on the traditional remedy and jerked a thumb towards the electric kettle.

'Go on, Dave,' he muttered, 'brew Mrs Tregaron a nice cuppa tea and make it strong. We could all do with one.'

CHAPTER THREE

LIKE A MAN who feels little pain from an amputated leg because the stump is anaesthetised, yet is tormented by an insignificant splinter in his thumb, the memory of those footsteps in the house nagged at Sally during the anguished weeks that followed. By degrees she learned how and where Mark had spent the hours before his death. At the office. At a Chinese restaurant. At Elaine Chan's flat.

She couldn't have heard him in the house, yet she knew she had. Auto-suggestion, said friends and relations, looking uncomfortable.

'After all, you were half-asleep, you said so yourself. And doped to the eyeballs.'

'Only aspirin. Hardly to the eyeballs.'

'Oh, well . . .' A shrug, an uneasy shying-off the possibility of occult mystery – a fetch, a ghost. Rapidly they would change the subject.

Soon Sally gave up trying to convince other people, but she knew that someone had been in the house with her that night, and who other than Mark? Who else had a key to the back door? There was no question of a break-in. Nothing had been disturbed, nothing was missing. She tried to put the matter to the back of her mind, but it continued to bother her.

The major pain of losing Mark was deadened at first by the efforts of neighbours and friends who rallied round with support and sympathy. Also by the feeling that she must keep going, for the boys' sake, at least until the Christmas holidays were over. When Tim and Willy went back to school in January she could indulge her grief, not before. So she forced herself to as near an appearance of normality as possible, and thought she had succeeded until she found nine-year-old William packing his school trunk four days before he was due back at school.

'No need to do that yet, darling,' she said, surveying with a degree of dismay the jumbled heaps of clean and dirty clothes, marked and unmarked laundry. 'I'll help you with it later on.'

He gave her a blue, flashing glance, lower lip jutting in a way that reminded her piercingly of Mark. 'I want to do it now,' he declared. 'I want to go back to school. It's horrid here at home without Daddy. I like school better.'

Sally's stomach seemed to drop as if in an over-swift lift. So much for her efforts to be a one-parent family. Timothy, at ten more tactful and sensitive to the moods of adults, saw her expression and turned savagely on his brother. His eyes flashed behind his heavy spectacles.

'Don't say that!' he ordered. 'It's not true and anyway it's not Mummy's fault that it's horrid. Say you're sorry or I'll really thump you.'

'I'm not sorry,' howled William. 'You're a beast and I hate you. I wish you were dead instead of Daddy. I do like school best.'

'Stop it, both of you.' Sally pulled them apart.

That evening she rang her half-brother Peter, a London solicitor and fervent Chelsea supporter.

'They never stop fighting. I'm sure it's because they miss Mark so much. If you could think of some way of taking their minds off it . . .'

There was no appeal more likely to please Peter. Instantly he put aside his clients' business and cancelled important engagements so that he could devise a strenuous programme of manly pursuits for his nephews. 'Leave it to me, Sal. I'll get them so damned tired they won't have the energy left to fight,' he promised happily.

When the boys had been whisked away, smiling and bemused, in Peter's Porsche, Sally went listlessly upstairs to begin the chore of packing for school.

Her elder son's squirrelling instincts were highly developed. She emptied conkers, marbles, ancient toffees and less easily identifiable treasures from his trunk and removed a shoebox full of letters, each one neatly returned to its envelope. All last term's mail, she thought, and riffled through the heap, wondering what she could jettison.

Her own letters; godparents' letters; Mark's letters. She picked up an airmail envelope dated November 23rd, realising with a small shock that it had been the very day Mark returned from Kenya. The very day he died.

'Darling Tim,' she read:
'Here are some sketches of the only elephant I've seen this trip. I wish you'd seen him too. He was stripping bark from a tree near your uncle's farm, which was pretty unwise of him since your uncle Matt is known to have an itchy finger in defence of his crops.

'This used to be a good place for elephant, but the ivory poachers have been busy and now they are rare. It makes me really angry. Of course the people who are most to blame are the men who pay so much for the ivory. A poacher can earn as much from selling one elephant's tusk as he could in a whole year of honest work, so it's easy to see why they do it. I've found out the identity of one of the buyers, at least, and I'm determined to put a stop to his activities. It will give me great pleasure, since I've never liked him anyway and once he did me out of a job! The elephants will be much safer when he's out of the way.

'I hope the Second XI won against Crosslanes, and that you are working hard at the Greek. Once you've got the alphabet the rest is relatively easy.

'Much love from Daddy'

Sally stared at the neat writing, feeling cold. Mark had wanted to see Fuzz Ferguson 'the minute he stepped off the plane'. But he hadn't managed it: Essex had been quicker on the draw. He had silenced Mark before he could reveal anything that might connect him with smuggled ivory. Elaine Chan worked for Essex. Had Mark gone to her flat that night to question her about Essex's illegal activities?

On impulse she dialled Fergcon's number, waiting with her heart pounding unevenly while it rang. No one had seen anything suspicious about Mark's death, and yet . . .

'Ferguson Construction. Can I help you?'

'I'd like to speak to Elaine Chan, please.'

'I'm sorry,' said the polite voice. 'Miss Chan has left this company.'

'Oh.' Sally felt jolted, as if she'd walked down a step which wasn't there. 'Can you tell me where to get in touch with her?'

'I'll put you through to Mr Essex's office. Perhaps they can help.'

But when she gave her name to the brisk voice that answered next, she felt the atmosphere chill at once. 'I'm sorry, but it is not our policy to disclose the addresses of our employees.'

'Surely she left a forwarding address? It's important.'

It was a mistake to let her anxiety be heard. The voice became still frostier. 'I'm sorry, I can't help you.'

'I see. Will you put me back to the switchboard?'

But when she asked for Georgina Rowell she met with the same blank wall. The operator was sorry, but Miss Rowell had left the firm at Christmas. She had no information as to where she could be contacted.

Sally stared out of the window at the darkening farmyard, the seed of doubt germinating, taking root. First Mark, then the two girls who had worked with him. It couldn't be a coincidence. Suspicion grew from a seedling into a vigorous plant. Essex had arranged for Mark to die.

Hatred rose in her heart like black bile, shocking in its intensity. Mark had been vain and impatient and a philanderer; he hadn't been the dream lover of her early imaginings, but he had been her husband. The gap his death left in his children's lives could never be filled. And because he had strayed too near the centre of his evil web, Martin Essex had arranged for his extinction as callously as a spider would throttle a fly.

She remembered his bulging pale eyes and soft hands at the funeral service, his glib phrases. 'Our deepest sympathy, Mrs Tregaron. A great loss to us all.'

Perhaps Essex himself had prowled the house the night Mark died, using his keys, searching for papers that might incriminate him. Sally shivered. Had he known she was there? If she had appeared in her nightdress to confront him, would he have disposed of her, too?

I've no evidence, she thought. I can't prove a thing. It's all guesswork and instinct. A letter to a child, my own memory . . . An evil man involved in an evil trade. She thought of elephants and the poachers who killed them for the sake of their gleaming tusks.

She felt as if she had woken from a long sleep. The soft blanket of dependency rolled back, leaving her shivering but wide awake, ready to take action. Carefully she folded Mark's letter and tucked it in her wallet, then searched through the heaps of notes of condolence untidily stacked on her desk. The one she needed was there, somewhere.

She found it at last near the bottom of the pile: neat, pointed Italianate script on old-fashioned black-bordered paper. The letter from 'poor Uncle Matt', expressing sympathy and inviting her to spend a month with him at Redstone Farm. '*A change of scene is sometimes helpful,*' he wrote, '*and it would give me great pleasure to welcome Janet's niece to my home.*'

I'll go, she thought. The scent may be cold but the trail begins there. I owe it to Mark to finish what he began.

Outside, a pale high January moon rode the storm-tossed clouds, but instead of bare branches lashed by a rising gale she seemed to see palms gently swaying. The muted roar of the chimney became the whisper of long grass, the yard a darkling plain bounded by faraway hills, where the shy dim forms of antelope and gnu, zebra and hartebeest bunched nervously for protection, encircling their young.

A shadow moved, detached itself from the shadow, yawned and stretched. Her brain knew it was Malachi, the black tomcat, stirring from his nest in the fertiliser sacks as night called him to hunt, but in her imagination the sacks became boulders and sinuous Malachi, prowling the yard, grew a lion's mane and twitching tufted tail. The king of beasts, slinking and menacing, snuffing the wind which carried the scent of foaling zebra or injured buffalo, waiting for the deepening dark that would hide his stealthy stalk.

She pulled the curtains across, shutting out the night, and sat down at her desk.

'*Dear Uncle Matt,*' she wrote,
'*Thank you for asking me to stay with you, I should like to very much . . .*'

CHAPTER FOUR

AT SUNSET THE bulldozers ceased their grinding roar and the nerve-stretching scream of power-saws was silenced. The trees which had fallen victim to the biting chains lay like a giant's game of spillikins, crushing the tangled vines, waiting for caterpillar tractors to push them away down the hill, along the fresh scar of track whose pitted surface was already churned into deep ruts by the passage of wheels.

The chatter, laughter and occasional squeals from the black work-gangs died away as the men swung loose-hipped towards the pick-up lorry and the evening's pleasures. Only the occasional flare from a bonfire, the odd shower of sparks as a half-burnt log collapsed into the ashy centre, and the thin pall of smoke hanging over the clearing still evoked the scent of man and the threat of his return.

Motionless in the shadow of a cliff, the old bull elephant waited, the big fan of his left ear pressed tight against the suppurating wound at the angle of neck and jaw. His trunk was raised, as it had been all day. The tip rested lightly against his knobbed forehead to ease the nagging pain as infection from his wound spread in a hot tight swelling, bigger than a football, along his nasal passages and sinuses, making each movement of his sensitive trunk a throbbing agony. Without his trunk he could not browse. Lately he had almost given up trying to fill the huge rumbling cavern of his belly and his skin hung in loose folds from his backbone on which each vertebra stood out in sharp relief.

He carried a great weight of ivory. One hundred pounds a side, the Wandrobo poacher gleefully reckoned as he fitted the arrow to his small light bow a month ago. The arrow had been tipped with viscous toffee-like ointment distilled from the *Acokanthus*, a slow-acting poison which would paralyse the nervous system by degrees; but the poacher's shot had been a poor one, and instead of piercing the skin behind the ear, as he intended, it had struck further forward and glanced off the angle of jawbone with no apparent effect. The poacher had cursed the *thahu* on the arrow that had spoiled its aim, and wondered gloomily how many sheep and goats the *mundu-mugu* would demand as payment for the ceremonial cleansing to lift the evil spirit. Brooding on the possible causes of the *thahu*, he had watched two hundred pounds of ivory depart at speed into the forest without making any serious attempt to follow.

Yet the poison had taken effect after all. At first it was a mere irritation that caused the old bull to rub frequently against trees and rocks and plaster his head with river mud in an attempt to stop the itching as he worked his way along the ridges of the Aberdare National Park. His rolling steps were directed, as they had been for many dry seasons, by a craving for minerals and fresh fodder to be found in a certain narrow ravine. For more than fifty years his migration had followed the same route; now that he was a lonely grumpy old warrior without even a couple of acolytes to attend him, habit still drew him towards his favourite haunt despite the worsening ache in his jaw and the rumbling void in his belly.

Once there had been many elephant in the forest, but now only small family groups browsed in the clearings or melted wraith-like into thicker cover when tourist minibuses churned up the muddy tracks shrouded in year-round mist which kept the forest fresh and green.

The old bull had been already full-grown in the fifties, when the Security Forces had used bombs and naphtha flares in the forest to flush the last of the Mau Mau terrorists from their hideouts. Even now the rumble of thunder and flashes of lightning which heralded the rains were enough to send him crashing headlong through the bush in remembered terror.

Then he had lived near enough to men to lose his fear of them, though he – and they – preserved a wary distance. Now in his pain, instinct drove him back to the place which had been safe for him as well as the terrorists: a steep ravine where the Security Forces had never penetrated and bombs never fell.

To this ancient Eden of yellow-blossomed cassia, purple-red kigelia and giant leadwood trees, where the violet-crested turaco flashed his brilliant flight-feathers as he swooped from branch to branch, generations of elephants had come to dig deep in the natural saltpan, sucking minerals from the mud. But now bulldozers and earthmovers were gouging out a new track at the lower end of the valley, clearing the trees in a wide circle round the saltpan, for this was where Benjamin Kariuki, rising star in the political firmament, had decreed should be the nerve centre of a new Game Reserve and Elephant Research Station.

Stars pricked through the dark like needlepoints stabbing blue velvet, and far away a buffalo bellowed, a single deep-throated roar that cut through the night's small squeaks and rustles. As if he had been waiting for a signal, the bull elephant rolled silently forward towards the saltpan.

For the past three nights he had eased his wound by shoving it deep in the healing salt-laden mud, kneeling down to strain with his hindquarters until he had pushed the infected side of his face beneath the surface, washing out the maggots that were eating him alive. There he knelt, suffering and ungainly, from dusk until dawn when the rumble of engines from below had driven him back into hiding.

Placing his big stub-nailed feet carefully, he picked his way over the newly-felled trees and skirted the smouldering fires, waving his trunk before him like the hand of a sleepwalker. At the lip of the saltpan he stopped, disconcerted, swaying from foot to foot, side to side, for his passage was barred. Glinting in the starlight, a newly-erected fence of strong chainlink surrounded the saltpan. It was topped by a strand of electrified wire that pulsed steadily, like a heartbeat.

The old bull raised his trunk. He had a short way with fences. He could snap off posts set in concrete as easily as he uprooted trees; even high-tensile wire would finally snap when he pitted his great strength against it. The ticking, however, was strange. Though his wound burned fiercely, urging him towards the cool, soothing mud, he took time to assess this new obstacle. For ten minutes he swayed on the spot, sizing it up, before reaching out a tentative trunk and sliding the fingered tip delicately along the top strand of wire.

An instant later the *thump* of the electric pulse sent an explosion of pain through his skull, and his trunk closed convulsively over the wire, fused to it until the charge was withdrawn. Squealing, he whirled, tail stuck straight out behind, knees bent and trunk raised in an agonised question mark as he crashed back into the trees. There he stood trembling, pressed against his rock, until the torment in his head gradually subsided into the familiar dull ache.

Twice more in the course of that night his burning wound drove him out to the saltpan to confront the fence, but each time his steps grew more uncertain. At the fourth attempt he no longer dared to touch the wire. His strength was no use against this enemy. Restlessly he paced back and forth until he had circled the entire pan in his search for a gap, but the fence was complete: there was no way for him to reach the mud which sucked and plopped gently, tantalisingly, calling to him to come and ease his wound. Baffled at last he stood before the fence, head sunk deep into his shoulders, eyes closed in dumb endurance as the hyenas giggled over their kill and the sky turned from violet to pewter to primrose with the approach of dawn.

When the growl of engines on the slope below heralded the return of the work-gangs, the old bull stirred at last. With measured rolling strides he covered the distance back to the shelter of the cliff, to suffer through another day in his long wait for death.

'Coming for a swim?' asked the tall stranger, stopping beside Sally as she stood in the flower-bright courtyard of the Norfolk Hotel in Nairobi, admiring the birds in the big cage built around a tree.

She turned, taking in wide shoulders that strained the seams of a faded Madras shirt, dark hair, a long, amused face with lively, curious eyes, a smile that was openly inviting. His gaze moved unhurriedly from her slim pale legs to her curly copper head, and she twitched an impatient shoulder. Dressed in a towelling wrap with a bathing-cap dangling from one finger, it was difficult to pretend she had any other destination than the pool.

'Yes.' She moved on and he fell into step beside her as if they were old friends.

'Good. It'll be lovely now. It gets a bit crowded if you wait until after breakfast. My name's Hamilton – Bay Hamilton. I think we came out on the same plane.'

'Possibly,' she said, walking a little faster. She was damned if she was going to be picked up before breakfast.

He quickened his pace to match. 'Haven't we met before?'

'I don't think so.' She took off the towelling wrap and hung it on a chair at the pool's edge. The early sun struck deliciously warm on her bare shoulders. She willed him to go away and leave her in peace. She couldn't cope with meeting people, fending them off, seeing the curiosity in their eyes. Damn the man, she thought. Can't he take a hint? Surely he's not another of those awful reporters? Not *here*.

'Do tell me your name,' he said, putting his towel beside

hers. 'I'm sure I've seen you somewhere.'

'Sally Tregaron,' she said quietly, and watched as wheels went click, click, click in his brain, bracing herself for the reaction when the penny finally dropped.

Her half-brother Peter had used his influence in the newspaper world to good effect, but he hadn't been able to kill the story entirely. He had managed to get *Whizzkid in Love-Nest Drama* toned down to *Sudden Death of Executive*, but the photographs had been there, big and bold on the tabloids' centre-spreads, as the story of Mark's love life and death were exposed to public gaze. No wonder he knew her face.

'Tregaron,' he repeated, glancing at her left hand. 'Of course, I remember, your husband died in a car crash. I read about it in some paper. I'm so sorry. You must have had a horrible time with those Fleet Street ghouls on your doorstep day after day.'

It was said so spontaneously that her instinctive hostility melted. Most people shied off the subject of bereavement, especially one that had been squalid and sensational enough to interest the gutter press. Yet though they didn't mention it, everything they said showed they were thinking of it.

She managed a smile. 'The reporters were pretty unbearable. I'm afraid I got in the habit of choking them off.'

'No need to apologise. Only sensible thing to do. Come on,' he said, dismissing the subject, smiling down at her with eyes which were not brown, as she would have expected, but a glinting pewter grew, 'I'll race you to the far end.'

Her spirits lightened magically. The sun shone, the birds sang. Bay Hamilton was no sensation-seeking reporter, but a good-looking and friendly man to whom the earthquake which had overturned her life was of no more interest than any other newspaper scandal.

'You'll have to give me a start!' she said, and dived quickly in, astonished to feel no shock from the water which was almost as warm as her own blood. Swimming in February! It seemed inconceivable that twenty-four hours ago she had been shivering in thermal underwear and fur-lined boots.

She was one of the world's slowest swimmers: when in a few strokes Bay overtook her she was happy to abandon the race and float idly, staring up at the blue sky with puffy, whipped-cream clouds. A couple of lengths were, in any case, enough to leave her gasping for breath at this unaccustomed altitude, so she soon hauled out to lie in the sun and watch him ploughing up and down with a steady, professional-looking crawl. She felt more alive than she had for months. In a way it was galling to discover that the grief she had believed to be unique responded so readily to the therapy which well-wishers had been trying to force on her ever since the tragedy.

'Have a break – a change of scene. Get some sunshine. Make new friends.' Stale platitudes, well-worn advice. It won't work for *me*, she'd thought.

Now it appeared they were right. Here she was, doing exactly what she'd been told to do, and the cure had begun. I'm nothing but a boring standard programmed auto-conditioned stocksize drip in the gutter, she thought, and held out a hand to let Bay help her to her feet.

'Let's get some breakfast. I'm starving,' he said.

Breakfast consisted of pawpaw sprinkled with fresh lime juice and substantial quantities of bacon and egg. Only when he questioned her about her holiday plans did her eyes shadow and a hint of her earlier constraint return, as she remembered it wasn't just a holiday.

'That depends on my uncle. I've never met him, you see.' She began to explain about poor Uncle Matt but he cut her short.

'Nolan Matthews of Redstone? Oh yes, I've heard the story. Poor fellow, they say he's mad as a hatter. That's probably a ridiculous exaggeration,' he added quickly, seeing the anxiety in her face. 'As a matter of fact, I'm working up there now on the Government's new Elephant Research Station.'

'Oh?' Her eyes were suddenly alert. 'What's your particular interest?'

'My firm's building the game lodge and various offices and laboratories.' He smiled. 'I'm interested in everything to do with elephants: counting them, measuring them, tracking them with radios, finding out why they behave as they do. I've always worked as a freelance before, but I met Fuzz Ferguson down in the Selous on a walking safari last year, and he roped me in for this job. He's a difficult man to refuse.'

'So you work for Ferguson Construction?' Sally fiddled with a slice of toast, breaking it into small brittle pieces.

He was surprised at her interest. 'Well, Lawne-Douglas Associates, actually. Fergcon gobbled them up about two years ago.'

'I remember.' She hesitated, then asked, 'Is Martin Essex your chairman, then?'

'He was, until he moved on to higher things. Why? Friend of yours?'

'Not exactly. I've met him. My husband used to run Ferguson Storage, you see.'

'Oh, of course.' He regarded her thoughtfully. What had he said to sharpen her attention so suddenly? She was trying to play it cool, but he sensed excitement fizzing just below the surface.

Sally felt like a child at a party who has spotted the first clue in the treasure hunt and wants to distract the others from seeing it.

She said at random, 'Is it a big job? What sort of area does a Research Station cover?'

'Not as big as we'd like.' He wondered if the question was as disingenuous as it seemed. 'Benjamin Kariuki's the moving spirit behind the whole scheme. Perhaps you've heard of him? He won a World Wildlife Award recently for his work in conserving elephant stocks. He picked the place to build the Research Station and got Government approval, but he's run into considerable opposition both from people who'd like to see him come a cropper politically, and from local farmers. The trouble is, there are two blocks of land right in the middle of the reserve where the farmers are not being exactly co-operative.'

Sally said carefully, 'Does one of them belong to my uncle, by any chance?'

'Right first time.'

Bang goes a promising friendship, she thought sadly. Now she understood what Mark had meant when he spoke of pressure on Uncle Matt to return his land to its original owners. Not – as she'd supposed – land-hungry humans, but the *real* original owners: elephant, buffalo and rhino.

She put down her knife and said with some heat, 'Surely there must be plenty of forest that can't be farmed without you having to grab poor Uncle Matt's few acres? I know elephants need a lot of room but there can't be any need to give them the farm he's worked for all his life. If that's what you want to do, I'm not surprised he's being uncooperative. I would be, too.'

The pewter eyes regarded her with some amusement. He said, 'It's the old story of Naboth's Vineyard, I'm afraid. Everyone covets the same few acres. From Benjamin Kariuki's point of view, your uncle is sitting like a dog in the manger on the ideal site for the headquarters of the Elephant Research Station.'

'And of course you're on Mr Kariuki's side?'

'I want the Research Station built – yes.'

'So that you can turn elephants loose on good farming land?'

Bay frowned. 'It's not a question of turning them loose. They're loose already. Nor, for that matter, is it good farming land. What we're trying to do is create a protected range where elephants can be studied. There's a great deal still to be found out about them before we can decide on the best policy for conserving them.'

'What sort of things?' Despite herself she felt a stir of interest.

'Nobody knows, for instance, how many elephants any given area will support, or what happens when numbers increase beyond the limit. There's a certain amount of evidence to suggest that they can stop breeding of their own accord when their range becomes overcrowded. That's got to be looked into.'

'Birth control?'

'Something like it.'

'I still don't see why you should pick on poor Uncle Matt's farm to do your research.'

'You will when you get there. As a farm, Redstone is barely viable. It's been neglected for years. In fact, that's probably why your uncle has been allowed to stay there so long. No one else wanted it.'

'Been *allowed*? But it belongs to him!'

Bay said dryly, 'In an African country, that's not a cast-iron guarantee that it'll always belong to him. However, up till now no one particularly yearned to sweat his guts out trying to make a living up there, so your uncle's little kingdom has been left alone.'

'Until you come along and try to snatch it for your elephants. I must say, I think that's the limit. If I was poor Uncle Matt, I'd fight you every inch of the way.'

'I'm sure you would. You'd rather the wild African elephant became extinct in your lifetime than your uncle was hounded from his farm – right?'

'Don't be ridiculous. Of course I wouldn't! Anyway, that's hardly likely to happen.'

He said seriously, 'Unless something is done now, the elephant *will* become extinct in the wild. You see, there's a double clash of interest: first with the human race, and then with the environment. Even if you create large ranges where elephants are protected, you still face the problem of feeding them. They're extremely destructive feeders. They uproot trees and bore holes in them. They strip off bark so that trees die. An area of forest where elephants have been feeding in the dry season looks like Passchendaele after the artillery finished with it. They're Nature's bulldozers, designed to open up overgrown areas so that other animals can graze there. As a system it works perfectly so long as there's always more bush for them to move to. When the bush runs out the trouble starts.'

'So your solution is to let them make Passchendaele out of my uncle's farm?'

He didn't smile. 'Broadly speaking, there are two schools of thought. One believes in non-interference, and the other in management.'

'Management? You mean shooting the surplus population? Making umbrella-stands and ivory knick-knacks?'

'I know it doesn't sound attractive, but the other system has drawbacks, too. The non-interferers argue that you should let elephants destroy their own habitat. They'd eventually convert forest and bush into open grassland on which most of them would starve to death. Then the woodland would regenerate – so the theory goes – and the surviving elephants would breed again. In a few hundred years the balance of Nature would be restored.'

'Back to Square One.' She thought it over. 'Which theory do you support? No, let me guess – you're a cropper.'

'Yes – up to a point. I don't think we've time to put the other theory to the test. But in order to manage the reserves properly, I think more research into elephant behaviour is urgently needed.'

'So that's why you want Redstone Farm?' And that's why you bothered to chat me up, she thought. I guessed there must be an ulterior motive behind all this. Naboth won't let you set foot in his Vineyard, but you think it's worth scraping an acquaintance with his niece all the same.

High time to change the subject.

'Are you married?'

'I was.'

'What happened?'

He shrugged. 'The usual story, I suppose. I was away from home too much. Sometimes I'd be working out here for two or three months at a stretch. My wife – my ex-wife –' he corrected himself quickly, 'found that absence didn't make the heart grow fonder. In the end she went off with someone who could give her the kind of life she wanted.'

'I see.' She, too, found it difficult to realise that her marriage was over. No doubt she'd adjust to it, given time. They said you adjusted to anything, given time.

'Children?' she asked.

'No, thank God.'

'You don't like children?'

'Let's say I don't like strings. I prefer to be a free agent and' – he held up a hand to forestall objection – 'before you embark on a lecture deploring such selfishness, consider how much more selfish I would be to drag a protesting wife and family from pillar to post in the wilds, while I satisfy my curiosity about the private lives of elephants.'

'Suppose they enjoyed being dragged from pillar to post?' she suggested.

'Camping in the bush for months on end, eaten by insects, infected with bilharzia, miles from the nearest shop or doctor? If there's a woman alive who enjoys that kind of existence, I have yet to meet her.'

'You can't have looked far,' she said with a touch of scorn.

He gave her a speculative glance. 'You could be right . . . Anyway, it wasn't what Marianna wanted. It was all a bit too bloody familiar. She was brought up here, you see, and by the time she was twenty she couldn't wait to get away. I can't complain: she told me so very early on. Said she was only marrying me to get away from Africa. Of course, I thought she was joking.'

'Of course. But she wasn't?'

He glanced at his watch, dismissing the subject. 'Now, what are your plans? I've got a free morning, and a car. I could show you a bit of the Nairobi Park. One of the rangers told me yesterday that there's a pair of rhino –'

He could see the refusal in her face, the prickles rising in automatic defence. 'I'm afraid I'm busy today. I've got to get things organised . . . Sorry.'

Yes, he thought, you look like an organised person. For some reason it annoyed him. Competent, self-sufficient, well able to take care of yourself. Definitely not cuddly. Definitely not my type. What I do for the sake of my elephants! he thought with an inward grimace. Benjamin Kariuki had suggested it would be worth getting acquainted with Mrs Tregaron, but obviously he hadn't realised the problems. Mrs Tregaron had Touch Me At Your Peril printed all over her. Her stand-offishness was provoking, even challenging. The contrast between that blazing hair and the ice-cool manner didn't seem quite real.

He tried once more. 'How about dinner tonight?'

She took time to consider the invitation, and he was almost sure she would refuse again. She stared out of the window at the bustling crowds, while he watched her clearcut profile with its short straight nose and strong jaw, and wondered if her hair was dark with a red rinse or red with a dark one. Either way it caught the eye: shiny and springy, almost too exuberant to belong to the pale face and shadowed eyes. She had a long, curvy, generous mouth that looked as if it would enjoy laughing and perhaps snapping out smart answers when its owner was not so busy wondering who the hell you were and what the hell you were after.

Finally she turned, looked at him directly, and the long mouth began to curl. 'Well, why not?' she said.

'I can't think of any reason.' She's hooked, he told himself with a flicker of satisfaction, but I'll have to play it gently. One false move and she'll be off downstream like lightning.

'You can tell me more about your elephants.'

'I'll look forward to it,' he assured her. 'Let's meet at seven-thirty in the bar.'

Serena Logie, wife of Fergcon's local representative, was plump, practical, and warm-hearted. She was also an enthusiastic gossip. Mark had used their home as a base during his last visit to Kenya. After a brief, startled silence over the telephone when Sally announced her arrival in Nairobi, she broke into hasty but sincere condolences.

'I wish I'd known you were coming,' she exclaimed when these ran out. 'It's too bad Jim's away up country – he'd have loved to meet you again. Can you make dinner? Oh dear! That doesn't give us much leeway. Why not come over and swim now?' Sally was glad to accept.

An hour later, she and Serena were lying comfortably on foam mattresses at the pool's edge, watching the tow-headed Logie teenagers launch themselves in complicated dives from the springboard.

'You want to know who Mark saw on that last trip?' Serena eased the perilously thin strap supporting her ample bosom to expose another square centimetre of well-oiled bronze skin. To Sally's relief she didn't seem to find the question odd. She frowned, searching her memory.

'Let's see: he spent a couple of days in Nairobi with Jim. Going through the books, they called it, but I said it was going through the Tuskers. Then Mark took off alone to Kericho in one of the office cars. He was away for several days, and I think he visited all our Estates in the area – I can give you the names. Then he went straight down to the Coast and saw the shipping agents. I know Jim offered him the use of the directors' bungalow at Dyali Beach, but I'm not sure if he went there or stayed in Mombasa. He came back to us, and spent another day on the accounts, and lunched with several bigwigs; then we gave a dinner party for him to meet more locals – and that was about it. He was only here for ten days.'

No mention of Uncle Matt or the Aberdares. Sally asked, 'Did he go to see anyone near Nyeri, do you know?'

Serena looked puzzled. 'I don't think so. We've sold all the tea interests up there. Oh! Wait a bit: you're quite right. He did go up to Dante for one night at least, to stay with that dishy van Ryn boy – what's his name? – Karel. That's right. Jim was surprised because Mr Essex had been through all the Dante books only a month or two ago.'

'But Mark went there all the same?' Sally felt a tiny frisson:

'Yes. Jim told him there was no need, but Mark said he'd like to see the place.' She laughed, showing strong white teeth. 'I think he really wanted a peek at Redstone Farm. It's where Nolan Matthews lives – reigns – I should say. One of our last eccentrics. Karel van Ryn's the only neighbour the old devil allows on his property. He finds it useful to have someone to run his errands, I expect. No one knows why Karel puts up with it, but perhaps he'll get his reward one day.'

Sally said diffidently, 'I meant to tell you before. That's where I'm going to stay. Redstone Farm.' Serena turned a look of amazement on her and she hurriedly added, 'Nolan Matthews is my uncle.'

'My dear girl! You must be out of your mind. He *never* has visitors – he's famous for it. He's – what's the word? – paranoid. Real persecution mania. Thinks everyone's out to get him. Well, you can't really blame the poor old boy. He's been very odd ever since the Mau Mau bumped off his wife and kids back in the fifties. But all the same, I'd draw the line at staying with him. Redstone's the back of beyond, you know.'

This information was hardly reassuring. Sally said doggedly, trying to convince herself, 'Uncle Matt sounds sane enough – on paper, anyway. He wrote and invited me: that's why I'm here.'

'Well! Wonders will never cease.' Serena gave her a shrewd look and added, 'It'll be one in the eye for Karel van Ryn when you turn up. A real live niece. No one thought he had any family left. I'd watch my step, if I was you. Dishy he may be, but that lad's got a temper, or so I'm told.' She smiled. 'Don't look so worried, pet. If you're thrown out on your ear you won't be the first to leave Redstone that way, not by a long chalk! You can always spend the rest of your holiday with us. We'd be glad to have you.'

The hypnotic pulse of the disco died behind them as Bay and Sally strolled across the night-scented courtyard, matching steps, his arm about her waist.

Remember why you're here, warned a voice at the back of her brain. Remember Mark. In so far as it was possible she drew away from him, and gently, inexorably, he pulled her back. The strength hidden beneath the smooth velvet jacket was exciting, possibly frightening. Into her mind flashed the image of Malachi, her big black cat, crouched belly to earth, tail waving softly, eyes intent. This man has been stalking me all day, she thought. What does he really want?

It was a shock to find herself attracted physically to a man she'd met only that morning. She didn't go in for that kind of casual romance. Obscurely she felt disloyal to the memory of Mark, because she still saw people through his eyes and it was easy to guess what his opinion of Bay Hamilton would have been. A drifter. Jack of all trades, master of none. She could almost hear Mark's tone of surprised contempt. 'That chap? My dear girl! I thought you had better taste.'

Further information had emerged during dinner at the Jacaranda Tree and dancing back at the hotel. Son of a sporting Northumbrian farmer, Bay appeared to have spent his boyhood either on a tractor or in the woods with a gun under his arm and a dog at his heels. As a man, the taste for an open-air life had persisted, turning him into a self-confessed nomad, footloose and fancy free. A taker of odd jobs in odd places, and a leaver of them when they threatened to become routine or the shadow of an office desk loomed.

A degree in zoology; a job in civil engineering. A spell with the World Wildlife Fund in Uganda; another spell as assistant to the greatest living authority on the identification of *Loxodonta africana* by means of skeletons, which had led to the start of a long love affair – with elephants.

'I'm hooked on them,' he said simply. 'To me they're the most fascinating creatures on earth. The more you find out about them the more you need to know. Hence this new Research Station. I've Fuzz Ferguson to thank for getting me in on the ground floor there – literally.'

'Where did you meet him?'

'Fuzz? He was on a foot safari in the Selous Reserve in Tanzania last year, when I was helping with an elephant count.'

'How on earth can you count them?'

Bay grinned, and the long dark face with its strong jaw and straight narrow brows became vital and attractive. 'Think of a number; double it; add fifty; halve it; take away the number you first thought of . . . We used to argue for hours over our totals. It's not a very exact science. Fuzz and I had a great time in the Selous.'

Fergcon's dynamic little Chairman was well known for his powers of persuasion and also notorious for finding a niche in his organisation for anyone he liked. Evidently Bay had been unable to resist the pressure he brought to bear. Reluctantly, by his own account, he had been recruited on to the payroll of Lawne-Douglas Associates and subsequently given the job of building Benjamin Kariuki's Game Lodge and Research Station.

'Just a temporary arrangement,' said Bay deprecatingly. It seemed to be a favourite phrase.

'Surely you've got a contract, though?' Mark had always

been meticulous about his contracts.

Bay laughed. 'Contracts are against my principles! No: we thought a kind of gentlemen's agreement would be simpler.'

'Simpler, certainly, but how binding is it?' Sally was astonished that anyone dealing with Fuzz Ferguson could be so naive.

He was amused by her concern. 'Who wants to be bound? I certainly don't. This suits us both perfectly. Just a temporary arrangement.' Then, as if even thinking about such things made him uneasy, he said, 'Come on, we're wasting good dancing-time.'

So they pushed on to the crowded pocket-handkerchief that was doing duty as a dance-floor. It was natural enough to clasp one another closely since there wasn't room to do anything else, and for a long, uncounted time they swayed in the noisy, smoky darkness shot with changing coloured lights, saying little while she tried not to imagine what it would be like to sleep with him. The heat and the din combined with the wine she had drunk at dinner to make her feel happy and giddy and quite unlike her usual self. She found herself wanting this evening to go on for ever and being well aware of how it was likely to end.

She felt out of her depth, as disoriented as the mouse which Malachi would pounce on, throw in the air, then drop in a fit of playfulness. Sometimes, faced with a choice between captivity or apparently limitless freedom, the mouse would run back to the waiting claws. She shivered.

'What is it?' he asked.

'Nothing. I'm a bit tired. Jet-lag catching up.'

'Of course,' he said at once. 'Let's go.'

Holding her hand, he pushed out of the crowd and led her into the star-bright courtyard. After the noisy disco, it seemed a haven of peace. Small squeaks and scuffles among the flowering shrubs told of another world about its nightly affairs. Bay steered her to a bench near the big birdcage.

'May I drop in and see you when you're up at Redstone?'

And get a foot into Naboth's Vineyard? She shook her head.

'Better not. I gather my uncle isn't keen on visitors. It would be a pity to waste your journey.'

'You could warn him I was coming.'

'I'd rather you didn't. Not until I know what he's like.'

He was silent, tense as a hunting cat, and she sensed frustration. Then he said lightly, 'In that case, we must make the most of tonight,' and took her in his arms.

For an instant he felt her recoil and contract like a startled snake about to strike. Then her body leaned towards him in a warm, natural response. His lips found hers, gently touching, exploring.

I should have escaped when I had the chance, she thought with a remote part of her brain. I didn't really want to. I've chosen the claws.

'Come to my room,' he murmured.

Again she thought, Why not? No one will know. No one will be hurt or betrayed. I'm a free agent. All she had to do was put her mind in neutral and abandon herself to the simple physical pleasure of feeling a man's mouth on hers, his hands moving over neck and shoulders, breasts and thighs, awakening hungry senses.

'No,' said a voice she hardly knew was her own. She tried to pull free, and for a panicky moment struggled against the velvet embrace which had suddenly turned to steel. So must the mouse feel when Malachi tightened his claws.

'Don't you want to?' Unhurriedly he released her.

'It – it's too soon.'

'Why should that matter?' She could tell from his tone that he was smiling. 'Getting to know someone isn't a question of time.'

Sally's pulse hammered unevenly and despite the night's warmth her body felt cold, cheated.

'I can't explain, but it does matter – to me, at any rate.

I'm afraid these – temporary arrangements – aren't in my line.'

His laugh was warm, genuinely amused. 'Aren't they? Oh well. I'll see you back to your room.'

'Don't bother.'

'I'd like to.'

In silence they walked back to the lobby and climbed to the first floor. She felt that her refusal had been stiff, ungracious; a bad end to the day which had started so well. He waited while she fumbled for her key, and she wondered if she would resist if he tried to force his way in.

'All right?' he said, as she fitted it in the lock. 'Good night then, and good luck. Enjoy your holiday. I'll drop in and see you if I get the chance.'

'No, don't –' she began, but he was gone, lifting a hand in farewell and strolling away down the long passage. Slowly she turned the key and went inside.

CHAPTER FIVE

BENJAMIN KARIUKI STOOD on the newly constructed platform of planks above the saltpan, staring down at the place where the buildings would soon rise out of the forest. Kariuki was a fighter, and he had battled long and hard to realise his dream of an Elephant Research Station deep in the forests of the Aberdare range. Not only did he appreciate the importance of Kenya's exotic wildlife to his country's flourishing tourist trade; he liked elephants for their own sake, having had in his youth unrivalled opportunities for getting to know them. To the huge pachyderms who had shown him their secret paths and warned him of danger he owed his life many times over.

Short and thickset, his crinkled hair was touched with grey at the temples, and his immense natural dignity enhanced by a gait so stately that he appeared to be leaning slightly backward. Kariuki was now a statesman respected by black and white alike, his murky past well buried under a sheaf of degrees and doctorates from Western universities. But now his heavy brow was lowered in a ferocious scowl which creased his eyes until they almost disappeared. His flared nostrils curled disgustedly as he surveyed the burly foreman of the work-gang whose powerful plaid-shirted form cringed with self-abasement.

The glistening expanse of fresh concrete foundation, the result of many days' labour, which had lain smooth as a sheet of ice the previous night when the gang left the site, had been ploughed and trampled into a sticky morass from which jagged lumps of setting concrete stuck up like smashed floes after the passage of an ice-breaker. The whole foundation would have to be hacked out and reconcreted, and Benjamin Kariuki was furious.

'Who is responsible for this damage?' he thundered, although he knew as well as the foreman did that there was only one way to account for the ruined concrete.

There was a long pause.

'Elephants have broken the fence,' faltered the foreman eventually.

'Did I not give orders that the fence should be electrified?'

'*N'dio, mzee.*'

'How did an elephant break an electric fence?'

There was another, even longer pause.

'How?' demanded Kariuki again.

'There is a *thahu* on the generator,' muttered the foreman, avoiding his eyes.

Kariuki experienced a sudden rush of longing for the old days when he could have signalled to aides who would have been standing behind the burly foreman. They would have stepped forward and strangled him, and so put an end to the matter. But those days were past: now other punishment must be devised. Mr Hamilton would arrive soon and wonder why the work was behind schedule. Someone must be punished or Kariuki would lose face. It was unfortunate that the foreman himself was too useful to be sacrificed in such a cause.

'If there is a *thahu* on the generator, a guard should be set,' he said more moderately. 'Was there a guard?'

'*N'dio*,' lied the foreman. He glanced furtively into Kariuki's face to assess his change of mood.

'Where was the guard when the elephants broke the fence?'

'He was sleeping. He was tired from working all day long.'

'You tell me this fellow can sleep while elephants destroy the fence?' Kariuki flung out a menacing hand.

'The guard was frightened and ran away,' amended the foreman, gladly shifting the blame to his mythical night watchman.

'Where is this man now?'

Hastily searching his mind for a suitable scapegoat, the foreman reviewed various men who owed him money or favours and chose an ideal candidate. Kipogo was a scoundrelly youth who had lain with the foreman's daughter and removed her second apron. Subsequently he had refused to pay the bride-price on the grounds that the girl had not been properly circumcised – a claim refuted both by her mother and the old crone who had performed the operation. The foreman decided that Kipogo should bear the weight of Kariuki's wrath.

'I will bring him to you,' he promised, happy to escape.

Kariuki guessed what was in his mind, but it didn't worry him. After all, every man had scores to settle. He nodded curtly and ordered that the perimeter fence should be strengthened. If the elephant tried to break in again, shots must be fired to scare him away.

The arrival of Nolan Matthews in the crowded noonday bar of the Norfolk Hotel caused the kind of stir associated in Sally's mind with the arrival of a fox in the henhouse.

As the rangy bush-shirted figure with its white mane and deeply-lined, deeply-tanned face stalked through the raftered entrance and halted, surveying the bar, a sudden hush fell on the noisy company. Even if no one actually turned tail and fled, there was a perceptible drawing-back of those nearest the door, to leave a clear passage down which the old man strode, looking neither to left nor right.

Sally, sipping mango juice at a corner table, keeping an eye on her packed suitcases, recognised him at once from old photographs. He was older, of course: scrawnier and swarthier than the man with his arm round Aunt Janet in the picture on her mother's dressing-table. There was a bitter twist to the mouth, and heavy eyebrows hid the expression in those deep-set eyes; the bush-shirt hung rather slackly from bony shoulders which must once have filled it properly.

'Uncle Matt!' she said into the silence, and heads turned as if jerked round by a string, to stare at her. Memories of the coroner's inquest with its blurred, gaping, inquisitive faces came flooding back.

The old man turned at the sound of her voice. For an instant he stood stockstill, rigid, as if taken unaware by some nerve-tingling echo from the past which stripped his defences away. He looked more than ever like a wild animal – wary, wily – caught in the beam of a flashlight. The guarded expression vanished, leaving his face astonished and so vulnerable that she felt a wave of pity. Her nervousness fled. This wasn't an ogre at all. This was just a lonely old man, isolated by pride and sorrow, who had rebuffed all overtures of help or friendship from his fellows until they preferred to turn their backs when he appeared.

'You're the image of Jan at that age,' her mother had often told her; but to Sally it had meant nothing. She had seen no special resemblance between her modern self and that slim girl with her dated square-shouldered dresses, her curly hair scraped into a towering beehive style, who smiled from her mother's photograph album. Nothing more striking than a general family likeness. The effect on Nolan Matthews, though, was startling. He seemed at a loss for words.

'Hello,' Sally said, moving forward to bridge the awkward pause, and at once the question of whether to shake hands or kiss this uncle she'd never met resolved itself quite naturally.

She took his hand and leaned forward, and without hesitation his leathery cheek bumped gently against her face. The first contact had been made, the first hurdle crossed. She felt an immense relief. Laughter and conversation were resumed throughout the bar. People turned back to their drinks and stopped staring. Although she was still aware of curious glances, they now seemed friendly, even admiring.

'How about a drink before we go?' she suggested, and Matthews nodded.

'Good idea.'

His voice was husky as if he were struggling with suppressed emotion, or perhaps he had lost the habit of small-talk. Again she felt protective.

'What'll you have?'

'What? Oh . . . anything.' He darted glances at her from beneath shaggy eyebrows.

She ordered two Tuskers and launched into a description of her journey to give him time to recover his composure.

The Tuskers arrived, ice-cold. He drained his glass and immediately signalled for more.

'You're the image of your Aunt Janet,' he said abruptly, and the act of putting his thought into words seemed to relax him. 'Sound like her, too. Gave me quite a turn. Sorry if I – well – ' He searched briefly for the appropriate words, gave up, and lapsed into silence.

'I know. My mother used to say so, too.'

'Ah. Penelope. Fine woman. All those years, she was the only one to keep writing. Kept me posted about the family. Sorry she died. Did you hang on to the house . . . Oxlees, Coxlease, some name like that?'

We'll have to plough through all this, Sally thought. It's an unavoidable part of getting to know one another. Where do you live? What do you do? It's as important as setting out your pawns in a game of chess. Only in rare cases dare one plunge straight in with the fighting pieces, and then the game usually ends in a rout. Like with Bay, yesterday. He tried to skip the groundwork and look what happened. With Uncle Matt, at least, she must take no short cuts.

The two black boys waiting by the Toyota truck piled her luggage in the back and were briefly introduced as Karanja and Waseru. They hopped in on top of the luggage, the engine coughed into life, and Matthews drove into the stream of traffic heading along Uhuru Avenue.

It took them most of the journey to bring Uncle Matt up to date on family affairs, and Sally's throat was sore from pitching her voice above the whine of the transmission before they reached the slopes of the Aberdare range of mountains and turned on to a dusty red murram track that wound steeply through dark trees.

The old man drove fast and said little, merely barking out a new question as soon as she finished answering the previous one. As he swung the Toyota off the tarmac on to soft red dust he turned and gave a shy grin that made him look far less formidable. She thought with surprise that he must once have been extremely attractive.

'Sorry to grill you like this – must think I'm the Gestapo or something. Change for me to hear an English voice, y'know. Better shut your window now, and keep the rest till later. This dust is the very devil in your throat.'

She was glad of the respite. After a mile or two of crashing over vicious potholes at twenty miles an hour, they took another left turn into what appeared to be a dry river bed between crumbling red banks. Once they passed a black man in ragged khaki shorts, weaving and wobbling along on an ancient bicycle. He jumped off and stood with head averted until the dustcloud passed. Skinny-legged *totos* herded goats beside the tracks, and they too turned away as the vehicle approached. The bends became tighter, the gradient steeper. Sally's ears began to pop. The tyres scrabbled for a grip on patches of bare rock, or sank into thick soft dust that would become a quagmire when it rained.

'Is this your front drive?' she shouted over the engine's roar.

'What? Yes. Only way in. Easier on a horse.'

She couldn't believe he'd have much trouble with casual visitors. No one in his senses would tackle this track unless sure of a warm welcome. The trees closed in, lush and green, a wall of vegetation interspersed with sedgy clearings.

She saw a movement on the right of the track and gasped. The black hump she'd spotted turned to display a haughty, aggressive head with an upturned rubbery muzzle. Its great horns swept upward like the bouffant hairdo of a fifties model.

Sally nudged Matthews and pointed, hoping he'd stop for a better view.

'Buff,' said Matthews, not stopping. 'Nasty-tempered sods. Never wound a buffalo. Either kill it stone dead or leave well alone, that's my rule.'

'You can't blame it for being nasty-tempered if you shoot at it,' she pointed out. 'I thought shooting was illegal, anyway.'

'Oh, it is. It is.' He gave a bark of laughter. 'But has anyone told the buffs?'

'You mean you still shoot them?'

He turned to give her a long considering look. 'Not one of those damned conservationist hot-air merchants, are you, my girl?'

It was difficult to argue over the engine-noise. 'If you mean am I against shooting animals, the answer's yes,' she shouted.

'Well, that won't last long when you try to farm out here,' he said, and changed into a still lower gear which made conversation impossible.

'When you try to farm.' Not 'if,' or 'Should you ever . . .' Just the simple bald 'When'. She wondered what made him think she wanted to.

'Nearly there,' said Matt, breaking a mile-long silence. She was glad to hear it. The truck bumped over a cattle-grid flanked by aggressively-lettered twin signs: HAPANA RAHUSA KWA WAGENI KUINGIA HAPA.

'What does that mean?' she asked.

'Keep out. No trespassers.'

She couldn't help laughing. They hadn't seen a single

human being since passing the goat-herding *watoto*.

Matt gave her a sharp sideways glance. 'No joke. If I didn't take steps to stop 'em they'd be swarming all over the place.'

'What kind of steps, Uncle Matt?'

'Usually put a couple of rounds over the black apes' heads,' he said. 'If that's not enough, I set the dogs on 'em. Used to get a lot of trouble with joyriding maniacs driving up to ask if I'd sell the place. Trying it on. They don't do that any more. Got the message.'

Sally was glad she had discouraged Bay from dropping in for a social call. The track climbed between tall stands of straight-trunked gum trees which gave off a delicious smell. Between these regular stands were weedy, rank-looking paddocks fenced roughly with cedar rails, many of them broken and roughly cobbled together with sagging wire. Small humped native cattle grazed side by side with Friesian-Hereford crosses. Many had scabs and sores. The stockman in Sally was not impressed.

'Are those yours?' she called, pointing, and Matt gave an indifferent nod.

'Rubbishy beasts,' he said dismissively.

Then why keep them? she wondered. They passed more fields with sheep and goats, untidy native shambas growing maize and cabbages which looked flourishing in contrast to the stunted irregular rows of coffee bushes and sparse cornfields. What a mess, she thought, suddenly depressed. Obviously the farm had been neglected for years, just as Bay had said.

They rounded a corner and as the ground dropped away before them she saw a long, low building set like a pink jewel in a smooth bowl of green velvet.

'Oh!' she exclaimed in surprise and pleasure. She had been beginning to imagine Redstone Farm as a tin shanty surrounded by parched earth.

Matt switched off the engine and in the blessed silence they sat and stared at the peaceful, graceful building basking in soft evening sun. In front of the pink-washed house and outbuildings, the hill which they had laboriously climbed dropped away in ridge after forested ridge until it flattened out to melt into the darkening plain below, while behind the farm rose a range of snow-capped peaks, a mighty escarpment over which the sun hung in a ball of fire.

'Like it?' he said, with that quick sidelong glance.

'It's beautiful. What a view! Can we get out for a moment?'

She felt for the doorcatch, swung it open, and was about to slide to the ground when Matt gave a low incoherent growl.

She turned. He was staring fixedly at the farm below, but his expression had changed. His lips were drawn back from his teeth in a snarl and his nostrils were pinched and white, giving him a mad, dangerous look.

'Who the devil's that?'

His hand jerked to the ignition. Hastily she slammed her door shut as he crashed into gear and the vehicle leapt forward, flinging the black boys into a heap among the groceries.

'What is it? What's the matter?' called Sally, alarmed at the way the truck was gathering speed until it hurtled down the winding track.

Matt didn't answer. The bared teeth and fixed eyes made him look completely irrational. She remembered Bay's casual: 'They say he's mad as a hatter.' It was beginning to seem horribly true. The truck rocked round a bend on two wheels and the boys moaned in unison.

'Stop!' She was now thoroughly frightened. 'You're going too fast.' She snatched at the handbrake between the seats, but he knocked her aside with a quick vicious blow that made her gasp with pain. It was like being struck by a twisted old branch.

'Those bastards,' he muttered. 'I'll get 'em this time.'

They hit the bottom of the hill and roared towards the farm, Matt's foot flat on the accelerator, his knuckles white as they gripped the wheel. Between the farmyard itself and the surrounding fields was a short narrow lane and another grid. Racing towards it from the opposite direction, obviously bent on escape, was a dust-covered Peugeot station-wagon with two men inside. It was plain that Matthews intended to ram it.

As the two vehicles roared at the grid on a collision course, Sally saw the faces of the Peugeot passengers. A scrawny African dressed in some kind of uniform was at the wheel, his hand flat on the horn, his mouth open, shouting. Beside him sat a rocklike chunky figure, also black, wearing a pale-blue suit and silvered reflecting sun-glasses.

The narrow lane was fenced. Even if the Peugeot braked it would have no room in which to dodge the heavy truck's onrush.

'Got 'em,' exulted Matthews in a low, savage snarl.

Sally felt cold with dread. He was stark staring mad and he was going to kill them all.

'Stop!' she screamed.

The vehicles were only fifty yards and converging on the grid when she reached for the handbrake again, and this time her fist closed round it before Matthews noticed. She jerked it upward with all her might. The truck slewed sideways and continued towards the grid with its front wheels off the track, raising a blinding cloud of dust. The oncoming car didn't hesitate. Scraping its length recklessly along the truck's side and wrenching off Sally's door in the process, it squeezed through the narrow gap, gathered speed, and roared off into the hills. For a moment the Toyota went on skidding sideways and Sally heard Matt's curses as he fought to get it under control. She clutched the back of her seat, waiting for the impact.

It came. The squat bonnet struck the stout bracing post to the left of the grid with a jarring shock that catapulted her against the windscreen. The side of her head hit the twisted metal of the door-frame, and she pitched forward into a roaring darkness streaked with flashing lights.

'Bloody apes! Bloody interfering bitch!' exploded Matt, jumping out and staring after the Peugeot in baffled rage. 'Why did you do that?' He turned furiously on Sally, and the anger faded from his face. 'Oh, my God!'

The boys were picking themselves out of the tumbled heap of luggage and groceries, rubbing their bruises.

'Karanja! Waseru! Come here. Pick up the memsaab with care and carry her to the house, *pese-pese*.' Even Matt could see that this was not the most auspicious way for his niece to arrive at Redstone Farm.

CHAPTER SIX

'BWANA, BWANA! Come and look!'

Bay Hamilton swam up through mists of sleep and opened an eye to see the sharp, animated face of Kidogo, his cook-boy, peering in through the tent's fly-screen in the pearly light of dawn.

He groaned. His mouth was as dry as the Kalahari and he wished he'd had the sense to leave the whisky alone last night. He and Clem Fairbrother, the black-bearded veterinary officer assigned to the area, had sat up late by the camp-fire, yarning about the ways of elephant and lowering the whisky level. Now Kidogo, whose uncertain English seemed to have broken down completely in the stress of the moment, was pouring out an excited flood of Swahili from which Bay gathered that during the hours of darkness the biggest elephant in the world had fallen into the mud of the saltpan and expired.

'Go and wake bwana Mira'a,' he ordered, struggling out of his sleeping-bag. Fairbrother's addiction to his villainous pipes had earned him the nickname of *Mira'a* – chewing-twig.

'*N'dio*, bwana.' The boy ran off.

Ten minutes later the three of them stood on the rim of the saltpan, where the rest of the work-force had already gathered, chattering excitedly as they stared at the fallen giant.

It was one of the biggest elephants Bay had ever seen. Even collapsed in an ungainly heap, half-kneeling, half-lying, it looked the size of a tank. Most of its head was buried in the mud, but the trunk rested on the rim of the hole it had dug, and as Bay watched intently he saw the fingered tip move very slightly, like a blind man groping for support.

'He's not dead yet,' he said, pointing.

'Soon will be unless we get him out of there,' grunted Clem, chewing the stem of his empty pipe.

'Dig him out? It's worth a try,' Bay agreed.

Together they prowled all round the trapped beast, stepping delicately on the saltpan's crust, studying angles, assessing possibilities. As they did so the trunk waved again, a mute appeal for help. The boys' chatter rose to a crescendo.

'It won't be easy,' said Clem. He tamped tobacco into his pipe. 'He's a big chap and he's pretty far gone. It looks to me as if there's some kind of infection around his ear, but I can't really tell because he's shoved it so far into the mud. Still, we've got the equipment we need to have a crack at dragging him out, and after that it'll be up to him. Are you with me?'

'All the way,' said Bay. 'What is it, Nelson?'

The burly, plaid-shirted foreman stepped forward, bursting with self-importance. 'This is the bad *ndovu* who has broken the fence. He has spoiled the concrete and done much damage. He must be shot. It is the orders of His Excellency.'

Clem made a rude noise. 'Balls to His Excellency. If the High Muckamuck wants this fellow shot he'll have to do it himself. I'm not putting a bullet through the brain of a fine specimen like this. There are few enough elephants round here as it is.'

'He can't have it both ways,' Bay agreed. 'Either you have elephants and put up with the damage, or you don't have elephants.'

'Where was our gallant night-watchman while all this drama was enacted?' asked Clem, looking round for the guard.

Bay laughed. 'Asleep on the job, of course! Either he's a

galloping case of *encephalitis lethargica* or he's been at your morphinomimetics. Right, what's our next move?'

They walked back to camp, planning the rescue, listing the equipment they would need. Ropes, sacks to pad them, water, hosepipes. Sedatives, antiseptics. The big JCB with the foreloading scoop. Two caterpillar tractors. Already the sun was gathering strength: at noon the unshaded saltpan would be like an oven. The first essential was to protect the mud-encrusted hulk from literally baking to death in the heat.

Bay called the boys together and issued orders. Once they understood what was planned they worked with a will, delighted with the break from routine. While one team laid a pipeline from the camp's water supply to the edge of the pan, another drove the JCB up the slope and began to scoop a path through the mud, along which the prostrate elephant could be dragged with ropes.

As soon as the pipeline was connected, Clem clambered cautiously over the treacherous surface crust, carrying a large wet gunny-sack and the trickling end of the hose. The sack he placed over the elephant's head as a compress which would also act as a blindfold should the patient recover enough to raise objections to their ministrations. The hose he inserted into the corner of the elephant's mouth and fed it in gently until a foot or so had descended into the gullet.

For ten minutes he held it there: then a convulsive heave and thrashing of the patient's tail warned that such proximity was dangerous. Clem withdrew to a safer distance from which he continued to spray the gunny-sack with water.

Meanwhile, Bay was supervising the digging which had run into problems. The mud was both softer and deeper than he had realised. Very soon the JCB driver's enthusiasm over-rode his caution and he ventured too near the edge which suddenly caved in beneath the machine's weight. The driver jumped clear, but with a loud squelch the JCB settled into liquid mud until it was as helplessly trapped as the elephant itself.

'Hell's teeth,' swore Bay. He sent two more drivers to bring up their machines.

Three hours later as the sun rose to its height, the site looked like a wreckers' yard. Two caterpillar tractors had joined the JCB in the mud, which plastered the entire work-force from head to foot. Chains had snapped, ropes broken, hopes been dashed and tempers frayed. Still the stranded elephant lay hunched in his self-dug grave, only the feebly waving trunk to show that he was still alive. In the heat the strong ammoniac stench from the hole was overpowering.

'It's hopeless,' said Clem at last. He tapped out his pipe on a rock with such force that the stem cracked clean across. 'Damn! How I hate machinery! If one small part breaks, the whole thing becomes US. I suppose I'll have to put a bullet through his brain after all. Kinder, really. Poor old chap.'

'Wait a bit, we're not beaten yet,' said Bay obstinately. The mechanical setbacks had only hardened his determination that the elephant should be rescued. 'Even if you shoot him we'll still have to get him out of there or he'll stink to high heaven.' He thought for a moment. 'Look, we'll have one more try. Do you think you can keep him alive while Nelson and I fetch that big crawler parked by the Redstone mailbox? I noticed it on the way up, and I think it would do the trick. It's far more powerful than anything we've got here.'

'Steady on, old chap. You can't take that,' protested Clem. 'That belongs to Matthews. He'd have your hide.'

'Perhaps he'll lend it to us.'

'Some hope. Old Matthews never lends anything to anyone. All the locals are scared stiff of the old devil: that's why he can leave his machines parked in the open.'

Bay said, 'We'll have to borrow it without asking, then. Come on, Nelson, round up a couple of boys and bring your mechanic's bag of tricks. I don't suppose he's left the key in her. See you later, Clem.'

He swung away down the hill. With a shrug Clem searched his pockets for another blackened pipe, filled and lit it, and turned his attention once more to his enormous patient.

Karel van Ryn drew his horse to a halt on the ridge overlooking the tall stand of blue gums that separated Redstone Farm from the Dante Tea Estate, and signed to Sally to do the same. All around the untamed forest of the Reserve stretched dense and unbroken, a green sea whose waves washed greedily right up to the shores of these two small islands of cultivation. Naboth's Vineyard, thought Sally. No wonder Bay longed to swallow them up in his Elephant Research Station.

She looked enquiringly at Karel, wondering what was on his mind. Since showing her the mailbox at the junction he had scarcely spoken a word.

'How do you get on with old Matt?' he asked now, giving her a glance that was both curious and confidential, an invitation to share secrets. 'Will you be able to stick it out for another week up there?'

Serena had described him as dishy, and it was easy to see how his wide shoulders and muscled legs, his tanned, sun-bleached, cowboyish good looks would appeal to a woman whose husband had lost his hair and his figure a decade before. Easy to see, too, that Mynheer van Ryn was far from being unaware of the effect his handsome face and powerful physique produced on most women, thought Sally rather uncharitably. He sat his breedy bay horse with a hint of swagger, and his wide, engaging grin seemed to invite indiscretions.

'Oh, we get on fine,' she said, disliking the hint of complicity, the suggestion of telling tales out of school. 'I'm really enjoying my visit.'

She thought he looked faintly disappointed. 'I heard he landed you in the ditch the moment you arrived.'

Sally laughed. 'Yes – it was quite exciting! I thought the brakes must have failed. It was amazing that Matt managed to keep the truck on the road at all.'

'That's not what Karanja told me,' said van Ryn. 'He said the bwana was chasing another car.' He cocked an eyebrow at her. 'If you hadn't grabbed the handbrake, someone would have been badly hurt. Perhaps even killed. Wasn't that more like it?'

'Karanja was in the back and couldn't possibly see what was happening,' she said firmly. 'You know how they dramatise things.'

'Nice for Matt to have someone to back up his story.' Again she was aware of the speculation in his glance. 'You don't scare easy, do you, Sally?'

'Oh, I was absolutely terrified. Gibbering!'

She remembered Serena's warning. Better not let him think she was usurping his privileges, threatening his position as Matt's link with the outside world. It was disturbing to learn that he had been questioning the servants: she wondered what they had told him about herself.

'That I very much doubt. Girls like you don't scare easy,' he repeated. 'Not when they're on to a good thing.' His blue eyes were suddenly hostile. 'I expect Matt tells you a lot about the old days. Big game hunting, and so on?'

She hesitated. 'Well, it's hardly my scene . . .'

'I'm sure he enjoys yarning about his exploits. It's a long time since he had a captive audience.'

Softlee, softlee . . . Sally produced a girlish shudder that was not entirely contrived. 'How all those trophies met their respective ends? Those poor stuffed heads with glass eyes watching you from every corner?'

Now she had hit the correct note. Van Ryn barked with contemptuous macho laughter. 'You don't like them? Your uncle was a famous elephant hunter, you know.'

'Well, I suppose I should be thankful the rooms aren't

full of tusks,' said Sally. Uncertain how long she could maintain the helpless pose he obviously liked, she gathered up the reins. 'Thanks for showing me the way.'

'Wait a bit.' He checked her cob with a hand on the bit. 'Don't you wonder what happened to all those tusks? Have you asked him?'

'I told you, I'm not interested in hunting stories. Anyway, it's illegal nowadays, isn't it?'

'And ivory's worth a lot of money.'

She stared at him, trying to guess his meaning. *Poaching*, Mark had said, *and your uncle's in it up to his neck*.

She said carefully, 'Are you telling me that Matt still shoots elephants, despite the ban?'

'I'm not telling you anything.' He glanced at his handsome gold watch and flicked an insect from his fringed suede jacket. Both looked expensive: too good to ride in. He was evidently a sharp dresser.

'Then why?'

He smiled. 'I'm suggesting you keep your eyes open while you stay at Redstone.'

'And tell you what I see?'

'It might be . . . profitable. For both of us. Very few people get the opportunity. You're a lucky lady, Sally.' He leaned towards her and she caught the whiff of spirits. 'You might consider why it is that your uncle chases visitors off his property, and why no elephant that steps over the Redstone boundary is ever seen again. Think about it. You're a clever girl: you might even come up with an answer.'

He raised his wide-brimmed hat in flamboyant farewell and wheeled his mare in a tight turn. Sally watched him canter away down the green slope and glance back to make sure she was watching before making a showy jump over the boundary rail. Leaving the reins loose on Caesar's neck she rode thoughtfully uphill towards the farm.

*

As Bay had guessed, the crawler tractor belonging to Nolan Matthews had a winch with twice the pulling power of any other vehicle on the site. It was equipped with an immense chain; with this attached to the doubled ropes thickly padded with vine-stuffed sacks, which Clem and his helpers had managed to infiltrate beneath the belly of the comatose, drugged elephant and fastened in a sort of harness across his spine, all seemed set for the big pull.

Digging beneath the patient had been a delicate, hazardous operation. Two men had been hurt, one with a dislocated shoulder when an unexpected convulsion from the elephant trapped his arm and only quick action by his workmates freed him alive.

Nevertheless, team morale was high as Clem gave the knots a final check and raised his arm, signalling to Nelson, at the crawler's controls, to take up the strain. Slowly the winch turned and the heavy links clanked as they straightened out. The harness tightened round the elephant's body and Bay, watching anxiously, saw the mud-encrusted skin pucker like a tomato about to burst as the padded sacks bit deeper and deeper into the flesh.

With a loud sucking sound, the head, body, and three legs came free, but the elephant's off-hindleg was still stuck in the mud and stretched out at an angle which seemed certain to pull the hip from its socket.

'Stop!' he shouted, dropping his arm.

'Quick, everyone!' Clem wielded his spade like a madman. 'Get that leg free before – he – slides back –'

They were all round the huge wrinkled body in an instant, burrowing with the single-minded fury of terriers at a badger sett. Some had spades and some scooped up the sloppy mud with bare hands.

'Hurry,' Clem urged. 'He can't stand this much longer.'

Had the elephant moved at that stage, he could hardly have avoided injuring one or more of his rescuers, digging and pushing and shoving in the confined space. Slowly the knee came into sight, the foot, the great stubby toenails.

'Haul away!' shouted Bay.

Nelson engaged gear, the ropes tightened and strained . . . and the whole grey-red body slid smoothly out of its hole and across the saltpan crust.

Whooping with triumph, the gang ran after it, guiding the ropes into the winch as Nelson wound it up close to where the crawler was parked beneath the shade of a group of kigelias. Then he slacked off the strain, and they all gathered round the inert mass in sudden silence.

'Is he alive?' It was hard to believe that any animal, even an elephant, could survive such treatment.

'We'll soon find out. I'll give him an antidote in a few minutes, but first I want a look at that wound.' Clem picked up his black instrument case. They all watched while he inspected the wound and swelling behind the elephant's ear, and called for water and carbolic.

'It looks like the work of a poisoned arrow,' he said, frowning. 'I thought the poachers round here had stopped using those damned things. He's been trying to disinfect the wound, poor old fellow. That's how he came to topple in. Look at the ivory he's carrying! Must be a hundred a side, at least.'

The work-force, almost as mud-covered as the elephant himself, was already exclaiming and pointing to the immense curved tusks.

'Has he got a chance?' asked Bay.

'Shouldn't wonder. These old boys are pretty tough.' Clem tapped his teeth with his pipe. 'I'll get that wound cleaned out and give him a few shots of this and that while he's out for the count,' he said at last. 'May be the only chance I'll get. You put the boys on to building a boma for him and mind they make it strong. Chap like this can bust his way through most things, and I'd like to keep an eye on him for a day or two. After that he'll have to take his chance.'

As Sally rode back up the hill after leaving Karel, she felt an extraordinary sense of well-being. She was hot, but not too hot. The sun struck pleasantly through her shirt; round the horizon high-piled clouds like mounds of whipped cream sailed proudly, their shadows softening the glare. After three hours in the saddle she was tired, but not too tired. Caesar was a cheerful willing ride: a chunky, liver-chestnut cob who could practically open gates without assistance.

Think of England now, she told herself. February Fill-Dyke. Fog, frost, mud, rain. Bare branches, bare fields, the bone-chilling damp of the Chilterns. Trains delayed, buses cancelled. 'Flu. Poor old Julian will be carrying bales of hay to hungry animals, eating woolly apples and sleepy pears. I hope that girlfriend of his can cook. Her nephew Julian, studying Agriculture at Reading University, had leapt at the chance to 'farm-sit' for her.

'It'll count towards my Practical,' he said. 'In fact, if you could see your way to staying abroad for a whole year, Sally . . .'

She'd laughed and said she doubted if it would come to that.

'Pity. Still, make it as long as you can.'

Julian and his tubby little girlfriend Jinty, with old Froud to act as anchorman, formed a team more than capable of dealing with any farm crisis. In fact, by Redstone standards, farming in the Chilterns seemed positively suburban.

Matt was waiting on the verandah when she rode up the last slope and dismounted. She handed Caesar's reins to Karanja.

'Good boy!' She patted the chestnut's neck and Karanja led him away.

'Did you get your letter?' called Matt.

'Yes, they'd both written. Lots of news. Tim had a trial for the Under-Elevens . . .' She broke off in surprise as she took in his appearance. Her uncle was resplendent in a white linen jacket and black bow-tie instead of the usual faded bush-shirt. 'You look too beautiful! What's up?'

'Thought a little celebration might be in order,' he said, darting a sidelong glance under the bushy brows, enjoying her surprise. 'Told Mbugwa to put a bottle of the Krug on ice. At least it'll do to wash down his damned cake.'

'Cake?'

He chuckled. 'You look just like your Aunt Jan! Got her to blame for the cake. Taught Mbugwa how to make it – he's never forgotten. Never had anyone to share the damned thing before.'

Light dawned. 'You mean, today's your birthday? Why didn't you tell me?' She felt the helpless confusion of those caught unprepared and presentless.

'Telling you now, aren't I? Seventy-five or near as dammit. Tell you the truth, forgot about it myself until that black rascal reminded me. Wanted to try out his cake on you.'

'Well, congratulations! Many happy returns!' She kissed him on both cheeks. 'Wait till I've washed off some of this dust and then we'll really celebrate. Champagne!'

'Took you long enough to get there and back. Lose your way?'

Sally hesitated. 'No. I met Karel van Ryn. He showed me where the mailbox is.'

Matt gave a derisive snort. 'Easy enough to find with a damned great yellow crawler parked on top of it! Hard to miss.'

'That was the odd thing – the tractor wasn't there.' She saw his disbelief and added, 'Karel was surprised, too.'

His lined features creased in an indulgent smile. 'You young people! Talking your heads off – probably rode straight past it.'

'I tell you it wasn't there.' Sally controlled her irritation. 'Anyway, we hardly talked at all. Karel seemed abstracted.'

'That boy drinks too much. Going the same way as his

father,' said Matt flatly. 'Poor old Dick couldn't hit a haystack at ten paces after a couple of Scotches. No head for the hard stuff.' He brooded for a moment. 'The tractor wasn't there?'

'Not a sign of it.'

'Then who the hell's moved it?'

Her uncle's face assumed a dark-red hue against which his white eyebrows stood out in alarming contrast. 'Nobody's got any damned business monkeying around with my tractor. Karanja!'

As Sally slipped away to bathe and change, she heard the storm of Matt's wrath break over the household, followed by great runnings and shoutings and revving of engines as a search party was sent to look for the missing vehicle.

The Krug was superb and the cake with its seventy-five candles was a masterpiece of green and white and chocolate icing. Sally made her uncle blow out the candles with a single puff, and wish, then she sang *Happy Birthday to You*. But her voice sounded thin and lonely, and it was a sad little party in spite of her efforts to inject an air of gaiety into it. She was haunted by the thought of all those other, sadder, lonelier birthdays when Matt must have eaten his splendid cake alone in silence. It would never have occurred to him to ask Mbugwa and Charles, the houseservants, to sit down and share it.

Once he roused himself from brooding over his missing tractor to say, 'We ought to have those young rascals of yours here to polish off the grub. Brace of schoolboys with good appetites would make short work of that cake. You'll have to bring 'em out here next time you come.'

'I'm not sure . . .' began Sally, but Matt was muttering aloud to himself as if he'd forgotten that she could hear.

'Had time to think it over now. Bound to accept, but can she cope? That's the puzzle: will she be able to cope?'

'Hey, I'm still here! What are you talking about?'

'Eh, what? Rubbish! Didn't say a word.'

Emboldened by champagne, she decided to call his bluff

It was by no means the first of these oblique comments.

'Yes, you did. You must have been thinking aloud. Wondering if I could cope with something. What was it?'

'Cope with the blacks, of course. No problem about running the farm: natural stockman – woman, I should say. Born, not made. But can you cope with the blacks? No good treating them soft; they take advantage of it. Keep 'em in their place, that's the ticket. My old father had a rhyme about it.'

He put down his glass and cleared his throat.

'If you gently touch the nettle, he will sting you for your pains. Grasp him like a man of metal: he from hurting you refrains. So it is with human nature: treat them gently, they rebel. Be as harsh as nutmeg-grater and the knaves will serve you well.'

He paused for applause. 'Sound advice, eh?'

Sally was torn between laughter and embarrassment. Charles, at his post behind her uncle's chair, had heard every word.

'Oh dear, I'm not much of a nutmeg-grater, I'm afraid. Nor a man of metal.'

'Rubbish. You can learn.'

'I doubt it.'

'You might have to if I leave you this place. Won't live for ever, you know,' he said aggressively, but she could see that he was disappointed by her reaction.

She said gently, 'I'm very grateful, and . . . honoured, but the trouble is I don't want to live here. My home's in England. There wouldn't be any point in leaving Redstone to me.'

'Don't be a fool, girl,' he snapped. 'Can't you see what you're throwing away? What have you got in England? Some rubbishy little smallholding with five acres and a cow? I'm offering you a slice of the finest country God ever made –'

He was interrupted by a sudden commotion outside the windows. Feet thudded, men shouted. There was the blast of a shot-gun from very close at hand, followed by the tinkle of breaking glass. From the kennel came the deep baying of the two Dobermans.

'What the devil?' Matt heaved up from his chair. He strode across to the gun-cupboard, removed a rifle and snapped it open.

'Visitors?' suggested Sally.

'More likely a jackal in the henhouse or a hyena after the calves. Stay where you are. I'll deal with this.' He hurried out, calling to Charles to loose the dogs.

Sally followed as far as the front door, but he barked at her again to stay inside, and uncertainly she returned to the dining-room. She had no great wish to see Matt shoot a hyena, and the thought of the havoc its lean jaws could wreak in the calf-pen was not a pleasant one. It occurred to her that the medicine chest might soon be needed, and she fetched it from the bathroom.

Outside the din continued, and she waited tensely for the sound of a shot.

Minutes crawled by and her curiosity became unbearable. The shouting had retreated into the distance: it sounded as if the boys had been formed into a cordon to beat through the rick-yard. She pushed open the french windows on to the verandah, and stood there silhouetted against the light, watching torchbeams flickering round the buildings. Faintly, from behind the barn, she could hear Matt's voice urging his dogs to hunt.

'Seek, seek, good dogs. Hansel, Gretel, leu in there. Push him out!'

The atavistic fear of the hunted sent a cold finger down Sally's spine. She wanted the hyena to escape. She imagined it slinking round the yard, red-eyed, slope-shouldered, waiting its chance to break through the cordon and lope away to the sheltering forest.

She stared into the dark. A shadow seemed to move under the verandah, rearing up on end. She strained her eyes, wondering if she'd imagined it. Then a scream rose bubbling in her throat and her heart nearly choked her as a tall shape sprang towards the guard rail, vaulted lightly over, and landed beside her.

A hard palm, sticky and salty, unmistakably smelling of blood, was clapped over her mouth, stifling her scream, while another pinioned her arms. She struggled in blind panic.

'Hush, Sally! Don't make a row. It's me.' The well-remembered voice was vibrant with laughter.

He waited a moment longer, then cautiously removed the hand that gagged her. She sagged in his arms, weak with shock.

'Oh, that's more like it!' His arms tightened round her.

Sally pulled away, hot with indignation.

'My God, you gave me a fright! I thought it was the hyena. What are you doing here!'

'Didn't I say I'd drop in and see you?' He was panting, she realised, as well as laughing, and now she could see him in the light filtering through the french window she realised that his shirt was torn and blood was running down one arm, dripping on to the polished parquet.

'You're hurt. Come inside.' She pulled him through the window into the electric light and exclaimed in horror. 'Was that the dogs?'

'No, just a bit of broken glass. No need to make a fuss. It looks worse than it is. Only trouble, those damned dogs are sure to pick up my scent once they get past the pepper. Can you strap up this hand for me, and then I'll be on my way?'

'But why did you come? I warned you. I *told* you not to.' She worked swiftly with lint and scissors, annoyed to find that her hands were not steady.

'Don't worry, it's only a scratch,' he said soothingly. 'I'm sorry I gave you a fright, and I'll apologise to your uncle if he'll call off his dogs long enough to listen. I came to thank him for the loan of his tractor. Brought a bottle.'

He reached inside the tattered shirt and pulled out a litre of malt whisky. 'Thought this might keep out the chill during the rainy season,' he said, laughing. He put it down on the table and inspected the remains of the birthday feast, leaning down to read the cake's inscription in Mbugwa's flamboyant copperplate: '*Happy Birthday, Bwana*!'

'Well!' said Bay, impressed. 'It looks as if I've come on the right day. That's one hell of a fine cake.'

She didn't offer him any. '*You* pinched his tractor?'

'I don't suppose he's even noticed, but I thought it only civil to come and explain,' he said gravely, though his eyes still laughed. 'Besides, it gave me an excuse to visit you. Let's have a look.' He turned her to the light and stared intently. 'Are you really all right? I've been worried about you, up here alone with the Ogre of the Aberdares. You hear such stories . . . I wondered if I should have let you come here at all.'

'You'd have found it hard to stop me,' she retorted.

'I'd have thought up some way,' he said calmly.

His assumption that she was incapable of looking after herself irritated her. She wasn't used to being protected. With Mark it had been the other way round: she did the protecting of his high-powered brain, his precious leisure. She kept boredom at bay, arranged parties and holidays. She made excuses when Mark broke dates. He could always be guaranteed to find time for a party which promised excitement or glamour. It was the humdrum functions – school play, family funeral, village fete – that he was always too busy to attend. At the inquest she had learned how he spent the time while she apologised for his absence.

She said rather more sharply than she intended to: 'I expect Ahab thought up the same kind of excuse.'

'To get a look at the Vineyard?' The grey eyes glinted.

'Isn't that the real reason why you're here?'

'Six of one and half a dozen of the other,' he admitted. 'I was curious to see old Matthews' hideout – but I also wanted to check that the Ogre hadn't eaten you alive.'

'Don't call him that! It's none of your business anyway. You can keep your nose out of my affairs – they're nothing to do with you. As you can see, I'm alive and well and in no need of your assistance.'

'Well, that's clear enough.' He considered her for a moment in silence. 'It must be the air up here.'

'What are you talking about?' She gave the bandage an extra tight turn and he winced.

'This sudden desire for privacy. This ferocious defence of territory. A lioness with cubs has nothing on you. You spend a couple of weeks up here and bang! Down comes the portcullis and up goes the drawbridge. Repel boarders. Keep Out. Entry Forbidden. No hawkers, circulars or income tax. Old friends strictly unwelcome.'

'You're not an old friend.'

He came closer, and instinctively she backed away until she came up against the edge of the table. 'What have you got to hide, Sally?' he asked, and the very softness of his question made it full of menace. 'What are you so scared of?'

'I'm not scared of anything except Uncle Matt finding you here and blasting off his gun at you. I told you, he doesn't like strangers, particularly people who want to hound him off his land so that elephants can trample his crops and tear down his fences. Can you wonder that he fights back?'

'*Cet animal est mérchant. Quand on l'attaque, il se défendre,*' said Bay with a wry grin. 'It's his method of fighting back that concerns me. Redstone Farm isn't exactly a healthy spot for elephants, is it?'

'I don't know what you mean.'

'I think you do.'

She turned away so he couldn't see her face. Coming on top of her conversation with Karel van Ryn, this inquisition was decidedly unwelcome. Matt couldn't be a poacher: she wouldn't believe it.

Bay took her by the shoulders, pulling her round to face him with a force that was unexpectedly frightening. 'Don't play with fire, Sally. Don't let him fool you. Matthews may be old, but he hasn't lost his claws, and it's the lame old lion with nothing to lose which needs to be watched.'

'You're talking rubbish!' Angrily she shook herself free and went on to the verandah. 'All Matt wants is to be left in peace to run his farm.'

'Then why has he asked you here? What was your husband doing on his last visit to Kenya, poking into matters which weren't strictly his business and asking a lot of awkward questions?'

Sally's heart gave an uncomfortable lurch. 'Please leave my husband out of this.'

'I'd be glad to if I was sure you weren't about to run straight into the kind of trouble he ran into,' said Bay bluntly. 'Don't pretend you don't understand me.'

'Mark's death was an accident,' she whispered, feeling suddenly cold. 'It was nothing to do with . . . with Uncle Matt. He was tired. He had a few drinks –'

'And within a few months his grief-stricken widow is back in the place he'd just left. Taking a holiday. It's no good, Sally. It won't wash. Why don't you tell me everything you know and let me sort it out?'

Because I don't trust you. I don't know that you're not part of the racket yourself. She leaned on the rail, saying nothing. The baying of the dogs became louder, closer. They had picked up the bloodspoor.

She said with a queer sense of relief, 'He's coming back. You'd better have your excuses ready if you don't want to feel the old lion's teeth. Matt's been vowing death and destruction on the man who took his tractor. If he hadn't sent half the boys to look for it they'd have nabbed you before now. Why did you take it?'

'We used it to pull an elephant out of the saltpan. We've got him penned up in a boma now – he was nearly a goner.' Bay spoke abstractedly, his attention focused on the bobbing line of lights which could now be seen between the two barns. 'No. On second thoughts, I'll be on my way. Look in and see our elephant some time – you might have a change of heart about the Research Station. Oh, and Sally –'

As she turned a questioning face towards him, he bent swiftly and kissed her on the lips. 'Thanks for patching me up,' he whispered. 'It was worth the journey just to see you.'

She didn't believe him – didn't want to believe him. It was obvious that he enjoyed the hunt. The danger sharpened his senses: the dark night was his friend. He was more than a match for Matt and his blundering dogs.

'Go away,' she said fiercely. 'Go away and stay away.'

He raised his head, listening; eyes narrowed, body tense. 'That's more than I can promise.' With a light, almost dancing step he moved out of the circle of lamplight, laid a hand on the rail and vaulted into the velvet darkness. She heard the soft thud of his landing and a muffled laugh. 'Exit the Demon King. Take care!'

His shadow melted into the night.

She stood for a moment longer at the rail. Moths fluttered against the windows, eager to sacrifice themselves on the light bulbs. Slowly her heartbeat returned to normal.

The search party was gathering together, cheated of its prey. The liquid sound of the boys' chatter made a background to Matt's louder, more emphatic voice dismissing them, sending them off to their shambas. The hunt was over, the quarry had escaped. Swiftly Sally picked up the scattered contents of the medicine box and stacked them neatly in place, then swabbed up the trail of blood leading from the verandah. She had just finished and picked up a book when Matt stamped in, his face scratched and the elegant linen jacket streaked with red dust.

'Some damned night prowler seeing what he could steal,' he said, pouring himself a glass of champagne and sitting down at table. 'Never got so much as a sight of him. He must have pushed off smartly when he heard the dogs. Hullo! Where did this spring from?'

He picked up Bay's bottle of whisky and a delighted

smile transformed his craggy features. 'Glenmorangie, by all that's wonderful! Thank you, my dear. That's extraordinarily kind of you. Nothing I like more. I haven't had a taste of the malt for years.'

CHAPTER SEVEN

'DEAR MUMMY,' wrote Willy.

'I hope you are having a nice time. On Wensday we played away to Ludgrove. We lost 6–2. I shot a goal. Uncle Peter took us to see Chelsea play and it was very exiting. Uncle Peter got exited and shouted a lot. I was swished for ragging by the Beast but he has spraned his rist and it did not hurt . . .'

Not again! thought Sally. She wished the Beast would pay less attention to ragging and more to spelling. She turned the page:

' . . . very much. It has rained a lot and the pitches are deep mud. When are you coming back?
　　Lots of love,
　　Yours sincerely,
William Tregaron'

She let the letter slip from her fingers and sat staring at the view, thinking about her sons. Below the verandah the trees had been cleared as a firebreak, and in this quiet glade forest animals went warily to and fro, ready to melt into the trees at the first sign of movement from the house above. Beyond the clearing, an emerald ocean of treetops stretched unbroken to the horizon. Where the field of ripe maize adjoined the forest, a bushbuck stood like a statue, his chestnut flanks plump with stolen forage.

'Shoo!' she called, waving her arms, and without haste the buck turned and trotted into the dark trees.

It was lovely to be on her own for once. Matt had driven off with Karanja before she was awake to inspect the tractor, whose mysterious reappearance had been reported. Glossy starlings, their splendid green and purple plumage glistening and iridescent, perched on the verandah rail, boldly soliciting crumbs from her breakfast tray. A warthog family trotted across the clearing, smart as standard-bearers on parade.

When they had gone, Sally put down her binoculars and read through Willy's letter once more, trying to see past the flat stilted sentences and into the mind of her younger son. *When are you coming back?* By that one phrase he betrayed how much he was missing her. She felt a pang of guilt. In the short term, the answer to that was very soon. But what about the long term? She tried to picture how they would react to life here at Redstone, were she to agree to Matt's proposal. Could she afford to turn down such a windfall?

In honesty she had to admit that Matt's proposition had come as no surprise. He was an eccentric old bully in some ways, but she found his transparency endearing. Although it had taken a few glasses of champagne to make him bring the subject into the open, she knew he had been flirting with the idea of leaving her the farm ever since she arrived. But should she accept the offer? She knew it would mean the end of her independence. If Matt was paying the piper he would want to call the tune.

No, thought Sally. I can't do it. I'd far rather work for my living than be dependent. Not even for the sake of the boys. Feeling more cheerful now that she'd come to a decision, she slipped Willy's letter back in its envelope and called to Charles to bring more coffee.

Matt returned at noon.

'Seen sense yet?' he demanded, stalking in as she was sunbathing in the hammock. 'Changed your mind?'

She shook her head. 'I'm sorry, Matt. I'm not likely to change it.'

'Stubborn as a mule,' he grumbled, but he didn't look downcast, rather the reverse. He stamped about shouting for food and drink: with a practised flick of the wrist he sent his hat spinning across the verandah to settle on the long spiral horns of a kudu, whose glass eyes stared mournfully down from the wall.

Sally found this new ebullient mood rather unnerving. He was as unpredictable as a buffalo, liable to charge in any direction but the one you expected.

She said, 'So tell me a bit more about Karel van Ryn. You said you knew his father?'

'All too well!' There was a long silence and she wondered if that was his final word on the subject. Then he added, 'Miserable bastard. Made life hell for his wife and kids. Don't you go setting your cap at young van Ryn, my girl. Bad blood in that family.'

Sally laughed. 'Because his father drank?'

'No! That came later, after he lost his farm. Drank himself into the grave, much to the relief of everyone else.'

'Then why–?'

'Give me a chance, girl; give me a chance! Old Dick van Ryn was a perfectionist – know what I mean? Had a farm up at Holyoak, on the other side of the ridge. Three hundred acres of arable and a dairy herd. Everything he owned had to be perfect. Best crops, best stock, best dairy produce. Used to mop up all the prizes at Nakuru – hardly worth entering if he did. Hard on himself and by God, he was hard on his sons.' Matt laughed grittily. 'Karel and Janni used to skive off here whenever they could give him the slip and I'd take them shooting – give 'em a bit of fun. They weren't bad boys. I've always liked boys. They said it was worth the hidings they got when old Dick caught them. Used to beat 'em black and blue: typical Boer – thinks the *sjambok's* the cure for everything.'

He took a swig of beer and went on, 'Karel was set on becoming a white hunter in those days. Even got Abercrombies to take him on as assistant one season. Thought he'd get rich and have film stars drooling over him.' He snorted derisively. 'Some hope! Then Janni, the one who should have inherited the farm, was killed by a wounded *chui* –'

'What's that?'

'Leopard. Some story that Karel turned yellow, funked going after it. Anyway, that was the end of his hunting. Safari outfit turned him off and next year – bang – *Uhuru!* Independence. Land League driving out the white farmers, grabbing their land. All Dick van Ryn's hard work gone for nothing. Truth is, he'd worked too hard for his own good. Doesn't do to have things looking too pretty. Holyoak was the first place they grabbed.'

'Oh – poor Karel.'

'He's all right,' grunted Matt. 'Manages the Dante, doesn't he? Earns a very decent screw, I believe. What more does he want?'

She said slowly, 'It can't be the same.'

'You're too damned right it's not the same. This is their country now and we've got to play by their rules. That farm was perfection in Dick's day. He wouldn't stand for anything less. Lawns, flowers, not a weed in sight. Everything polished until it dazzled you. Look at it now! Goats in the shrubbery, chickens on the lawn, mealies growing where the mem had her rose garden. Enough to break your heart. The sister married to get away from it all – can't blame her. Dick drank himself to death in two years; the wife went back to Holland and died in a bin. End of story.'

He drained his coffee cup and stood over her impatiently. 'You planning to sit there all afternoon?'

'Well . . .' she smiled teasingly, 'it might be nice.'

'Got something to show you,' he said. 'Something young van Ryn would give a bit to see. Come on.'

'I really ought to write some letters.' She was comfortable on the verandah. Out in the drive the Toyota shimmered in a heat haze.

'Damn your letters. They can wait. Put on some good strong shoes – those sandals are no use. I'll give you ten minutes.'

He was overbearing, remorseless. Once the buffalo had decided on his charge he was impossible to resist. Sally sighed and went to change her clothes.

Dressed in canvas ankle-boots, a long-sleeved shirt, jeans, and a wide-brimmed hat, she joined him as he was placing a rifle across the gunrack behind the truck's front seat. A waterbottle was strapped to his belt and the loops of his bush-shirt were filled with long-nosed bullets.

'You're not going to shoot some animal?'

'Good God, girl! Never knew such a squeamish female. You're as bad as your Aunt Jan. She'd have had the place knee-deep in four-footed friends if she'd had her way.'

'Are you?'

'Not allowed to, am I?' His grin was mischievous. 'Not unless it attacks us . . . or something. Gun's strictly for self-defence. Satisfied?'

Karanja appeared and asked a question. He was curtly dismissed. This expedition, it seemed, was to be for her benefit alone.

'Where are we going?' she asked, getting in beside him.

'Wait and see.' They roared over the cattle-grid in a cloud of dust and headed for the hills.

By British standards, the valley road leading up to Redstone Farm was rough. Soon she realised it was a motorway in comparison with the steep, wheelmarked track over sedgy, tussocky grass that the truck now tackled. Matt drove without speaking, eyes hooded, jaw set in concentration as he hauled the vehicle round hairpin bends overlooking frightening drops. The knotted knuckles of his hands showed white as he gripped the wheel, and beneath his rolled shirtsleeves the sinews of his arms stood out like knitting-needles.

Sally clung to the doorframe with one hand and the gunrack upright with the other, and wished very much that she was sitting peacefully on the verandah. The pitching motion of the truck was as nauseating as a boat in a swell.

So suddenly that it was like stepping into a cathedral, the

cedar forest closed round them. The straining engine sounded profane in the cool, green-tinged gloom. Twigs shook as monkeys made an indignant retreat before the mechanical intruder; in places the trees pressed so close that branches snapped across the windscreen and clattered against the roof as the truck forced a passage. Moisture sluiced down the windscreen from dripping leaves. Sally saw that her uncle's foot was stamped flat on the accelerator, even so, the labouring engine could only manage a walking pace.

'How high are we now?' she shouted.

'Bamboo starts at nine thousand. Nearly there. Then we have to walk.'

Her heart sank. She'd hoped they could drive all the way, despite Matt's warning about the shoes. A country ramble lost its charms when every step bristled with unfamiliar perils.

A few moments later he stopped in the middle of dense bush and switched off the engine. The forest silence surged in through the open window: dark, mysterious, heavy with menace. Sally shivered. She didn't want to leave the fuggy, familiar haven of the cab and plunge into this strange inimical world. She felt out of her depth. Ignorant of what was normal and what dangerous, which plants would prick or sting, of places where snakes might lurk. Ignorant, even, of what she should do if they encountered wild animals. She had no confidence in Matt as a guide and protector.

Like a non-swimmer required to cross a river of unknown depth, she hung back trying to think of excuses while Matt stamped around pulling branches across the track until the Toyota was entirely hidden from below.

'Why are you doing that?'

'Keep your voice down! Better still, don't talk. Don't want everyone in the forest to know we're about.'

'*Everyone*? Who?' Unseen eyes seemed to gleam from the thickets, watchful, hostile.

Matt frowned, glancing from side to side, sniffing the

wind. 'Don't talk so loud. You'll never make a hunter. Come on.'

'I don't want to make a hunter,' she muttered resentfully.

Matt loaded the rifle, eased the breech shut with a barely-audible snick, and slung it on his shoulder. 'What are you hanging about for?'

Without giving her a chance to answer, he ducked under a curtain of vines and vanished.

Oh, hell! thought Sally. She had no choice but to follow. She cast a longing look at the squat, sturdy shape of the truck beneath its tangle of greenery, and hurried to catch up with Matt, who had scrambled down a bank into a small, steep gully, and was examining a pile of dung at the bottom with keen interest.

'Buff. Some hours ago,' he murmured.

To Sally's eye the dung looked ominously fresh. She wondered how far buffaloes wandered. They might be standing only a few yards away, hidden in the thick scrub, shadows among shadow. She moved closer to Matt.

'Could you hear if they were near?' she whispered.

'Depends. If they're feeding you hear 'em. Sometimes when they're resting you can walk right up to 'em without hearing a thing. Come on.'

Now the forest, which she'd thought so silent when encased in the strong steel shell of the Toyota, seemed to hum and pulse with hidden life – all unfamiliar, all potentially dangerous. A squawk made her jump as a flash of scarlet and turquoise swooped low over a clearing. A tree convulsed with noisy movement as a troop of monkeys fled, their splendid black-and-white tails streaming behind them. An impala barked, standing poised for flight on legs as slender as willow wands.

'Don't make such a row,' muttered Matt, silently stalking ahead.

The going underfoot was treacherous. It was impossible to move without a certain amount of noise. Bamboo and brushwood obscured deep pits; thorns snatched at her clothes and stabbed viciously, vines reached out sinuous fingers to trip and strangle. She pressed so close to Matt for reassurance that twice she bumped into him when he stopped unexpectedly.

'Don't tread on my heels, girl! Give me a bit of room.'

'Are we nearly there?' Despite the damp forest chill she was sweating with nerves and exertion, panting in the thin air. A rotten log snapped loudly when she trod on it, causing a sudden eruption in the bush to their left and an ominous snort.

'There they are. Keep still.' Matt glared at her.

Sally froze against the nearest tree, remembering that sulky arrogant head she'd admired from the safety of the truck; the heavy sweeping horns. She had no wish to confront a buffalo on foot.

For what seemed an age they listened to grunts and crashes which came from all directions, uncomfortably close. Once or twice Matt raised the rifle to his shoulder and she waited tensely for him to fire; each time he silently lowered it again.

'They've gone,' he whispered at last.

'How can you tell?'

But again Matt was moving on, and she was obliged to follow, venting her anxiety and discomfort in silent curses directed at his bony oblivious back.

By the time they had crossed a ridge, descended a precipitous wooded slope oozing water, and emerged from the trees in a valley full of head-high fern, she had worked up such a fine heat of indignation that at first she failed to notice the effect of the exertion on her uncle. From behind his stride seemed as relentless as ever, his shoulders as implacably set while she struggled along at his heels, tripping and swearing and swatting at insects.

When he halted at last, leaning half-doubled up against a rock, something strained in his attitude made her look at him with sudden misgiving. His whole attention seemed to be concentrated inward: like a man who detects a mechanical fault in his car, he was waiting and listening for the giveaway symptom again.

'Matt!' she said sharply, breaking his rule of silence. 'Are you all right?'

He winced, either at the intrusion of a human voice or at some internal pain. For a moment he didn't reply.

'Matt?'

Looking closely at his face, she was alarmed. Seventy-five, had he said? She was less than half his age, yet her legs trembled with exhaustion from climbing and sliding and stumbling. How must he be feeling? His skin had a greyish tinge and the rat-trap mouth that habitually snapped shut after each staccato pronouncement now hung slightly open, as if he needed air. Feeling her eyes on him, he turned slightly away, hunching a shoulder.

'Be all right . . . in a moment. Don't fuss. Chest feels . . . a bit tight, that's all. Altitude.'

Oh, no! she thought. Scraps of first-aid jumbled her mind.

'Give me the gun,' she said. 'There. Sit down and drink some water.'

He didn't move. 'Come on, Matt,' she urged. 'Do as you're told for a change.'

It was hard to keep her voice calm as she pushed and manoeuvred his stiffly-held body into a comfortable place in the blue shadow of a rock. It was like handling a puppet, and when his back touched the rock's support he sagged suddenly, as a puppet does when the strings are loosened. His head tipped back, so that his hat was pushed over his eyes, and his mouth opened still more, breath rasping.

She bent down to take the waterbottle from his belt, and as she did so a long green sinuous shape uncoiled from the ledge of rock a foot from Matt's head and poured itself on to the ground. For a moment it regarded her, tongue flickering, flat head raised; then the long body stretched and contracted like elastic as it writhed away and vanished under an overhanging rock.

Sally stood transfixed, unable even to scream, staring at the spot where it had disappeared. With shaking hands she unscrewed the bottle top and splashed water on Matt's face. She held the bottle to his lips, urging him to drink, but after a few seconds he pushed it away.

'No need to soak me,' he mumbled. Though his voice was slow and slurred, the return of tetchiness was comforting. 'Don't waste the stuff. All we've got.'

With unpleasant force, his words brought home to her the nature of their predicament: miles from help, with no food, no medicine, and very little water. All they had was a gun which she didn't know how to handle. Oh God, thought Sally, even if I could leave him, would I ever find my way back to the truck?

She remembered Karanja asking if he should accompany them, and his curt dismissal. At least someone knew where they had gone. Presumably, if they failed to return, he would raise the alarm.

Or would he? Everything she had ever heard about black servants emphasised their fatal lack of initiative, their cautious inborn attitude of wait-and-see. It would be quite out of character for simple respectful Karanja to come hunting for the bwana who had expressly ordered him to stay at home.

Anxiously she watched Matt. After a while his complexion began to look more normal, and he roused himself to say, 'Sorry about this. Must have tackled that last slope too fast. Be all right in a minute.'

'Don't worry,' she said. 'Take your time. There's no rush.'

As she spoke though, it struck her that there *was* a limiting time factor: sunset. She glanced at the sky and then her watch. Already it was twenty minutes to five. It had taken them well over an hour to walk here from the truck. To return would take at least as long – probably longer if Matt had to husband his strength. She couldn't possibly drag or carry him: he was too big. Not only did darkness descend with frightening swiftness so near the equator, at this altitude the temperature plummeted as well. After sunset cedar fires, bright and aromatic, burned in living-room and bedroom alike at Redstone Farm. Out here in their light cotton clothes without so much as a blanket between them, they might die of cold.

Oh Matt, she thought, what have you got us into? Fear rose like a tidal wave, smothering common sense. She sat fighting it, willing it to ebb. Think what to do. Do it. That was the only way to keep panic at bay.

She stood up and Matt opened his eyes. 'Where . . . you off to?'

'I'm going to collect wood for a fire. Have you got matches?'

He nodded. 'Good girl. Can't stay here. Go on to the cave.'

'Cave?'

'Cliff's full of 'em. I keep a few bits and pieces there. Handy.' He was quiet for a few minutes, gathering his strength, then went on, 'Mickey Mouse used to hide there during the Emergency. Kikuyu won't go near the place. Too many bad spirits.' His eyes closed.

Mickey Mouse? Mau Mau? Why should he want to show her a terrorist hideout? She watched him for a moment, then turned and went over to a clump of fallen trees. She snapped off dry brittle branches, making as much noise as she could to scare off snakes. And other unwelcome visitors. It was humiliating to discover how quickly her enthusiasm for African wildlife evaporated when she was reduced to level terms with animals. Rhino, elephant, buffalo, leopard, hyena – she was scared stiff of them all. Soon her bare hands were scratched and bloody, and insects buzzed maddeningly round the small wounds, but she had a good heap of firewood.

Carrying loads, she made four trips back to the rock

where Matt lay. He had slipped farther down until he lay on his left side. She unbuckled his cartridge belt so that he could lie more comfortably. He seemed to be asleep. She concentrated on building up a stock of fuel that would see them through the hours of darkness and pulling up armfuls of dead fern for bedding.

While she worked, the sun slipped lower behind the cliff and set the dark treetops ablaze with its dying rays. The blue sky faded to grey streaked with orange and primrose. Purple shadow moved swiftly out from the cliffs until only their overhanging summits still basked in a rosy glow. Moths began to swoop and flutter in the gathering gloom. There was no longer the least hope of getting back to the truck that night.

'Matt,' she said urgently, squatting down beside him and patting his cheeks to rouse him, 'Wake up, Matt. It's getting dark. Can you show me where your cave is?'

He groaned and shifted, then settled back to sleep. Sally searched his pockets and found the matches, but she wasted half a dozen before her small wigwam of dried twigs flared into a blaze. Once alight, though, the fire took hold quickly, and she kept stoking it until sparks showered high into the air.

Already it had grown nippy, and she was afraid that one side of Matt would scorch while the other froze. The answer seemed to be a second fire. She spent the last few minutes before total darkness in hauling more wood supplies from the dead trees.

It was tantalising not to know the whereabouts of Matt's cave. His 'bits and pieces' might include all sorts of useful equipment. It could be within fifty yards or half a mile: she had no means of telling.

As she toiled back to the makeshift camp for the last time, bent double under her load of firewood like a Kikuyu woman, the winking flames mocked her with an illusion of cosy cheer. There ought to be a billycan propped on three stones, heating thick sweet camp tea which tasted of smoke and had floating tea-leaves that stuck to one's teeth. There should be juicy steaks sizzling in a blackened skillet, potatoes baking among the embers, human faces glowing with firelight and open air to smile a welcome. The prospects of a full stomach, a yarn, a song, a warm sleeping-bag.

Instead . . . My first safari, she thought, and likely to be my last. Her stomach growled: lunch seemed a lifetime away.

She picked up the rifle and examined it. As a teenager she had shot rabbits with Peter's .22; although this was so much bigger, the principle was the same. She made a cushion of fern to act as an elbow-rest and took a few practise aims through the telescopic sight. If the worst came to the worst, she thought she could scare off nocturnal visitors.

Wild animals feared fire. She kept herself busy stoking the two separate blazes, pulling out half-burned branches and thrusting them deep into the red-hot heart. All the time she felt like an actor on a brightly-lit stage. Outside, in the vast black amphitheatre of the night, her audience watched. A hungry, predatory, puzzled audience, and by no means a silent one. Hyraxes screeched gratingly in the rocks, and down by the muddy stream frogs kept up their nerve-battering chorus of croaking, occasionally falling silent for no reason and then breaking out again. Those were background noises, identifiable and familiar after three weeks in the country.

Less pleasant and less easy to pinpoint were eldritch yelps and howls, gruff barks and a shrill – almost human – scolding.

Monkeys, thought Sally, and got up to put another branch on the fire. Probably baboons. It might be a leopard causing the commotion among them. Faintly the sound of a rasping cough was borne on the wind, and she shivered, holding her arms clamped round her. *Night is for hunting* . . . Presently, if the leopard's hunt was successful, she would hear a scream cut off abruptly.

Matt moved and she turned hopefully, longing for a human voice.

'How are you?'

'Cold,' he muttered. 'Bloody awful place to camp. Sorry. Can't move my legs.'

She rearranged his stiff limbs and heaped bracken over him. It was hard to be sure in the flickering firelight but she thought one side of his face had dropped, dragging down his eye and mouth. It would account for the slurred speech.

'How's that?'

'Better, thanks. Keep up the fire. Don't want – visitors.'

'Don't worry, I'll chase them away,' she said with forced cheerfulness. A moment ago she'd been almost certain that a darker patch of shadow had moved just beyond the circle of firelight.

'Pity we left – your malt behind.'

'It certainly is.'

He didn't speak again, but lay with eyes open, staring at the stars.

It must have been an hour later that the shadow beyond the fire moved again and this time she saw it clearly. Her heart hit her ribs with a fierce jolt as she recognised the slinking sloped back and cocked ears.

'Matt, wake up! We've got visitors!' She tried not to sound hysterical.

'Wha . . . Whassat?'

She peered into the blackness, shielding her eyes to see past the flames. 'There's a hyena. Oh, God! There are two – no, three. The place is swarming with them.'

'Throw – something.'

Sally seized a burning stick from the fire and hurled it towards the circling shapes that moved in and out of her vision like sharks preparing an attack. It looked as if they were egging one another on to come in closer. The stick landed near them in a shower of sparks and a long plume of smoke. The hyenas moved back, but not for long. When they advanced again it was more boldly. She could see their speckled hides quite distinctly, and see the blood on some of the long blunt snouts. They must have killed already that night.

She threw another stick and was pulling a third from the fire when something at the corner of her eye made her spin round. Framed in the gap between the two fires, a hyena crouched, its ugly muzzle and bat ears lowered as it sniffed at Matt's bracken-covered boots.

'Get off!' she yelled, running forward to beat it away with the flaming brand.

The attacker lifted his lip in a snarl and melted backwards out of her reach. He stood broadside on, head turned assessingly towards her, one paw lifted, hindquarters crouched. The speckled coat was red-tinged in the firelight and she could see bare patches left by old wounds. She snatched up the rifle and flung herself to the ground in a firing position.

Without conscious thought she fitted the stock into her shoulder and thumbed off the safety-catch. Only when the heavy recoil hammered against her collar-bone was she aware that she'd actually pulled the trigger.

The explosion shattered the night. With a yowling wail the hyena sprang high in the air, twisting and snapping at its belly. It writhed on the ground, and like a leprous speckled wave its companions flowed over the wounded beast, tearing it limb from limb with concentrated ferocity. Sally felt sick. She looked at the rifle with loathing and her teeth chattered uncontrollably.

'Good shot,' whispered Matt hoarsely. 'Didn't think you . . . had it in you. Reload now, quick as you can. They'll be back.'

CHAPTER EIGHT

GAME ASSISTANT MARCUS Githende laid his hand gently on Bay's arm. 'I hear poachers,' he said with great emphasis. 'You will come and see.'

Bay regarded him thoughtfully. Clem had warned him there might be some attempt to get him away from camp long enough for the rescued elephant to 'escape'. His brooding, squealing presence made the Africans uneasy and they had taken to blaming him for every setback, from mechanical failure to bad weather.

'They'd like to see the back of poor old Babar, but they'll have to lump it for a day or two,' said Clem cheerfully. 'That wound's clearing up nicely but the antibiotics won't do a blind bit of good unless he finishes the course. I'll let him go when I think he's ready and not before. Just watch out that no one dreams up a pressing reason for you to leave camp in the next forty-eight hours, or I'll bet you a monkey Babar won't be here when you return.'

He'd clapped Bay on the shoulder and driven off, promising to join him for supper next day, and soon after Marcus Githende had arrived with his patrol of wiry hardbitten rangers packed into a battered Daihatsu with holes cut in the roof for better viewing, and they had established themselves in a camp on the other side of the saltpan. He sent a courteous message inviting Bay to share his fire: as the swift darkness fell, Bay stuck a bottle of whisky in his pocket and sauntered over to join his host.

It had been a good evening. Githende's deep slow voice told tales of men and beasts that grew ever more impossible as the level of whisky sank. Elephants were his passion. As a young man he had hunted them in the old way with bow and arrows. Later he had achieved brief fame as the star tracker for an expensive safari outfit. The hunting ban obliged him to turn his skills in another direction: now he hunted the poachers who preyed on his own former quarry and at this, too, he was successful. He had helped to clear Tsavo of the Somali gangs which wreaked havoc among the elephants there, and when Benjamin Kariuki assumed control of the Elephant Research scheme, one of his first moves was to put Githende at the head of the local antipoaching units.

He was a lean, lined, sharp-faced Liangulu, trim in khaki shorts and polished boots, with the alert sagacious expression of a top-class gundog. Bay hadn't expected the attempt to lure him from camp to come from such a quarter.

However, Githende had made no secret of his disapproval of their action in rescuing the elephant.

'When this *ndovu* is ready to die, he must die. It is wrong to build him a *boma* and feed him medicines,' he said sternly. 'You must take down this fence and let him go.'

Bay wondered how much was his training speaking and how much the persuasion of Nelson, the foreman, who had been advancing exactly this argument ever since the elephant was pulled from the mud. No interference with the balance of Nature: that was the rule of the parks.

'We don't plan to keep him much longer,' he explained. 'Just until he's finished the course of penicillin. Fairbrother thinks he'll do all right after that.'

'It is wrong,' repeated Githende, but he made no further reference to their large captive as they ate beans and rice companionably by the blue-smokey fire.

Instead he talked of the great days of safari his father had known, when forty porters would carry one bwana's creature comforts into the bush; when vast herds of game roamed the grasslands and Voi was a forest instead of a dusty desert set with skeleton trees. He talked of tracking buffalo and lion, of nights watching for leopard upwind of a zebra's stinking remains; of film stars and Italian counts and industrial barons who wanted trophy heads to adorn their walls. Somali tribesmen with poisoned arrows and hungry families. 'Big men in Government' who coveted rhino horn and hippo meat and the shining tusks that commanded huge prices in Hong Kong and Canton.

The elephant population of Africa was dwindling fast. A recent survey estimated that there were only a million and a quarter left in the entire continent.

Githende said gloomily, 'My son's son will say, "Father, tell me, what is an elephant?"'

'Not as bad as that, surely? Think of the new Reserves. And people – your people – are starting to see their wildlife as a national resource rather than a national larder. That must be a hopeful sign. Besides, think of *waziris* like Benjamin Kariuki. He's doing all he can to conserve elephant stocks.'

'It is too late,' insisted Githende.

Silence fell between them. Bay yawned. The long day's work and the whisky combined to make him sleepy. Here in the hills, the night air nipped.

'Listen!' exclaimed Githende. He stared into the dark trees. 'I hear poachers.'

Bay listened. The usual night noises: shrieks and giggles, whoops and screams. Nothing out of the ordinary. 'I can't hear anything,' he said.

'Yes, there were shots. Not far away. We will go now and catch them. Come.'

He shouted orders and the rangers shook themselves out of their blankets, grabbed their guns and were ready with the eagerness of a pack of hounds released from kennels. They piled into the truck.

'Come,' urged Githende, but Bay didn't move.

'I'll stay here, thanks.' He would have liked to go with them and see the anti-poaching patrol in action, but Clem's warning had been plain. Over in his thorn stockade the elephant rumbled disapproval, his shifting bulk a pewter blur in the starlight.

'No, you must come. It is orders.'

'Whose damned orders?'

Githende looked unhappy. 'Orders of the *waziri*.'

That meant Benjamin Kariuki and he carried a lot of clout. Bay felt sorry for Githende: it was no joke for him to be caught like this between the devil and the deep blue sea. He thought of a way out.

'Nelson?'

The big foreman loomed out of the dark. As usual he had been standing near enough to overhear their conversation.

Bay said, 'I'm putting you in charge of the camp while I'm away. You will be responsible for guarding the elephant until I come back. If anything happens to him, I'll have your hide. Understand?'

'*N'dio*, bwana.' Nelson wouldn't meet his eyes. Bay wondered if it had been wise to make his suspicion so plain, but he couldn't withdraw the threat now. Githende was fretting to be off.

'See to it, then,' he called, and slammed the truck door. His last sight of camp was the bull elephant standing with ears spread, trunk raised, a picture postcard impression of Wild Africa.

When they left the truck after a mile of bumping and struck off along a narrow game-trail, Bay's worry that this was a put-up job faded and instead a primitive excitement possessed him. Nine-to-Five Man, who fought his battles armed with telephone and calculator, and filled his cooking-pot with plastic-wrapped packages from supermarket shelves, was replaced by a fiercer, wilder incarnation: the most dangerous beast of all.

Silently they moved in single file, the trackers ranging ahead, shadows under the star-bright sky. They crossed a deep dry ravine and scrambled up the other side. Over a ridge, across a stream, into another gully; here the patrol paused to regroup, the trackers pointing ahead.

'He is there.' Githende's white teeth gleamed. Bay wondered at his use of the singular: poachers usually operated in gangs. He stared in the direction of the pointing hand.

A few hundred yards uphill, against the black shadow of a cliff, two small points of light flickered, tiny as candles in a cathedral. Faintly a thread of smoke was borne to them on the wind.

Githende sniffed, then turned a puzzled face to Bay, as disconcerted as a hound that winds cat instead of the expected fox.

'I do not understand this.' He was suddenly downcast.

'What's up?'

'There is fire, but no meat.'

Indeed, the smoke was free from the pervading greasiness of charred flesh. It hung on the night air with the clean tang of a garden bonfire. Bay could see questions building in Githende's mind, the mounting fear of the unknown. Why should a poacher light a fire unless he had something to cook? Only a spirit would do such a thing and a man was unwise to interfere in the affairs of spirits. This was an evil place, as all men knew . . .

His dash and enthusiasm had drained away, and the rest of the patrol was affected. Bay felt it was time to offer encouragement.

'Let's see what they're up to.'

The suggestion was not well received. The men shuffled their feet and muttered uneasily, suddenly reluctant to approach those twinkling fires. Bay's earlier anxiety returned with a rush. Perhaps this *was* all a blind, a ruse to take him away from camp so that an 'accident' involving the elephant could be engineered.

He said, 'Is this where the shots came from?'

Githende consulted with his second-in-command, a rangy youth called David. 'The shots came from here,' he agreed.

'Right. Come on, then.'

Without waiting to see if they would follow, he pushed

forward through the head-high, acrid-smelling fern fronds, careful still to move as quietly as possible. A dip in the ground hid the fires for a while, and when he breasted the next rise he was less than forty yards from them. He leaned on a boulder, recovering his breath after the stiff climb, and surveyed the ground before him with eyes now well accustomed to the dark.

In the open space beneath the cliff, the twin fires blazed merrily, but they appeared to be unattended.

Odd, he thought.

A shadow moved among the boulders, slinking, heavy-shouldered. Barely had he identified it as a hyena than he saw the starlight wink on something else: the wicked, slender barrel of a rifle. The fire was not unattended after all.

Hastily he ducked behind the boulder.

A split second later – a bare heartbeat later – he felt the heavy bullet smash into the rock with an impact that nearly stunned him. The crash of the explosion made his ears ring and the sharp tang of cordite drifted across the intervening space. He lay still as death. It had been a close thing: too close for comfort. Sweat trickled clammily down his spine as he realised just how near he had come to being blasted apart by that bullet.

'Damn! Missed!'

'Reload,' growled a deeper voice. 'Wait till he moves. Aim lower . . .'

'Sally!' shouted Bay, standing up beside his boulder. 'What the *hell* are you doing?'

In the stunned silence that followed his shout he distinctly heard the snick of the rifle-bolt. Before he realised what she was doing, flame spurted once more from the rifle's muzzle and chips of rock sprayed up all round him, cutting his arms and legs in a dozen places.

'For God's sake, Sally!'

He sprinted forward. She was reloading yet again, her eyes dark hollows in the dead-white triangle of her face, when he seized the weapon and wrestled it from her. She gave a despairing moan and her hands dropped to her side. The next moment Githende and his rangers surrounded them, chattering and exclaiming at the sight of the old bwana crumpled on the ground, the girl and the gun and the few scraps of bloody fur which were all that remained of two hyenas.

'My God, you nearly did for me then!' He took her hands, which were rigid with cold or shock, and shook her gently. 'Try to pick your targets with more care next time.'

'There isn't . . . going to be . . . a next time.'

'Why didn't you stop when I shouted?'

She pushed back her hair with a dazed, uncertain gesture. 'I thought you were a ghost. I couldn't believe you were real. Matt told me to shoot at anything that moved, and keep shooting. He's ill. He had some sort of an attack. I thought he was going to die – we were both going to die.'

Her eyes were wide with remembered terror. Bay said briskly, 'All right, stop worrying. You're safe now. We'll carry him back to the farm.'

Matt's colour was bad and he seemed to be unconscious when at last the truck bumped over the cattle-grid and ground to a halt in the drive. It had taken nearly two hours to carry him back to the vehicle. With much eye-rolling and worried exclamation, his house-servants carried him to his bedroom and hovered anxiously, waiting for orders.

'Brandy,' said Bay, and took charge of the delicate operation of getting it down his throat. Githende and his men prepared to leave.

'Don't you want to go with them?' asked Sally doubtfully. 'I can manage now – really I can.'

'Good lord, no,' said Bay. 'I wouldn't dream of leaving you here on your own. You've had a hell of a day – you must be all in.'

Grateful though she was for his support, she couldn't suppress a flicker of uneasiness at Matt's possible reaction to the uninvited guest.

For several hours the patient's condition showed no change; but just before dawn when Sally had fallen into an exhausted sleep in an armchair, Bay Hamilton woke from a doze to find two fierce blue eyes glaring at him in the lamplight.

'Who the devil are you?' growled Matt.

At the sound of his voice Sally woke and was out of her chair in a flash. 'How d'you feel?' she asked, putting her fingers to his pulse, but Matt brushed her away like a troublesome fly.

'Who's that fellow and what's he doing here?' he demanded loudly.

'My name's Bay Hamilton. I was with the party that found you on the hill,' he said easily, but his hands gripping the chair back tensed.

'And what were you doing there? You've got no damned business on my land.'

Sally drew in her breath sharply, but Bay said in the same quiet tone, 'I wasn't on your land, Mr Matthews. We heard Sally's shots from the Reserve and came to see what the trouble was.'

Matt's complexion darkened and his nostrils took on the pinched, dangerous look Sally knew too well. 'Then you can get back there as fast as you came,' he snarled. 'I don't want you here, spying on me, worming your way in. This farm's no part of your damned Reserve and I've made sure it never will be. Go on, get out! You and your kind aren't wanted here!'

He ended with a kind of croak, as if breath was too scarce to say all he wanted to.

'Don't worry, Mr Matthews. I'm going,' said Bay, controlling his temper with an effort. He stalked out of the room.

Sally struggled to get out the words which seemed to have jammed solid in her throat. For the first time, she felt bitterly ashamed of Matt.

'Charles, look after the bwana,' she managed to choke out, and ran after Bay.

'Don't go!' she called. 'Come back. He doesn't mean it.'

He was already running lightly down the porch steps, but he turned – reluctantly, she thought – and came towards her.

'Didn't you hear him?' he asked in a hard, cold voice she hadn't heard before.

'Don't go,' she repeated. 'I'm – I'm sorry. He's not himself.'

'From all accounts, that was an entirely characteristic performance,' he snapped. 'What's more, it's not so very different from what you said to me yourself a few nights ago. Don't you remember? "Go away and stay away" were your words on that occasion unless my memory's at fault.'

'Well, now you see what I meant. I didn't want you to run into Matt without warning. That's what I was trying to explain, but you wouldn't listen,' she said with some spirit. 'He's an old man and he's liable –'

'He's an old fraud,' said Bay roughly. 'If he's taken you in with his bullying and bluster, you're a fool; and if not –' His mouth snapped shut.

'Go on,' she said tightly. 'Finish the sentence. Tell me what I am.'

There was a moment's silence, then Bay said quietly, 'I'm beginning to think you're tarred with the same brush as your uncle. You'd rather hang on to this miserable place and let it go to rack and ruin than sell out to the blacks. It wouldn't bother either of you if elephants disappeared from Africa in the next two decades; you'd still have a few run-down acres to call your own.'

'If you think it's such a miserable place, why are you so anxious to grab it? Why can't you do your research somewhere else?'

'For the simple reason that you can't dictate to elephants where they should live. They wouldn't be truly wild if you could. When your uncle hacked Redstone Farm out of the forest, he cut straight across one of their migratory routes. Elephants have used the same trails for hundreds of years, and there's no way to stop them doing it. If your uncle would leave them a corridor between his fields and the escarpment it would be better than nothing; but he won't even consider it.'

'Of course not. Why should he give up any of the land he cleared and felled and cultivated? It's all he's got,' said Sally doggedly, though she felt that the concession of a corridor for the elephants was not, perhaps, something Matt should have refused. Unfortunately he was not a man to do things by halves, and nor, it seemed, was Bay. A head-on collision between their personalities and interests was inevitable.

Again he stared at her in silence as if wondering if any further argument would convince her: then he said: 'All right. If Matthews wants a fight we'll see he gets one. We've tried to persuade him the easy way and it's got us nowhere. From now on I warn you we're going to play rough – and believe me, we can be every bit as rough as he can.'

'You won't scare him with that kind of talk,' she said scornfully. 'The Mau Mau couldn't drive him from this place and I don't see a bunch of hot-air merchants like you and Benjamin Kariuki succeeding where they failed.'

'It's not a question of scaring him. Kariuki's a powerful man. If he chooses to throw the book at Matthews he could get a compulsory purchase order on this place, and there'd be no arguing with that.'

But Sally hadn't wasted her morning in Nairobi. From two separate sources she had heard of the power struggle within Kariuki's own Ministry, the palace revolution that threatened to topple him. His enemies complained that his grandiose conservation schemes were a waste of land and money and the country could not afford them.

'I doubt if he'd be able to,' she said coolly. 'He'd have the whole farming lobby up in arms against him. According to my information, your Mr Kariuki's got his hands full fighting off cuts to his Ministry's spending without stirring up any more hornets' nests jut now.'

'You know nothing about it. You're talking through your hat,' said Bay, but she had the feeling that her words had struck home. He added, 'I suppose you're in line to inherit the old boy's property? Well, if you want my advice, don't get any fancy ideas about selling up at home and trying your hand out here. Kenya's a tough place and farming's one of the toughest jobs going.'

'Women have managed to run farms very successfully here,' she said lightly, aware that he was being deliberately provoking and sternly resisting the temptation to lose her temper. That was what he wanted. 'I expect I could manage. I won't really know until I try, will I?'

'Redstone Farm is hardly le Petit Trianon,' he said dryly.

She gave him her sweetest smile. 'And I am hardly Marie Antoinette. Now, if you'll forgive me, I ought to go back and look after Matt.'

'Of course. I'll be on my way.'

She hadn't expected him to give in so easily. It seemed out of character. She said uncertainly, 'Won't you have something to eat before you go? Breakfast?'

'Strangely enough, I seem to have lost my appetite. Don't bother to see me out – unless you're worried that I'm about to indulge in some more spying activities. Perhaps you'd like to let the dogs out to make sure I've really gone?'

'Oh, I think I can trust you that far,' she said and went quickly up the steps into the house before she added anything she might later regret. She wanted nothing more to do with Bay Hamilton, but she had an uneasy suspicion that she had not seen the last of his attempts to infiltrate Matt's domain. If he meant what he said about playing it rough, she guessed it would be difficult to head him off.

With a surprising feeling of isolation she watched him cross the lawn and disappear into the trees, and remembered too late that she had never thanked him for saving her life.

CHAPTER NINE

PEOPLE COME IN all colours, thought Karel van Ryn.

From his cluttered tin-roofed office set a little apart from the main hangar-like building that housed the tea factory, he watched his workers go off duty, a chattering multi-hued stream of humanity: bright shirts, vivid skirts, black faces, brown faces, flattened noses, aquiline noses, thick lips, thin lips, crisp wool, straight oily hair – an endless variety on the human theme heading for hearth and home, beer-gourd and shamba at the end of a working day.

Black and brown and pinko-grey, he thought. Some, like McKinnon, are white with a touch of red. Some are true-blue and some are yellow. That's me. I'm yellow. Still yellow as the day the leopard killed Janni and I ran away. Yellow as the time the buff came for old Matt and I hadn't the guts to fire at him.

Across the gap of years he seemed to hear Matt's bellow: 'Shoot, damn you! Shoot!' and then the horrible bumping, grinding sound. He'd been eighteen, a man, but he couldn't squeeze the trigger. He'd lain sobbing with shock and self-disgust, thinking Matt had been trampled to a pulp and afraid to go and look. Then he'd felt a hand on his shoulder and nearly jumped out of his skin.

'I'm sorry,' he'd blurted. 'The gun must have jammed.'

Matt had given him a long look. 'All right, boy,' he'd said. 'No need to pitch me a yarn. I know what happened.' He'd held up a hand, forestalling protest. 'Not your fault if you've got no guts.'

'But I want to be a white hunter!' The glamour attached to safaris had dominated his dreams since he was eight.

'Not made of the right stuff,' said Matt. 'Forget it.' He opened his mouth as if to add more, then closed it with a snap. He had never taken Karel hunting again.

The bitter realisation that he'd been judged and found wanting was as sharp now as it had been all those years ago. In his heart he knew that Matt was right. When it came to the crunch, he would always turn and run.

Even now, when he couldn't get a pair of tusks for love or money to keep that bloodsucker Essex off his back, and he knew there was a bull carrying a good weight of ivory penned up in a boma at the Elephant Research Station, he doubted if he dared shoot it. Anything small and timid he shot without a second's hesitation. Even Matt admitted he was an excellent marksman. But just looking down the barrel at that big domed head and spread ears, knowing what it could do to him if he missed the vital spot, was enough to bring on the shakes.

All the same, he had to try. There might not be another chance. Sam Kamau, on whom he had relied for enough ivory to keep Essex satisfied, had recently been bitten in half by a crocodile, and because he had been poaching on van Ryn's behalf at the time, his brother Nelson had turned nasty and was trying a spot of blackmail. Nelson had become a dangerous liability. He had an insatiable thirst for whisky and his demands for money to buy it were ever more frequent, his behaviour ever more insolent. Nelson had outlived his usefulness and must be silenced.

Someone knocked at the office door. 'Come in,' called van Ryn, pulling a heap of papers towards himself. 'Ah, McKinnon. Everything in order?'

'I had to throw out half the leaf brought in from K Block today,' grunted the assistant manager. He was thickset, low-browed, and strong as a bull, and had a knack of getting instant obedience from his work-force. He had been discharged from the Metropolitan Police Force after beating up a prisoner in the cells, and had come out to Kenya to make a fresh start.

'Too dry?' asked van Ryn.

His assistant nodded. 'All stalk. The drought will do for the whole of that slope if we don't get rain soon. I'll put the boys on to covering the bushes tomorrow, and we'll have to hope for the best. The forecast's promising.'

'Oh?'

'They've had rain at Kazera, not a lot but better than nothing, and it's said to be coming our way. Are you working late?'

'Damned paperwork.' Van Ryn gestured at the heaped desk-top. 'Don't worry about locking up. I'll see to that.'

'Thanks.' McKinnon stamped away.

As soon as he saw his assistant's car churning up the hill towards the cluster of management bungalows, van Ryn unlocked his personal filing cabinet, poured himself three fingers of vodka from the bottle in the top drawer, and settled down to juggle with figures, trying to decide which debts must be settled immediately and which could wait. His quarterly pay-cheque was already fully committed to his sister's bills, and there were statements of account ranging from the plaintive to the openly threatening from tailors, jewellers, and bookmakers.

So what am I to live on? he thought. I can't refuse Marianna. Left on her own with no one else to turn to, she's bound to depend on me. She's always depended on me. But money had a way of running through Marianna's fingers like sand.

He drank again and thought, those skinflints in London don't pay me a tenth of what they should. They salt away all my profits. I ought to have it out with them. If I resigned it would make them sit up.

But the failure of his last attempt to negotiate a pay rise was uncomfortably fresh in his memory. London had sent out that bastard Mark Tregaron, with his X-ray eyes and uncanny flair for figures. He had made mincemeat of van Ryn's claim for more money and given him a rough ride over the Dante accounts. He'd ended by as good as telling him he'd be lucky if he wasn't prosecuted for embezzlement of Company assets. There'd been no hope of an increase in salary from that quarter, nor was there now Martin Essex was in the saddle.

Mr Martin Bloody Essex. Van Ryn knocked back more vodka. Five years ago it had seemed providential that Marianna had been staying at Dante, resting between marriages, when Essex paid the tea estate a routine director's visit. His reptilean eyes had fixed on Marianna's lush blonde beauty like an anaconda confronted by a gazelle, and when she realised that a word from Essex would be enough to throw open to her the salon doors of several top couturiers, the result was a foregone conclusion. Marianna wasn't choosy.

Very soon she had Essex eating from her hand, drinking from her shoe, and offering financial assistance to her brother. Van Ryn had only to hint that Marianna's extravagance was making things difficult for him, and Essex offered at once to lend him money.

He'd brushed away the question of repayment. 'When you can afford it, dear boy. No rush. Interest? Nonsense. But if you could see your way to putting the odd tusk in with your tea, I'd really appreciate it. Address the chests to me personally, that way there's no fear of them falling into the wrong hands.'

Fool that I was! thought van Ryn now. Five years ago, with the hunting ban newly imposed and everyone expecting it to be taken off as soon as the herds began to build up their numbers, the odd tusk was not too hard to come by. Then the price climbed steeply as supplies dwindled and the anti-poaching patrols tightened their grip. Now it was difficult, expensive and dangerous to send Essex his yearly toll of ivory, and what had begun as a friendly arrangement had turned into a threat as Essex put on the screws. Send me ivory or else.

Or else was unthinkable. Marianna's fling with Essex had run its short, predictable course and now she was shacked up with an Italian film director. Her brother was on his own to deal with Essex's ultimatum: send me ivory or I shall put the Dante Estate on the market and throw you out on your ear.

The figures were dancing before his eyes. With a curse, van Ryn downed the last of the vodka and held the bottle to drain over his glass. He shoved all the papers back in the file, relocked the cabinet, and walked outside to draw deep breaths of night air.

A half-grown boy was squatting patiently by the door, waiting for him.

'What is it?' he asked curtly in Swahili.

'I bring a message, bwana.'

'Give me your message.'

'It is from Nelson Kamau. He sends you word that the bwanas have left the camp and he is waiting for you.'

'Is that all?'

'*N'dio*, bwana.'

Van Ryn waved him away and drove back to his bungalow. He shouted for his houseboy to bring him coffee, strong and black. In the gunroom he unlocked the cabinet which housed his father's arsenal and selected a double-barrelled Westley-Richards .470, and the .38 Special revolver which had been issued to farmers at the beginning of the Emergency. To these he added the narrow-bladed simi, or stabbing-knife, which Matt had given him for his twelfth birthday. Gulping down the scalding coffee he went out into the night.

Nelson was waiting when van Ryn reached the building-site two hours later, after parking his truck well off the track and finishing the journey on foot.

'*Jambo*, bwana! You have brought me *tembo*?' he demanded at once.

'I'll give it to you later.'

Nelson scowled. 'Give it now.'

'No,' said van Ryn firmly. 'The elephant first.'

Nelson's scowl vanished, replaced by alarmed rolling

eyes. 'You must not shoot the elephant here. It is too near the camp.'

Van Ryn knew he was right, but said sharply, 'Don't tell me what to do, *nugu*! You will cut the fence and let out the elephant; then I will follow and shoot.'

He watched, covertly fingering the simi while Nelson hacked at the thorn bushes until he had opened a section large enough for the elephant to pass through. Then they retreated to the shadow of one of the kigelias, waiting for the captive to discover his escape route.

They waited a long time. Inside the boma, the elephant rumbled and gurgled as he moved about, browsing on the lower branches of trees. The moon bathed the clearing in a silver light, and every small noise signalled danger to van Ryn, who knelt motionless, the rifle propped against the tree-trunk, nerves stretched as he watched the hole in the fence.

An hour crawled by. The moon turned from silver to gold. For an instant van Ryn closed his eyes to refresh their sight, and when he looked again the elephant was standing in the open. He had passed through the gap in the fence without a sound in the mysterious way of elephants. Now, as if realising the need for silence was past, his ears flapped wide and the snaking trunk rose. Three rending trumpet blasts tore the night apart, painful to hear: a threat and a challenge.

That'll keep the Kikuyu in their huts, thought van Ryn with satisfaction. He touched Nelson's arm. 'Come on. We'll follow.'

Nelson stood as if nailed to the spot. 'I am waiting here,' he announced, and van Ryn knew he would not budge. The big bull had begun to move purposefully across the clearing, his swaying gait devouring the ground with deceptive speed. There was no time to argue, no time to allow himself second thoughts.

'Look out!' exclaimed van Ryn urgently, pointing over Nelson's shoulder. As the foreman turned, he knifed him cleanly through the back ribs, driving the simi's slender blade in an oblique line through lungs and heart until the hilt ran up tight against the plaid shirt. It slid in as smoothly as a gaff through a salmon.

Nelson gasped and gurgled, choking on blood, and whirled with clawing hands on his assailant. He was a huge man, and though van Ryn was certain that the simi had done its work well, he knew a moment's fear that the gorilla-like arms would crush him before Nelson's heart stopped beating.

He stepped back quickly, jerking away from the fingers which had fastened with desperate strength on his shirt. For a moment they struggled, then the material ripped and van Ryn broke free. Groaning, Nelson sprawled on his face. His back humped convulsively as he tried to elbow himself up again. Then with a gusty sigh the life went out of him.

Van Ryn bent cautiously to retrieve the rifle which had been knocked over in the fracas. He watched for further movements while the dark stain round the simi's handle spread to encompass the whole back of the plaid shirt. Nelson did not stir. Hastily van Ryn pulled down a curtain of vines, concealing the corpse, and hurried after the elephant.

Forging steadily over the broken ground with no more difficulty than if it had been smooth turf, the big bull would soon have outdistanced his two-legged pursuer had he not stopped now and again to forage round certain trees whose cherry-like fruits seemed a particular favourite. Three times in the course of the next hour he offered a perfect shot, but each time van Ryn let it pass, telling himself there would be an even better – closer – chance if he waited long enough.

But even as he made this excuse to himself, he was aware that his old problem still lurked near the surface, ready to pop up the minute he put the rifle to his shoulder. Knifing an unsuspecting man was one thing: shooting an elephant quite another. Van Ryn knew, and fought against the knowledge, that as soon as he tried to focus on that vital spot behind the shoulder, his heart would begin to pound so hard that his whole body would shake, his breath come so short and fast that he could no longer fill his lungs. Stag fever, some people called it. Hunter's shakes or trigger paralysis. Whatever the name, the effect was the same: a dose of adrenaline so powerful that it numbed the whole system, making it impossible for him to fire the gun.

They crossed the gully separating the eastern end of the game reserve from Redstone land, and skirted the shoulder of a hill. It was ground van Ryn knew well, having often tramped behind Nolan Matthews as a boy, in search of wild pig and dikdik, but in the light of the waning moon it looked strange and hostile. They reached the edge of the forest and plunged into the trees, the elephant following what was evidently a familiar trail, shouldering through moss-draped branches and huge boulders, no sound coming from his big feet which were muffled deep in leaf mould.

Stumbling now, disoriented by the thin mist that rose in vapour from the sodden ground, van Ryn began to believe that the elephant was taunting him, knowing his weakness and mocking it. Why else did he allow his pursuer so close, posing frequently as if inviting a shot? The head loaded with the ivory that would get Essex off his back, at least for the time being, was only forty, fifty, sixty yards away. One shot and the tusks would be his, but van Ryn, bedevilled by his old failure, his old disease, could not shoot.

They came to a deep ravine where a waterfall roared, tossing spray fifty feet high. This was the Python Pool, below which Matthews had dammed the river, stocking the resulting reservoir with rainbow trout. As a boy, van Ryn had often bathed there. The elephant paused to drink, a perfect target, while long minutes passed.

Van Ryn sprawled on damp leafmould, legs spread in a firing position, rifle braced against a tree-trunk. His teeth chattered, a red mist swam before his eyes, and his fingers were numb, floppy and useless as if with frostbite. Try as he would to hold the rifle steady, the pillar of the sight waved uselessly, frustrating his attempts to aim. He put it down and took deep breaths. He thought of all the ivory would mean to him. Picked up the rifle again and found that, ghostlike, the elephant had disappeared.

His last chance – vanished.

Soaked in sweat as well as moisture from the dripping undergrowth, van Ryn stumbled downhill past the reservoir, heading for Redstone Farm. He knew he'd been deceiving himself: he could never hunt his own ivory. He was yellow. Like the jackal, he must scavenge the leavings of others.

That meant discovering Nolan Matthews' hoard. Somewhere on the land he guarded so jealously, the old man must have hidden the spoils of all his poaching forays. Elephants that strayed on to Redstone land were never seen again. The Kikuyu regarded Matthews with superstitious awe. Sam Kamau had refused pointblank to set foot over the Redstone boundary. He had told van Ryn it was well known that bwana Matthews had a great store of tusks hidden, but he had utterly rejected the idea of searching for it. For years van Ryn had swallowed old Matt's insults and run his errands, hoping the old man would give him a clue to where the hoard was concealed. Now he could wait no longer.

It was mid-morning when he reached the farm, having hidden his rifle in the quarry beyond the cattle-grid, but it soon became clear that neither the breakfast nor the interview he hoped to have with Matthews would be forthcoming.

Charles, the house boy, agitated out of his habitual calm, told van Ryn that the old bwana had been taken ill the day before and was now in the clinic. The memsaab was in the office, busy with the telephone. It was a great *shauri*. Should he call her?

'I'll find her myself,' said van Ryn quickly. 'I'll just have a wash first.'

In the cloakroom beside the porch, he stripped off his sodden bush-shirt and exchanged it for one of the clean ones hung on the pegs, knowing that Charles would add the torn and filthy garment to the daily wash in which he took such pride. He was about to leave the house as quietly as he had come, when the office door opened and Sally came out.

She stopped short, looking anything but pleased to see her visitor. She had had only three hours' sleep before the arrival of the doctor and his announcement that Matt must be taken to his clinic outside Nyeri for immediate tests had thrown the household into fresh confusion. Only the promise that she would cancel her air-ticket home and stay at Redstone until he returned had persuaded her uncle to obey Dr Savundra's orders; but when he was at last convinced that she was not going to desert him, such a look of relief crossed his lined, leathery face that she could not regret the promise.

'Good,' he'd said, and allowed himself to be carried to the Indian doctor's dust-covered Mercedes without further objections, while Sally's mind began to run in circles, wondering how she could rearrange her plans.

As they were about to drive off, it finally occurred to Matt that staying on might be less than convenient for Sally. He said gruffly, 'Good of you to hold the fort like this. Take care of yourself.'

'Don't worry,' she said, tucking a rug round him. 'I'll manage all right.'

'What about your boys? Don't want to spoil their holidays.'

'I thought,' said Sally slowly, 'I might arrange to fly them out here – if you wouldn't mind.'

'Mind? My dear girl, I'd be delighted. Nothing I'd like more. Tell you what – I'll pay their fares.'

'Oh, goodness, no need for that,' she said, embarrassed.

'Only fair,' he growled, and slammed the door, cutting

off further protest. He waved as the car bumped slowly away in a cloud of red dust, and Sally went indoors to wash her face before starting a prolonged wrestle with the antiquated telephone.

This unheralded visit from Karel van Ryn was the last thing she wanted, but she made a determined effort to inject welcome and warmth into her tone as she said, 'Well, hello! What brings you here?'

She wondered why the dogs hadn't barked at his car. He must have entered the house while she was on the telephone. He certainly seemed very much at home. She noted that he hadn't shaved that morning, but his hair was slicked back damply as if from a recent wash.

'I gather you've had a spot of bother here. Matt taken ill? I'm so sorry. Anything I can do to help?'

Just a friendly, neighbourly visit. She mustn't get into the habit of regarding every casual caller as a threat. She was getting as bad as Matt, she scolded herself, and smiled at Karel with more conviction.

'Thanks very much, but I think everything's more or less under control now. He's going to spend a week having tests in the clinic, and I've said I'll stay here and keep an eye on things until he comes home.'

'Won't that wreck your plans?' he objected. 'I thought you were flying home the day after tomorrow.' He added a little too eagerly, 'If it'll help at all, I'll come and stay up here while Matt's away. I know my way around.'

'Goodness, no! I wouldn't dream of putting you to such trouble,' Sally exclaimed. A flicker of disappointment crossed his face.

'But it'll be lonely for you. If anything went wrong –'

She laughed. 'Why should anything go wrong? If it did, I'd be most grateful for your help, but I think I'll be able to cope. I rather enjoy being on my own, as a matter of fact.'

He shrugged, and strolled across the hall and out on to the wisteria-shaded porch, buttoning his khaki shirt and replacing his hat. 'Oh very well, if you really feel you'll be all right in such an isolated spot. Tell me, what happened exactly?'

She told the story of Matt's collapse as briefly as she could, and he listened intently, leaning against the porch-rail, his hat tipped down so that only a slit of bright blue eye gleamed beneath the shadowing brim.

'Why had Matt taken you up in the hills?' he asked when she finished. 'Damned odd place to take a walk. You could have been in real trouble if that patrol hadn't found you.'

'I know. It was . . . quite frightening.'

'Why go there?' he persisted.

'I don't really know. He said he wanted to show me something. You know how he loves surprises, secrets . . .'

'Up in the hills?' He bent his head to light a cigarette. The bright gaze watched her through the smoke: curious, assessing. 'Didn't he say what it was?'

'I'm afraid not.' Instinct prompted her to look deliberately vague. Karel van Ryn was just a little too interested, too pressing. She wondered how long he had been in the house before she met him.

He picked up a pebble, flicking it idly from hand to hand. 'Could you find the place again?'

'Oh, no. I've got a hopeless sense of direction, and you know how confusing that forest is. Everything looks the same.' She paused, watching him carefully, and added, 'Why not ask the game assistant – what was his name? – Githende. He'd know just where we were.'

Van Ryn laughed, but he didn't sound amused. 'Oh yes, he'd know. Secretive bunch of bastards, those wardens. I wouldn't trust any of them, least of all Githende. Anti-poaching unit! That's a joke.' His shoulders slumped fractionally. He looked tired and a little haggard. 'Well, if you're sure you don't need my help, I'll be on my way.'

The drive, she realised, was empty. No car – that was one reason why she hadn't suspected an intruder. Expected a visitor, she corrected herself hastily, and thought: talk about the territorial imperative! I'm getting as possessive about this place as Matt himself. Ashamed that she hadn't offered him refreshment or been more welcoming, she tried hastily to make amends.

'You came on foot? Shall I get one of the boys to drive you home? Actually, there is a slight problem I'd like your advice about. I've arranged for my sons to fly out next Friday, and unless Matt's back by then – which seems a bit optimistic – I won't be able to meet them at Nairobi. D'you suppose one could hire a taxi to come up here?'

He was immediately eager to help. 'I'm going to Nairobi next week. I'll meet your boys off the plane and bring them up here.'

'Really? Isn't that a lot of trouble for you?'

'No sweat.' He laughed, once more relaxed and handsome, his fair hair shining in the sun as it began to dry. She revised her opinion. It wasn't nosiness that made him ask those questions; simply concern for Matt and, by extension, for herself. He was a direct, practical man who belonged to the country and understood it. She would be a fool to turn down his offer of help.

'I'll look in tomorrow and see how you're getting on,' he promised, 'and in the meantime if there's anything you want – anything you're worried about – just send one of your boys over with a message.'

'Thanks very much,' she said with genuine gratitude, glad that he hadn't questioned her competence to manage alone but chosen this tactful way to assure her of support. 'Now, can't I offer you a lift home? One good turn –'

'Don't bother. I'll take a short cut home across your pastures. Remember me to Matt.'

For the second time that morning she watched a man swing quickly down the hill, but instead of the feeling of anxiety and isolation that had accompanied Bay's departure, she was now conscious of a certain pride. *Your pastures*. For the moment, at least, they were hers, and she was determined that on the completion of her stewardship, Redstone Farm should no longer be the miserable place

Bay had thought fit for nothing but return to the bush, but a flourishing agricultural unit. That would make him change his tune. Full of hope and resolution, she returned to the empty house.

CHAPTER TEN

CLEM WAS WAITING by the boma when Bay returned to the site, pipe clenched between his teeth, dark eyes angry.

'Why did you let him go?' he demanded without preamble. 'I told you he needed two more shots.'

'Why –? Oh!' Bay took in the broken fence, the trampled bushes. 'You mean he's gone?'

'You have it in one.'

'Damnation!' said Bay; and then, 'I'm sorry. I thought he'd be safe enough. I told Nelson I'd skin him alive if anything happened to old Babar when my back was turned.'

'That's probably why they've both vamoosed,' said Clem dryly.

'Both of them?'

'Look around you.' Clem waved his pipe at the idle work-gang, watching from the shade of a giant fig tree. 'The elephant "escaped" during the night, and as a result Nelson has thought of some pressing reason to disappear as well. Probably even now two good tusks are on their way to the coast. Pity. He was one of the best bulls I've seen around here. I'd have liked to give him a few more years. Too bad.'

'I'm sorry,' said Bay again. 'I suppose I shouldn't have left camp. You warned me. Trouble was, Githende shanghaied me on to his anti-poaching patrol when he heard someone blazing away on the far boundary.'

'You should have told Githende to take a running jump,' said Clem. 'Put-up job. Oldest trick in the book. Poachers, my foot! He's probably sharing the profits. I've had my suspicions of Githende for some time – too glib by half. I suppose when you got to the scene of the alleged crime there was no sign of the poachers. There never is.'

'Well, not exactly . . .' said Bay, but Clem wasn't interested in further explanations. Together they inspected the smashed stockade and questioned the men, who declared with one voice that they knew nothing. Nelson had sent the night-guard to his shamba and told them he would watch the elephant all night long, as the Bwana Mkubwa had ordered. No one had heard him leave, but in the morning the fence was broken and the boma empty – and Nelson had gone too. They had followed the elephant's tracks around the saltpan and down to the river, but found nothing.

'Go and search the other bank,' ordered Clem, and turned to Bay with a shrug. 'That's their story and they're sticking to it. Up to their necks in it, no doubt, every man Jack of them. God! Sometimes I hate this damned country.'

Though his manner towards Bay was still frosty, he thawed enough to accept the offer of a Tusker before driving back to Nyeri. They had drained a can apiece and started on a second when shouts from the far bank of the river attracted their attention.

Clem groaned. 'More fudged evidence, I expect. We'd better see what it is.'

The stream was no more than thigh-deep, and they waded across to join the searchers, who were standing in a tight bunch staring down at something half hidden behind a curtain of vines. Flies buzzed angrily as they rose in a sheeny, green-black cloud and then settled again. With murmurs of dismay the Africans moved aside to let the white men pass.

Nelson Kamau was not on his way to the coast with a load of poached ivory. He lay sprawled face down on the red earth in the shadow of the vines, with a moving blanket of flies almost obscuring the sticky dark stain which had spread across his bright plaid shirt. His hands were flung out before him, the fists clenched, and his purplish lips were drawn back from his big teeth in a ferocious grimace. Between his back ribs protruded the handle of a knife.

'My God,' breathed Clem. He knelt swiftly and turned the dead man on his side, brushing away flies, then shook his head. 'Dead some hours. Murder. Better send for the police.'

He issued terse orders and two of the boys ran back to camp. The others stood round, their expressions closed and wary. Nelson had not been popular. He had frequently used his position to make life uncomfortable for his underlings.

'Poor chap.' Bay stared down at the burly, plaid-shirted body, remembering how Nelson had urged him to have the elephant driven out of camp. If he had done so, would the foreman be alive today?

He said quietly, 'What do you make of it, Clem? It doesn't add up to me. I can't see Nelson risking his life for that elephant. All he wanted was to get rid of it. Yet it looks as if he must have challenged some intruder and got a knife in the back for it.'

Clem shrugged. 'That's for the police to decide.' He stood up and felt in his pocket for a pipe. 'All right, boys, carry him back to camp before the ants get at him.'

'Wait a minute.' Bay bent down and gently loosened Nelson's clenched fingers. In his hand was a scrap of khaki cotton a few inches square, with an inverted pleat and a buttoned flap. Silently they examined it. A line of holes showed where the stitches had ripped.

'It's a pocket,' said Bay after a moment.

'Looks like it. Find someone with a pocket missing from his bush-shirt, and I'll go nap you've got your murderer,' said Clem quietly. 'I think I'd better take charge of this. We don't want it to vanish too before the *askaris* get here.'

*

Stock farming is much the same wherever you do it, thought Sally with a certain complacency as she rode up to the hill pasture where the sheep were folded a week after Matt had been taken into the clinic. The climate might be different, the animals themselves might be different in shape and colour, but their basic needs were the same: food, shelter, water, supervision. A degree of love. Given these essentials, most animals flourished.

In the past week she had learned a lot about Redstone, and also about herself, and she was now certain that if Matt was to offer her the farm again, she would not refuse. Already, thanks to her efforts, the appearance of the whole place had improved. She had set the boys to repairing fences and digging out irrigation channels and ditches. Rusting machinery had been dragged from its concealment in patches of weed, and the weeds themselves ruthlessly cut down. She revelled in having an apparently limitless supply of labour to call on, and the shamba-boys seemed to accept the orders of their new boss cheerfully enough.

At home in the Chilterns she had done all the farm work herself with the occasional inept assistance of Mark, but since he was by temperament no hewer of wood and drawer of water, physical labour soon bored him. An excuse would be found to leave the job in hand, and she would toil on alone, spending days over small tasks which two skilled men could have finished in an hour.

True to his promise, Karel van Ryn had dropped in daily with advice and news. She had begun to look forward to his visits. He knew where Matt's machinery was kept and how it worked, and she had begun to feel quite at ease with him.

'You're managing better than I expected,' he said one morning, watching as the boys drove the cattle into a home-built crush she had designed for purposes of medication. 'I bet those scrubs of Matt's have never been dosed for worms in their lives.'

'A step in the right direction?' she asked, smiling.

'I'd say so. Even if the beasts are hardly worth the expense.'

'I know. That Border Leicester ram is about the only decent animal on the place,' she agreed. 'But there's no reason why we shouldn't upgrade all the livestock, starting with the cattle. I might buy a Hereford bull. Matt says Herefords used to do well here.'

He watched her hand move over the back of a purring tortoiseshell cat that had jumped up beside her. 'You like animals, don't you?'

'Oh, yes. Though of course the crops are fascinating, too.'

'You're planning to stay here, then? Permanently?'

'Well . . .' She glanced up quickly, but his face expressed only polite interest. 'Nothing's settled, of course. But while I'm here I might as well do what I can.'

He regarded her thoughtfully. 'You're a great surprise to me.'

'In what way?'

He gave her his disarming smile. 'Don't get me wrong, but I wouldn't have expected Mark Tregaron's wife to know one end of a cow from the other.'

'I hope you're not disappointed,' she said lightly.

'By no means. Just . . . surprised.'

'Did Mark tell you he was married to Matt's niece?' she said cautiously. 'He stayed with you recently, didn't he?' She watched him carefully but his face remained unreadable. Only the hard brown hand gripping the rail beside her seemed to tense a little.

'No, he didn't mention it. He asked a lot of questions about Redstone – but then he asked a lot of questions about everything. He gave the books a proper going-over, in fact. I know I shouldn't say so to you, but these directors' visits are the bane of my life!'

'They must be. Especially when you get two so close together.'

'Two?'

'Yes. Didn't Mr Essex pay you a visit just before Mark did?'

'Where on earth did you get that idea? Essex hasn't been near the place for years,' said Karel, laughing. 'He's much too high and mighty to bother with routine inspections.'

'Oh, but I heard –' Abruptly she stopped as she noticed the hand on the rail tighten until the knuckles showed white.

'What did you hear?'

'Only that he enjoyed coming to Kenya,' she said lamely, and the hand slowly relaxed. She wondered why he had lied. Of course he had no idea she'd spoken to Serena Logie; even so, Essex's visit could not have been secret. 'Of course, China's really more his line, isn't it?' she said to cover her mistake. 'He collects those lovely carved ivories – all Chinese work. I wonder where they get tusks to carve nowadays? Mark told me they're still turning them out as fast as ever.'

'I wouldn't know,' said Karel shortly and changed the subject.

Now, riding up the hill with Karanja loping beside her, Sally's thoughts slid into the familiar groove. She could see both ends of the thread that stretched between Redstone and Martin Essex's office, but the shadowy figure holding them together was still unrecognisable. Who was the missing link? Although Matt made no bones about admitting responsibility for clearing the area of elephants – even seemed proud of doing so – he denied that he had ever sold ivory, and also denied all knowledge of Martin Essex.

'Never heard of the fellow,' he declared categorically, and she believed him.

On the other hand Karel van Ryn knew Essex, and so did Bay. Matt contemptuously dismissed her suggestion that Karel might hunt elephant. 'He hasn't got the guts. Yellow as a custard. He's never shot an elephant in his life – nor likely to.'

And Bay? Tough, ruthless, but 'hooked on elephants' –

or so he claimed. Hooked on the conservation of Africa's vanishing wildlife, just as Fuzz Ferguson was.

Sally well remembered Mark's account of how Ferguson had bearded the ageing Lion of Kenya, Jomo Kenyatta, in his den and berated him for allowing his family to grow rich on the proceeds of poached ivory. He had threatened to withdraw all his firm's business from the newly-independent country unless steps were taken to stop the trade in animal parts.

Few Europeans could have spoken their minds on such a subject without getting a severe mauling, but Fuzz emerged unscathed from the interview, having made his point. A year later Kenyatta announced a ban on all game hunting, soon followed – when the curio shops continued to flourish – with a total ban on the sale of animal parts. Poaching was forced underground, but no one would claim it had stopped. If she could give Fuzz Ferguson chapter and verse of the poaching racket that started here in these hills and led to Essex's office, Fergcon's Chairman would have no hesitation in showing his subordinate the door. Too late to save Mark. Too late to do anything but assuage her angry desire for revenge.

She squeezed Caesar's sides and hustled him into a canter, hurrying up the slope towards the wattle-sided fold in which the sheep were penned at night. There was a surprising amount of noise coming from it, enough to convince her something was wrong.

'Obadiah!' she called through the barrage of bleating. 'Jimmy! Where are you?'

There was no answer from either of the cheerful round-headed *totos* who herded the flock.

'Here, hold him!' Sally dismounted quickly and gave Caesar's reins to Karanja. She ran forward and pulled open the wattle hurdle that formed a gate for the pen.

At first glance nothing seemed seriously amiss, though the ewes were crowded tightly into one corner of the pen, obviously scared. They shoved against one another, making the wattle hurdles bulge, and from the thick of the flock came a piteous incessant bleating, a tone that she recognised instantly. An animal in pain.

With a cold dread she pushed aside the packed woolly bodies, heaving the frightened ewes out of her way until she could see what was hidden in their midst.

The Border Leicester ram was still alive, but barely. His handsome high-nosed head had two bloody holes where the eyes should have been and his ears were gone. He blundered in pathetic charges against the side of the pen, trampling on the tangled mess of his own intestines which spilled from the gaping slash in his belly, bleating all the time.

Sally felt sick. Fighting off waves of nausea, she pushed her way out of the milling ewes.

'Give me the gun.'

'But, memsaab –'

'Don't argue.'

Tears streamed unchecked down her cheeks as she put the 12-bore against the back of the ram's skull, which twisted desperately to get away, fighting for life although hope was gone.

'Sorry,' she whispered, and squeezed the trigger. The ram dropped like a stone. She stared down at the mutilated remains through a veil of tears, and the smiling face of Kenya that she had come to love dissolved once more into the dark inimical country of her childhood fears. The place where Aunt Janet had been brutally hacked to pieces – harsh, bloody, savage.

'Devils!' she sobbed. 'Cruel, cruel devils. How could they hurt him like that?'

Karanja touched her arm. 'Come, memsaab.'

She took a deep breath and got herself under control. 'Not until I've seen the herdboys. Where are they?'

'They have run away, memsaab.'

'They won't run far,' she said grimly.

But although they searched the shambas and questioned

the boys' parents, no trace could be found of either Obadiah or Jimmy. Sally appointed two new herdboys and had the ewes driven down to a fold within sight of the house, but that night for the first time since she arrived at Redstone, she found it difficult to sleep.

'Why would anyone do such a thing?' she demanded of Karel when he brought up the mail next day. He noticed that although her letters included a bulky envelope in an unmistakably childish hand, she had not attempted to open it. She looked pale and worried.

'It's not easy to understand the workings of the African mind,' he said slowly.

'You think it was Africans, then?'

'Certain of it. Typical Kikuyu ritual slaughter.'

She shuddered. 'Horrible. But why? You've lived here all your life. You must have some idea. Why mutilate Matt's best ram?'

She's rattled, he thought. It doesn't take much to crack that shell of self-confidence. Underneath she's just a woman like all the rest of them.

He said, 'Well, if you want my guess – and I emphasise that it's only a guess – it's someone's way of paying off a grudge.'

'Against Matt?'

'More likely against you.'

Her eyes widened, shocked. 'But what have I done? I've only just arrived –'

'Which makes it perfectly possible that somehow, quite without meaning to, you've trodden on someone's toes,' he said gravely. 'Oh, I'm sure all your boys seem very friendly and obliging on the surface. I'm afraid that's the Kikuyu way. Smile at your face and stab you in the back. Only they don't usually stab you – they take it out on something that belongs to you. Something helpless, for choice.'

'Like the ram.' A dark minefield seemed to open up in front of her; a gallery of smiling faces and murderous hearts.

'Like the ram,' he agreed.

When he had gone, she moved mechanically through the day's work – ordering, supervising, planning; but the pleasure she had felt yesterday in improving the place had vanished. She fought against the instinct to appeal to Matt for guidance and at length suppressed it. He was making good progress at the clinic. If he became worried and demanded an early discharge from Doctor Savundra's care, that good might be undone.

Twice she had visited him in the pleasant one-storeyed clinic with its wide verandahs overlooking a garden ablaze with flowering shrubs, where women in bright headscarves sang softly as they hoed the geometrically-planted flowerbeds. He was sharing a room with a young man of whom little could be seen since he was swathed in a cocoon of bandages from which only a single baleful blue eye opened from time to time to survey a section of the room. Drips and bottles surrounded his bed and both legs were strung up in a complicated hoist. His plight seemed to amuse Matt.

'Car accident,' he explained. 'Silly young sod overtook a lorry on the inside. Came off second-best.'

Barefoot, shaggy-headed, wearing striped flannel pyjamas despite the heat, Matt seemed somehow diminished in the bright modern room, like a mangy old lion removed from his comfortably dirty bone-strewn lair and confined in a clean symmetrical cage.

'Terrible place,' he confided. 'Never give you a moment's peace. Always waking you up and washing you and sticking needles in your bum. Food's filthy, too.'

In spite of his grumbles, she could see that the rest was doing him good. The blue look had gone from around his nostrils and the drooping eyelid was back in place. She knew it would be a mistake to allow him home before the doctor's treatment was complete: news of the ram's death would have to wait.

Two days passed without incident, and she was begin

ning to think that the grudge, whatever it was, had been forgotten when a noise outside her bedroom window just before dawn brought her to startled wakefulness. A high-pitched yowl that ended in a choking cough. Like a flash she was out of bed and across the room, and just as she opened the french window on to the verandah a heavy, limp object whirled over the rail and landed with a thump across her bare feet. Numbly she stared at it.

Something that belongs to you. Something helpless, for choice. The tortoiseshell cat satisfied those conditions. Her amber eyes stared unseeing at the dawn mist; her teeth were bared in a terrified snarl; and round her neck was a length of orange baler-twine tied in a noose so tight that Sally could not get one blade of her nail-scissors beneath it and had to sever it by sawing from the top.

Quickly as Sally had reacted, she was too late to save the cat. Too late, also, to see her murderer. There could be no doubt that this attack was directed, not at Matt who cared nothing for the kitchen cats, but at her, the memsaab, who had singled out this particular cat for favour and fed it scraps from her plate. For a long time Sally crouched on the verandah beside the limp tortoiseshell body, and when at last she straightened up it was not to call for Charles to take away the corpse for burial. I'll say nothing about it, she thought. I won't let anyone know that I care. And I won't make any more pets about the farm – it's as bad as signing their death warrants. I'll show them they can't drive me off this way.

Using the small spade Matt kept for his geraniums, she scooped a small grave in the flowerbed below the verandah and replanted petunias on top of the cat's body. She wiped the spade and replaced it, and went shivering back to bed to await Charles' seven o'clock arrival with her cup of tea.

All that day she watched and listened, waiting for some mention of the missing cat, but none of the farm staff appeared to have noticed its disappearance. Work on her new project, the rebuilding of the calf-pens, proceeded smoothly with none of the usual mechanical hitches, the shamba-boys greeted her with cheerful smiles; the whole early-morning episode might have been a bad dream.

As darkness was falling Karel van Ryn drove up to the house and she invited him in for a sundowner.

'I've brought you some good news,' he announced, spinning his hat across the room to land on the kudu's horns in direct imitation of Matt.

'Oh?'

'The old boy's been passed fit. You can go down and fetch him home any time after tomorrow.' He buried his nose in his tankard, regarding her over the rim. When he had drained it he set it carefully on the table beside him and said deliberately, 'I wish I could be pleased about it.'

Oh Lord! thought Sally. Clearly as a ribbon of road unrolling before her, she saw the course the conversation was about to take, and like the driver of a brake-less car she could do nothing but steer and hope for the best. She remained silent.

'Don't you wonder why I'm not pleased?' said Karel with a touch of impatience, as if she had missed her cue.

The chocks were gone: the car had begun to move.

'Surely you're glad he's better?' She forced a laugh. 'I'd have thought you'd be glad to stop driving up and down this frightful road, looking after me. Redstone owes your car a new set of springs!'

'I'd drive twice as far twice as often to see you.'

'You're too kind,' she said mechanically. Here came the first corner.

'That's where you're wrong.' He left his chair and planted himself beside her on the chaise-longue. 'I didn't do it out of kindness. I'm not that kind of chap. I did it because I wanted to be near you – and now I'm sorry because I won't have the excuse to see so much of you when Matt comes home.'

'You'll still be welcome. You'll always be welcome.' Sh

had been at such pains to persuade him that she was no threat to him; now, it seemed, she had succeeded too well.

'That's not enough.' He leaned closer. 'I don't want to be just a friend, Sally. We've a lot in common – have you thought of that? Together we could make a real go of this place. It's a long time since I've felt able to . . . to talk to a woman as I can to you.' He saw her involuntary glance at the glass he'd left on the table. 'No, it's not the drink talking, I promise you. I'm sure Matt's filled you in on my father's sad history. I've wanted to say this ever since I first set eyes on you – ever since I realised you're the woman I've been looking for all my life.'

'Karel, don't –'

His arms were about her shoulders, pulling her towards him. She couldn't reject him brusquely after such a build-up. Something warned her he was not a man to take a rebuff lightly. She felt the touch of his lips on hers and waited for the thump of recognition, the quickening pulse that would tell her love was possible. It didn't come. His arms tightened round her, his lips forced hers apart, and instead of excitement she was conscious of nothing but the hope that he would release her before she gave in to the temptation to slap his face. For Matt's sake as well as her own she felt it would be unwise to make an enemy of him.

To her relief he let her go. 'I need you,' he said huskily, and she cursed the still small voice at the back of her head that informed her coldly that this was all an act. Of course he was acting: it was the time-honoured way for the male to capture his female. I need you and you need me. Together we'll conquer the world. Joint-heirs to Matt's estate: they had, as he said, a lot in common. It would be a thoroughly suitable, sensible match to make with a good-looking, acceptable father-substitute for her sons.

Though she despised herself for shirking the issue, which he knew would be better nipped in the bud, Sally fell back on the time-honoured female response to an inconvenient declaration.

'I'm sorry, Karel – I really am – but it's too soon for me to think about anything of the kind. It's such a short time since Mark died. I still feel numb.'

He rose, and stood looking down at her with an expression that was hard to interpret. Scorn? Irritation? Impatience? A mixture of all three. 'All right, I'll accept that – for the moment,' he said. 'But don't forget, will you? And don't leave it too long.'

He moved restlessly about the verandah. 'Where's that little cat of yours tonight?' he asked. 'I've got so used to seeing her sitting on your lap, it seems odd without her.'

Sally looked vaguely round, hoping to conceal the sudden painful jolt of her heart, very conscious that Charles was standing in the shadows, waiting to announce dinner.

'Oh, somewhere around. In the kitchen, I expect. She likes getting under Mbugwa's feet when he's busy.'

'The cat is not in the kitchen, memsaab,' said Charles from behind her chair.

'You've made quite a pet of her,' said Karel.

'Not really. I don't believe in getting fond of particular animals,' said Sally clearly. She wanted the message to get home and knew Charles could be relied on to spread it. 'I think it's wrong to treat animals like human beings – it never works.'

'Quite right.' Karel sounded amused. 'That's the mistake those damned conservationists down at the Reserve are making. They shoot their research elephants full of dope, kit them out in radio-transmitters and thermometers and God knows what else, turn them into walking laboratories, in fact. They get them so damned tame they'll practically eat from your hand, and then squeal blue murder when some farmer shoots them for raiding his crops. Stands to reason they'll raid crops if they've lost their fear of man, and whose fault is that?'

'Well, I suppose one could make a case for finding ou

more about them,' she began, but he cut her short.

'Don't you believe it! Any old hunter could tell you more about elephants than those boffins down at the Research Station, for all their drugs and electronic gadgets. Don't let them pull the wool over your eyes. You're on our side, Sally – mine and Matt's – and don't you forget it!'

Though his tone was pleasant enough, the hint of coercion in the words made her hackles rise. 'I'll make up my own mind about that, if it's all the same to you.'

He gave her a measuring look and said in a more conciliatory voice, 'Sorry – I didn't mean to lay down the law, but I can't forget how new you are to this place. I wouldn't like you to do anything you might regret later on.'

Ashamed of the snap, she invited him to stay for supper, but he refused the offer with the excuse of work to do. When they had agreed the details of where and when he was to pick up her sons in Nairobi, he drove off leaving her to eat her solitary meal in the pleasant knowledge that soon Matt would be home and responsibility for Redstone Farm would be off her shoulders.

She celebrated with a modest half-bottle of wine and went early to bed, dreaming that she was back home in Oxfordshire, baking a batch of scones for the boys' tea while outside the kitchen window they worked in the woodshed, splitting kindling. She could hear the irregular thump of their hatchets, and cracks of falling wood. Her oven was too hot, and though she struggled with the damper, she could smell the scones burning. She tried to open the oven door, but it had stuck and smoke began to filter into the kitchen. Woodsmoke . . .

Now she knew she was awake, but oddly the dream went on. She could still hear wood splitting; still smell smoke. Moonlight bathed the room in a soft golden glow and that was wrong, too, she thought. Moonlight was silver, not gold. She raised herself on an elbow and stared through the window. Suddenly the glow became a stream of orange sparks, shooting heavenwards.

Fire!

With frenzied speed she flung on clothes and ran outside to the porch. The barn in which the seed-corn was stored in readiness for planting after the rains adjoined the stables, and it was well ablaze. She could hear frantic whinnies from Caesar and the three mules which shared the stables with him, and already rolling clouds of smoke made it impossible to see where the door was.

There was no time to summon help. Charles and Mbugwa were sleeping at their shambas near the cattle-grid, along with the rest of the farm staff. Every minute the flames licked higher, while the blast of heat reached the porch where she stood.

Sally whirled round and ran indoors. Grabbing the towels off the cloakroom rails, she soused them in water and tied one over her mouth. Carrying the others she ran to the stables. She bent double to duck under the billowing smoke-cloud, and scrabbled desperately for the door-bolt. It was almost too hot to touch, but holding it through the towel she managed to shoot it back and flung open the door of Caesar's loose-box. He erupted through the opening, a wild-eyed thunderbolt with sparks in his mane, nearly trampling his rescuer in his desperation to get outside. He was free, but the mules were tied up in their stalls, pulling back with strangled squeals of terror against the ropes that tethered them, their sharp hoofs scrabbling on the packed earth floor. They were wild with fear, flinging themselves against the narrow partitions that boxed them in, and she could not get to their heads to untie them.

At the end of the barn a rafter split with a loud crack and the wall adjoining the stable collapsed. Smoke poured thickly into the building. Sally's eyes streamed and stung; even with the filtering towel to breathe through she felt she was going to suffocate.

The only way to get at the mules' heads was by climbing along their manger from the back of Caesar's loose-box. Balancing on its narrow edge, she leaned over the partition and grabbed the headcollar of the mule nearest the flames. The knot was pulled too tight to undo, but from this angle she could touch the terrified animal's head as it strained backwards. Praying that it would not plunge forward and brain her, she worked her fingers beneath the headpiece and, with an effort that left her knuckles skinned and bleeding, forced the strong hempen band forward over the long ears. The mule, suddenly released, sat back on its haunches, then whirled round and clattered towards the door.

Two to go.

She pulled up the towel which had slipped during her struggle with the rope, and plunged over into the darkness of the next stall, whose occupant had collapsed and lay kicking and grunting, its tethered head twisted at a perilous angle and the headstall already half off, dragged over one eye. A jerk from Sally and it, too, was free; yet it made no effort to rise. Twisted gut, she thought: it can't get up, poor brute. Nevertheless, she lashed at it with the halter rope, feeling her strength ebb and a panicky desire for fresh air possess her. The mule grunted hopelessly and stayed where it was.

Outside she could hear men shouting and the hiss of water hitting flame. Assistance had arrived, but too late to help in her lonely struggle. Any moment now the main beam supporting the stable roof would go, and when it did there would be no escape for anyone inside.

Leaving the comatose animal she hurried on to the last stall, which was farthest from the fire but contained the biggest and worst-tempered of the Redstone mules, named Satan. As she leaned over the partition to undo his headcollar, he lunged at her with long yellow teeth, as if holding her personally responsible for his plight. She dodged back, striking her head on the partition.

Leave him, urged her brain. Get the hell out.

Beams cracked overhead and an oven-blast of heat made her senses reel. She had a sudden awful conviction that this was it: she would never get out alive. Again she forced herself to seize the headstall and this time Satan didn't try to bite her but stood shaking, coat dripping, eyes glazed. Between them and the door rose a sheet of flame.

Leave him. Save yourself and leave him. He'll die anyway. Weakly Sally leaned against the mule, heedless of his teeth, her fingers tearing at the headstall. If only she had a knife. Suddenly the strain on her fingers eased. The rope had been slashed and Satan staggered backwards. Sally felt herself grabbed and slung across the mule's bony withers, then he was moving forward, being urged into the wall of flame by a blackened madman who shouted and belaboured him until he put his ears back and charged through the fire which had become the lesser of two evils.

Cold air hit her like an icy douche. Her throat was too raw to speak as willing hands lifted her from the mule. She sat where they had placed her, limp as a rag doll, and watched her rescuer run back to the barn.

'No – oh, no!' she sobbed dryly; but a moment later he emerged, driving in front of him the last of the mules, just as the stable roof began to cave in slowly like a dented hat, and the whole interior became an inferno.

The yard was full of people. The shamba-boys had formed into long lines to fetch water from both the stream and the well and throw it on the flames. She wondered at their prompt and efficient organisation and then became aware of the source of it. Standing in the middle of the yard, directing operations, was Karel van Ryn.

Sally dragged herself upright and went towards him, suddenly conscious of how she must look. Conscious, too, of the sting of scorched skin and a sickening smell of charred hair. He saw her coming and turned a smoke-blackened face towards her.

'It's all right – we'll soon have it under control!' he shouted. 'Leave it to me. We're lucky with the wind, otherwise the house would have gone up too. Charles, look after the memsaab.'

She croaked a protest but he insisted she should go inside. 'Take care of the wounded if you like,' he said with a laugh. 'That's more up your street than mine. Come on, Karanja, keep those buckets moving.'

She realised with a shock that he was enjoying himself. As she smeared ointment on the bruises and burns the shamba-boys had collected when the fire-fighting was at its height, she wondered at Karel's timely arrival. Could he have seen the flames from Dante? If he had, could he have driven up so quickly? She doubted it.

Nearly an hour later he joined her and downed three Tuskers in quick succession. By then Sally had washed off the worst of the soot and grime, but her anxiety to know the cause of the fire burned even more painfully than the areas of scorched skin.

Karel wiped his mouth with the back of his hand. 'Good job I was there to take charge,' he said. 'No use relying on Africans in a tight corner. They're too liable to panic and let the whole place go up in smoke.'

She was astonished at his complacence. 'Who did it?' she demanded. 'How did it start? How did you know we had a barn on fire?'

Karel stretched his long legs out in front of him and didn't answer for a moment. Then he nodded as if a guess had been confirmed.

'I'm afraid you've got an enemy, Sally,' he said gravely. 'Someone who doesn't want you here and will stick at nothing to get rid of you. I thought so when your ram was killed. Now I'm sure of it.'

'But how did you get here?' she repeated. It seemed the most important thing to know.

'Oh, I've been doing the rounds here every night,' he said easily. 'I was afraid there might be more trouble to come, and I was too damn right.'

'You mean you've been prowling round Redstone in the dark every night?' She didn't even try to suppress her outrage. 'Why didn't you tell me?'

'Because I knew you wouldn't like it,' he said promptly. 'I admire your independence, Sally. You've got a lot of guts. All the same, I didn't care to think of you up here on your own without a man to protect you.'

'I've got Charles and Mbugwa. I don't need any more protection,' she said angrily.

He smiled. 'Believe me, Sally, you do. You need someone who knows the ropes. Take tonight: your seed-corn was an obvious target. As soon as I saw the petrol cans stacked against the barn wall, I guessed what was up.'

'Then why, in heaven's name, didn't you stop it?'

The handsome face twisted in a scowl. 'Because the bastard got at me first,' said Karel savagely. 'Take a look at this.' He pushed back the hair from his forehead and she saw a bluish swelling about the size of a bantam's egg.

'I saw him about to put a match to a train of straw behind the barn and shouted at him; and he came at me like a tiger. Knocked me cold. When I came to, the barn was going up like a torch. There was only one thing to do and that was get help – fast. I ran down to the shambas –'

'It didn't occur to you to wake me?'

'I thought you were safest where you were.'

Sally said slowly, 'I suppose you didn't get a good look at – at the man you call my enemy. You didn't know him?'

'Yes, I did,' said Karel with a satisfaction that was almost smug. 'I knew the bastard all right. He was wearing one of those black balaclavas, but he swore at me and I recognised his voice at once.'

'One of the farm staff? Not . . . not Charles?'

'Good God, no. Why would Charles do a thing like that? No, I'm afraid you've made a worse enemy than poor old Charles. It was that chap from the Research Station, Bay Hamilton. Used to be married to my sister. Treated her badly – very badly. Oh yes, I'd know that bastard's voice anywhere.'

CHAPTER ELEVEN

SALLY HAD NO difficulty in locating the track that led up to the site for the Elephant Research Station. The turning lay a couple of miles beyond the Redstone mailbox, beside which the big yellow crawler tractor was parked, and the freshly-gouged red scar of track ran back at a sharp angle towards the Redstone boundary. They're building it right on our doorstep, she thought, and the old resentment rose within her. They've got the whole of the Aberdares to put it on: why do they have to stick it right under Matt's nose? No wonder he's furious.

She passed several tree-loaded lorries parked driverless beside the track, but when at last she drove into the bowl-shaped clearing of the site itself, it seemed deserted. On one slope were huts, cook-fires, washing lines – all neat and permanent-looking. Living quarters for the workmen. Across the dip from them rose the foundations of the lodge.

Sally parked the Toyota in the shade of some trees and stared around, wondering where everyone was. In the white heat of anger that followed Karel's revelation last night, it had seemed obvious that her first move must be to confront Bay with her knowledge and threaten legal action if any more damage occurred at Redstone Farm. Now, in the hot brooding silence of the deserted building-site, she was less sure that she should have come alone.

Ahead of her was the saltpan from which Bay had told her they rescued the elephant. And stole Matt's tractor to do it, she remembered. Mr Hamilton's grasp of the laws of property seemed tenuous, to say the least.

The pan was simply a dry-looking expanse of mud scored with cracks like crazy paving. The twisted roots of trees lay jumbled round it, giving the place a sinister, surreal appearance. The air was oppressively, ominously still, and flies buzzed maddeningly about her head. Sally walked forward and stood by it, listening to the slow sucking and plopping of mud below the crust. Now she could see marks where the big body had been dragged across the surface. She followed where they led, and came to the thorn stockade which had been built to house the enormous patient. A strong ammoniac smell hung round about the prickly perimeter, but the fence was too high for her to see in.

She walked round it, and came presently to a break in the fence: a narrow slit between two thorn bushes, just wide enough for her to squeeze through. For a moment she stood listening, wondering if she dared go in. She was curious to see the rescued elephant; besides, it might provide a neutral opening for what promised to become a highly charged confrontation.

Again she scanned the clearing, hoping to see someone who would know where to find Bay. Apart from the croaking of frogs and the low drone of insects, there wasn't a sound. The sun baked down on the saltpan. The whole world seemed asleep, stunned into a heavy noonday torpor, yet her skin prickled a warning of unseen eyes watching every move she made.

Curiosity battled with caution. Curiosity won. It was too tantalising to be so close yet unable to see. Moving carefully she eased forward through the gap until she could see the far side of the stockade. Nothing. Inside the fence the smell of elephant dung was throat-catchingly strong. Flies swarmed on the balls of droppings scattered about on the trampled red earth, and heaps of branches which had evidently been thrown in as fodder lay stripped of leaves and bark around the perimeter, but of the elephant there was no sign.

The boma had been constructed round a clump of thick trees. Sally stood just inside the fence, letting her eyes adjust to the dim light. After the glare in the clearing, the blue shadows of trunk and branch were difficult to penetrate. She knew how easy it was to overlook cows or horses if they stood perfectly still among trees. An elephant, whose survival might depend on its powers of camouflage, would no doubt blend into its background even better. For several minutes she examined every foot of the enclosure that came within her field of vision, trying to distinguish the curve of a back, the glint of an eye – but she could see nothing. Strangely, the sensation of being watched grew stronger all the time. She couldn't see right round the enclosure. Trees got in the way. From where she was standing, quite a slice of the stockade was hidden. The elephant must be over on the far side, blending with its background. If she was to move a few yards to her right she should get a better view.

With her heart hammering hard, Sally edged sideways along the fence, ready to turn and flee at the least movement in the shadows beyond the trees. Carefully she worked round the enclosure, growing bolder as more of the ground was revealed and the possible hiding-place of the elephant narrowed into a single patch of shade.

When the sound came it was from a totally unexpected direction: behind her. Sally swung round. In the stillness the crash of breaking twigs sounded very loud, but it came from outside the boma. Her heart lurched uncomfortably and she struggled to understand. Was the elephant outside, trying to get in? Impossible. It must be some trick of acoustics, she told herself firmly. The great pachyderm was moving in the thick bushes on the far side of the stockade. Perhaps he had spotted her.

After an instant's frozen fear, Sally fled back towards the gap by which she had entered. Like a runner in a nightmare, her legs seemed leaden, uncooperative, and when she reached the place where she thought the gap should be, it wasn't there.

Frantically she cast up and down the barrier of thorns, hysteria mounting as she realised she was trapped. Then, as she stopped to look more closely at the barricade, she saw what had happened. There was a new thorn tree jammed in among the withered old ones; what she had heard was someone blocking the gap, sealing off her way of escape. Who? Why? She couldn't guess. Like a gladiator in an arena, she was stuck in this stockade along with a bull-elephant, and there was no way out.

Disregarding the thorns which stabbed at her skin and clothes, she tried to force a passage through, but the trees had been dragged into position so that their dense flat tops overlapped in a double thickness that was absolutely impenetrable by anyone clad in less than full armour. She fought her way a foot or so into the prickly barrier, but was then forced to back out with arms and legs streaming blood.

The pain brought her sharply to her senses. Whoever had barred her escape must still be there on the other side of the fence.

'Who's there?' she called in a low, urgent voice. 'Let me out!'

There was no answer, but she was convinced someone listened. She looked apprehensively over her shoulder, half expecting to see the looming grey bulk sway out from beneath the trees, but nothing moved.

'Let me out!' she called a little louder. She tried to sound calm and authoritative, but the note of hysteria was detectable to her own ears. 'I have a message for Mr Hamilton.'

Still there was no answer, though she heard the soft jabber of Africans conferring. She cursed her inability to speak Swahili. Perhaps they couldn't understand her.

'Fetch bwana Hamilton!'

There was a movement among the branches of the

obstructing tree and her heart leaped. They were going to do as she asked. All the anger and fright of the past minutes were swamped in a tidal wave of relief as she saw the gap opening by slow degrees.

A deep voice called, 'Come out here!'

Sally needed no urging. Crossing her arms over her face to avoid the thorns, she squeezed through the narrow slit and emerged, blinking, into the sun's white glare.

A semi-circle of black faces confronted her: a dozen or so tough, burly Africans ranged shoulder to shoulder, barring her path. Muscles bulged beneath shirts and cotton singlets. They wore faded jeans or khaki denims and looked extremely hostile.

'*Asante, asante sana*. Thank you very much.' She smiled at them but they didn't respond. Their eyes were fixed, not on her scratched and dirty face but on her bosom. A low murmur changed to a menacing growl, and before she realised what was happening, her arms were grabbed from behind.

'What are you doing? Let me go!' She tried to wrench free and yelped with pain as her arms were jerked upward, nearly dislocating the shoulder joint.

'Stop it!' she gasped. 'Mr Hamilton . . . *Oh!*'

Indignation turned abruptly to fear as a big black man wearing a tee-shirt with *Million-Dollar Man* stencilled across the chest stepped forward and began systematically to unbutton her bush shirt, starting at the neck and working downward. Underneath she wore nothing but a broderie anglaise bra.

Rape, she thought numbly. They're going to rape me and kill me just as they raped and killed Aunt Janet. No one knows I'm here. No one will ever know what happened to me. Oh, where is Bay? She fought and struggled with the strength of desperation and managed to slip her hands from the grasp of the man behind her, but before she could run a single step the rest of them were on her, wrestling her to the ground. Million-Dollar Man sat solidly across her ankles while his mates stripped off her shirt. The sun struck her bare skin with hammer force.

This is it, she thought. This is the end. She shut her eyes and waited almost calmly for the onslaught.

It didn't come. There was some more soft, rapid consultation, then Million-Dollar Man slung her bodily over his shoulder and walked away while the rest of the gang began to amble towards the distant huts as if they had lost interest in her. One of them carried her shirt like a trophy.

Million-Dollar Man headed for the elephant's boma.

'You staying here,' he said with great emphasis, setting her on her feet and pushing her towards the gap in the fence again.

'No. No!' She kicked and fought in a panic. 'Not in there!'

Almost casually he raised a hand the size of a Bradenham ham and hit her an openhanded blow that sent an explosion of fireworks spinning across her vision. It was followed by red rage. She no longer cared what he did to her if only she could hurt him first. She didn't care if he killed her.

Into her mind flashed the memory of Sarge, the bulletheaded ex-NCO whom her enlightened headmistress had employed to instruct the girls in self-defence. 'The first thing you've got to get rid of,' Sarge would tell the goggling fifth-formers, 'is the notion that you can't fight because you're female. That's a load of . . . nonsense. Any female can defend herself against any man if she knows how to go about it. She's got a lot of sharp edges in her anatomy and a man's got a lot of soft spots. My job is to show you where those are.' He would pause and fix his audience with a beady, lizard-like stare. 'You'll find the knowledge a comfort when you walk down Whitechapel on a foggy night and hear footsteps behind you.'

She hadn't thought of Sarge for years, but now she deliberately let herself go limp, and Million-Dollar Man grunted with satisfaction. As he bent towards her, she drew her knees up to her chin and kicked him with both feet in the stomach and groin. He doubled up, gasping, then grabbed her roughly from behind as she scrambled to her feet.

She knew he expected her to pull away, so instead went into reverse, stamping on his bare insteps and raking the soles of her stout brogues across his shins. Like a man who has bitten into an apple and found it full of wasps, he bellowed and let her go.

Sally jabbed the point of her elbow into his solar plexus and was off at full speed, jinking like a snipe. If she could hide, get back to the truck . . . She hadn't a hope. At Million-Dollar Man's roar, the rest of the gang turned and came after her in great bounds, their faces alight with the thrill of the chase. She sold one a dummy, handed off another . . . and was then pulled down as three of them tackled her together. She lay gasping and winded, hugging the remains of her brassiere across her breasts. Both shoulderstraps had snapped in her fight for freedom.

This time Million-Dollar Man was taking no chances. Muttering darkly he took out a length of cord and tied her wrists behind her back. Then he pushed her roughly ahead of him through the gap in the boma fence and gave her a shove that sent her sprawling in the dust.

'We are coming back soon,' he threatened, and she saw his bare feet pad away. Moments later shouts and the crash of twigs told her the fence was being replaced, leaving her trapped. The voices faded and silence fell on the clearing.

Sally sat up and the cord fell away from her wrists. It had not been knotted. She was painfully conscious of the state of her clothes, or rather the lack of them. Her shirt was gone, her jeans torn, her bra a technical write-off. It was no use telling herself that a single layer of cotton would have been little protection against an enraged elephant: the fact remained that without a bra she felt at a disadvantage. As Adam and Eve had discovered, being naked in a jungle was no joke. Psychology apart, there was a strong practical need to cover her skin. After sitting in the sun for a few minutes she realised that it was a more immediate threat to her health than either wild elephants or lustful natives. Unless she got into shelter quickly, she'd be joining Matt in his clinic with a classic case of sunburn.

The bruises she'd collected from her brush with Million-Dollar Man were beginning to ache. I'm out of practise for that kind of lark, she thought and got up stiffly. She limped across to the nearest trees, which were near the fence and had low, inviting branches. Allowing the remains of her bra to slip down round her waist, she caught hold of the lowest and swung herself astride it. Thereafter it was easy to scramble high enough to get beyond the reach of any questing trunk. She drew her knees up to her chest and wedged her back against a fork in the trunk. Then she settled down to wait.

'We are coming back soon,' he'd said. How soon was soon? The sun slipped sideways and blue shadows lengthened. The stunning heat of noon gave way to a mellow evening glow and small animals that had dozed away the middle of the day emerged to stretch and scratch and think about supper. Sally tried not to do the same. It seemed a very long time since breakfast.

In any other circumstances she would have enjoyed watching from her lofty perch as oblivious forest creatures went about their affairs below.

When there were no humans about the saltpan was evidently a popular evening rendezvous for animals. If only the tree she sat in had been a little nearer to the boma fence, she might have climbed out along a branch and risked a jump to freedom, but as it was, only a flying squirrel would have been successful in such a leap. She sat and watched the activity round the pan, and wondered what her captors planned to do with her. Worse than her hunger was thirst. It took considerable self-restraint to prevent herself licking constantly at her parched and cracking lips.

Mongooses darted here and there with sinuous gliding movements that seemed closer to snakes 'than mammals'. Two of them met from opposite sides of a rock. They leaned together, like a pair of short-sighted old women peering at a knitting pattern, drew back and hurried on their separate ways. A family of warthogs trotted importantly from the bush like standard-bearers leading a parade, heads up, tails erect, trotters moving with military precision. As if at a signal, they lowered their heads to rootle briskly in the mud, then wheeled smartly and resumed formation – adults fore and aft, piglets in between – to return to the forest at the same well-drilled pace. She wondered if everything in a warthog's life was done by numbers, or if their immaculate parade-ground behaviour was reserved for public appearances. She felt like clapping her approval as the smart little procession disappeared offstage.

Her back was getting stiff. She shifted to a more comfortable position and found herself staring directly into a pair of round, aggrieved eyes in the next-door tree. The sizeable grey lump which she had taken for part of the tree now revealed itself as the back view of a large owl with very fine tufted ears, which had swivelled its entire head round in the manner peculiar to owls in order to stare haughtily at her over its shoulder. It blinked, revealing eyelids of a surprising powder pink, waited a moment as if hoping she would vanish in a puff of smoke, then opened a single eye in patent disapproval.

Apologies seemed in order. 'I'm sorry, I didn't mean to disturb you,' she said aloud. 'I'd really much rather not be here, believe me.'

This was altogether too much for the owl, which spread large grey wings and was gone silently with a flash of white underpinnings. She wondered what it had been and whether she'd ever get the chance to look it up in Matt's bird-books. Her vigil was beginning to seem endless; she thought it more than likely that her captors had forgotten all about her.

Once more she glanced towards the cracked surface of the saltpan and caught her breath. While her attention had been diverted by the owl, the biggest elephant she had ever seen had swayed silently from the trees, not inside the boma as she would have expected, but outside in the clearing. He was only a few yards from her, just where she would have tried to jump down had the branches been longer.

The smell of elephant rose to her nostrils: not the sharp ammoniac pungency of dung, which had been with her all afternoon, but a warm musky animal scent that was almost delicious and almost revolting, but in either case absolutely unmistakable. He must have heard her voice addressing the owl, for his huge crinkled ears, somewhat scarred and ragged at the edges, were spread wide and his trunk raised in a challenging question-mark. With surprising agility he swung round to test the air again, standing sideways on to her, and she saw the great drooping tusks, one hanging lower than the other; the curved back and haunches coated and crusted with red mud. The evening sun also highlighted a less natural-looking stain: behind one ear was a vivid violet splash more than a foot in diameter. Sally stared at it. There was no mistaking that particular colour: the modern vet's standard answer to inaccessible wounds on intractable animals was to administer a quick squirt of antibiotic spray from an aerosol can – the bright colour told you soon enough if you'd hit the target – then to leap for safety before the patient expressed disapproval. Her heart thudded with excitement. This must be the rescued elephant she'd come to see, but what was he doing outside his enclosure?

She had a grandstand view of him. For several minutes he stood motionless except for the gently waving ears, then apparently reassured that nothing threatened him he picked a leafy branch and tucked it absentmindedly into his mouth, rather as a compulsive eater faced with a knotty problem might believe his brain worked better if his jaws were moving. It was soon apparent to her what his problem was: he yearned to wallow in the saltpan but was afraid to venture on to the crust. With feet gathered close together, trunk outstretched, he swayed on the edge until she feared he would topple over. Now and again he lifted a foot as if to walk forward, but each time replaced it without advancing.

She had plenty of time to observe his splendid physique, for the mighty domed head was almost directly below her. She could even see his beautiful sweeping eyelashes. His backbone stuck out like that of an old horse and there were deep hollows over his eyes. All the same, his movements were fluid and graceful as if he made them in time to some ancient rhythm whose pulse no one else could feel, speedy yet unhurried, wary yet unworried, the lord of creation before whom all lesser creatures must give way.

Except man, she thought. A foolish lump rose in her throat, it was hard to explain exactly why. The elephant was so magnificent; he believed himself secure in the armour which millions of years of evolution had tailored precisely to fit him – and yet he was the most vulnerable of all Africa's great animals.

What a target, she thought. What a simple, inviting target for the trophy hunter of yesterday or the poacher of today. And how much do they want out of that mass of bone and muscle, skin and nerve and sinew? Just the tusks – one tiny insignificant part of that magnificent whole. It sickened her to realise how easily all that physical splendour and serenity could be destroyed by a modern rifle.

As if to illustrate her thoughts, two small upright figures crept from the bush beyond the saltpan and began to steal closer to the motionless elephant. One a black man in the greenish Game Department uniform, the other a white man with his face half hidden by a broad-brimmed floppy hat. She would have known that walk, those quick, controlled movements, at a greater range than the two hundred yards or so that separated them.

So Bay had returned: but what in heaven's name was he doing? She watched them creep from rock to rock, bush to bush, hidden from the elephant but plainly visible to her. Sometimes they lay flat, wriggling across an exposed stretch of ground; sometimes they stood pressed against tree-trunks, blending into the dappled pattern of sun and shade like a pair of hunting leopards.

As they came nearer she recognised the African as Marcus Githende, the Game Assistant who had found her with his patrol. He carried a rifle slung across his shoulder. Karel van Ryn had hinted that Githende poached on his own account. She wondered if Bay knew of this, and decided he could not. A dedicated conservationist would hardly lead a suspected poacher up to so much ivory on the hoof.

She chewed at her cracked lips, impatience mounting as the men continued their slow, painstaking approach. They could see the elephant clearly enough – were they trying to count his eyelashes?

A deep rumble from within the elephant warned that he sensed danger. He pulled a tussock of grass from the bank, dusted it against his knees, then dropped it and swung round nervously, testing the air. The leathery flap of his ears so close beneath her sounded like a ringmaster's whip. He walked a few paces forward towards the rock where the men crouched, and to her horror she saw Bay reach behind him and take the rifle which Githende had unslung from his shoulder.

For a shocked moment she could hardly believe what she was seeing. Bay, the conservationist, was kneeling beside a tree, the rifle in his hands, and as she watched he raised the stock to his shoulder, steadying the barrel against the tree-trunk, aiming through the telescopic sight.

'Stop!' she screamed. 'Don't shoot!'

Her voice sounded hoarse and cracked, but it had an electrifying effect on the elephant. He gave a great start which sent shockwaves through the ground and crouched for an instant with knees bent, head swinging wildly in search of this new danger.

Then he squealed, a raw primitive sound like a blast on a paper-wrapped comb heard through a megaphone, curled up his trunk and stuck his tail straight out behind. With ears outspread like sails he charged towards the rocks where the two men lay. Sally saw Githende fling himself flat, and a moment later there was the deafening crump of a heavy rifle.

The elephant slithered to a halt only yards from the rocks, wheeled and squealed and fled back to the boma. He crashed through the thorn fence as if it had been tissue paper, and Sally had barely time to realise that he was coming for her tree before he struck it a blow that split the fork down the middle.

The branch she was clinging to splintered and broke. She lost her grip and fell slowly through the lower branches to land on the packed red earth in a crumpled heap. As she lost consciousness she heard the blast of a second shot.

CHAPTER TWELVE

SHE OPENED HER eyes to darkness and a strong, familiar smell. Lavender, she thought. Some kind of cologne or aftershave lotion. Exploration traced the scent to a folded cloth soaked in the stuff which had been placed over her forehead and was dripping stickily past her ears. Her hair clung to her neck. She pushed the cloth away and saw that she was lying in a tent, comfortably furnished with a camp bed, chest, washstand, and even a primitive dressing-table made of square-lashed poles surmounted by a small round mirror. The windows were darkened by mosquito netting, although through the flap the sun shed a mellow glow on the clearing. Some way off she caught the silvery glint of water.

Under the tent's awning, between her and the daylight, Bay sat at a writing table, scribbling busily as he transferred notes from scraps of paper to a thick ledger.

She studied his dark, absorbed profile. This was a view of Bay she hadn't seen before. Without the animation lent by speech or laughter he looked tough, uncompromising, distinctly formidable. A man who would pay little heed to the conventions demanded by civilisation – if, indeed, he heeded them at all. A man who would not let anything stand in the way of what he wanted. Redstone Farm was what he wanted. If Karel was right, and Bay had struck the match that fired the barn, did it follow that he had also murdered her animals? Little as she wanted to believe it, the only other possibility – that two people could be engaged in a vendetta against her – seemed so far-fetched as to be ludicrous. With her own eyes she had seen him shoot the elephant.

She sat up clutching the blanket round her bare shoulders, and pushed back the netting, ignoring the swimmy feeling in her head as it came upright.

'Did you get a good pair of tusks?' she said abrasively into the silence. 'Was it worth shooting that elephant?'

The pen slowed, stopped. He closed the ledger and swung round to face her. 'Did I *what*?' A muscle twitched in his jaw.

'I saw you shoot it. You can't deny it.' Sally's head ached fiercely and she had a choky, unstable feeling, as if she might start crying. The image of the great bull elephant crumpled into a grey ruin like a collapsed dirigible was painfully clear in her mind's eye. She said again, 'I saw you.'

'You did nothing of the kind.' The pewter eyes glinted, bright and menacing as the spark of an electric fuse. 'No one has shot an elephant. And now, if you feel sufficiently restored, perhaps you'll be good enough to explain just what you're doing here. We don't encourage people to drift in uninvited and start poking around. It was lucky you didn't get hurt.'

And then when she said nothing, speechless with indignation at this attack, he added, 'Come on, there must be some reason. I don't suppose you came all this way just to thank me.'

She wondered if she had misheard. 'I've nothing to thank you for,' she snapped. In the circumstances she thought her reply remarkably restrained, but something – hope or expectation – faded from Bay's expression.

'No,' he said reflectively, 'I forgot. You like to do things all your own way. I expect you'd have preferred to stay in the stable until it collapsed on top of you rather than accept help from me.'

'*You* slung me across that mule?' Far from feeling grateful she was suddenly furiously angry. Against all the evidence she had hoped that Karel's guess would prove to be mistaken: that the voice he claimed to recognise had not been Bay's. But instead of denying that he'd been at Redstone last night, he was actually boasting of it.

'I did. I thought it was time you had some fresh air. It was getting a trifle warm in there.'

'Thanks to you,' said Sally bitterly. 'Well, I suppose it's reassuring to know that your idea of rough play stops short of murder. Even your friend Mr Kariuki might find that a bit much to swallow.'

Bay frowned. 'What are you talking about?'

'You know well enough. I can't claim that you didn't warn me, either, but I never dreamed anyone would fight that dirty. That's why I've come here today: to tell you to lay off – you'll never win that way. If there's any more damage to Redstone, I'll take you to court and all your powerful friends won't be able to save you.'

If she had hoped to worry him with this threat, she was disappointed. 'Now this is getting interesting,' he said. 'Tell me why you think I'm responsible for damage to your uncle's property. What kind of damage, by the way?'

'You set fire to the barn. Can you deny it?'

'Certainly. I deny it most strenuously. Who said I did?'

'Karel van Ryn.'

'Even more interesting. As you're no doubt aware, van Ryn and I are not on the best of terms.' He paused. The shadow of his broken marriage hung between them. Then he said evenly, 'Tell me exactly what van Ryn said to you. Go on – don't be frightened. I'm not going to eat you.'

'I'm not frightened of you.'

'Then why are you shaking like a jelly?' He laughed – a short, unpleasant, distinctly unamused laugh. 'You're pretty thick with van Ryn, aren't you? I hear he's practically taken up residence at Redstone. While the cat's away –'

'He hasn't. And if he had it would be none of your business.'

'Ah, but I think it might be. If it comes to my word against his, I wouldn't like to think you were in any way biased. I'd like to be sure of an impartial hearing.'

'All right, I'll tell you just what Karel said. Apparently he has been coming up to Redstone every night since Matt went to hospital. Sort of beating the bounds. I didn't ask him to. I didn't even know he was doing it. Last night he saw a man in a black balaclava lighting a train of straw that led to the barn. He shouted to him – and the intruder went for him and knocked him out. He says it was you.'

'And I,' said Bay softly, 'say it was him. There you are: my word against his. Which of us do you believe?'

'Karel, of course. You can't fool me, Bay. Not after what I saw today.'

Abruptly he rose, towering over the bed on which she sat, and she checked an involuntary movement of fear. 'Let's get one or two things straight, shall we?' he said pleasantly enough, but anger was only just below the surface. 'You think you saw me shoot an elephant, but you're wrong. What you actually saw was me looking through the telescopic sight to check the wound behind old Babar's ear.'

'I don't believe you.'

'That's the truth!'

'There's no need to shout at me. What about the shots?'

'I'll tell you. The first was to stop umpteen tons of elephant crashing down on top of me and Githende when you stampeded the poor old fellow by screeching in his ear. You scared him out of his wits.'

'And the second?'

'That was Githende blazing off at the sky to stop him trampling *you* to pulp. Satisfied?'

She wasn't in the least satisfied. She had a curious, dreamlike feeling that this conversation was not proceeding in the way she had planned. Her accusation had been brushed aside and now she, in turn, found herself accused.

She made an effort to get back to the right tack. 'Why did your boys attack me if you've nothing to hide? Does every woman who visits you get stripped and thrown into a stockade, or was I just unlucky?'

Bay said coolly, 'It's not every woman who comes here wearing a bush-shirt like yours. Where did you get it?'

'My bush-shirt?' She stared at him as if he'd gone completely crazy. 'Why on earth do you want to know that?'

'Tell me where you got it.'

She shrugged. 'It's nothing special. Actually it isn't even mine. I took it off the cloakroom pegs. It was the only one that fitted me.'

'Ah. Now we're getting somewhere. Were the others too big?'

'How did you guess? What's all this about?'

He said deliberately, 'On the night I left camp to fetch you and your uncle down from the hill, Nelson Kamau, my foreman, was murdered. Somebody opened the fence of the boma, let the elephant escape, and stabbed Nelson, who was guarding him, through the heart.'

He paused.

'Well? What's that got to do with me?'

'You don't seem . . . exactly surprised.'

'What d'you want me to do?' she said angrily. 'Throw a fit? You tell me a man I never even knew existed has been killed – how am I supposed to react? All right, I'm sorry to hear your foreman has been killed – murdered – but I repeat, it's nothing to do with me. It was probably the result of some tribal squabble. Why are you looking at me like that?'

'Because Nelson had something in his hand when we found him. A piece of material. Can you guess what it was?'

'Of course I can't.' Sally's face had become very white and she clenched her hands together to stop them shaking. She could see where these questions were leading. Charles, who washed and ironed and mended all the Redstone laundry with fanatical zeal, had tried to stop her wearing a shirt with a missing pocket, but she had laughed off his objections. Nobody would notice, she said. It seemed she should have listened to him.

'He was holding the pocket of a bush-shirt,' said Bay remorselessly. 'I think that tests may well prove that it came from the one you were wearing this afternoon. Now do you see why my boys were so anxious to lay their hands on it?'

She was silent, thinking back to that morning when Matt had been taken to the clinic; when she'd met Karel van Ryn coming out of the cloakroom with his hair slicked down. Buttoning his shirt.

Bay said, 'I don't know what your game is, Sally, but I advise you to pack it in before you get hurt. Go home. You don't belong here. Redstone Farm is no place for amateur lady agriculturalists, and I wouldn't recommend setting up house with Karel van Ryn, either.'

'You're very free with your advice.' She kept her temper on a tight rein.

'I hope you'll take it.'

'I'll go home when I'm ready. Not a moment before.'

'May I ask when that will be?'

'When I've found out what I came to find out.'

'You little fool!' he said explosively. For a moment she feared he would resort to physical violence, but instead he got up and stood outside the tent, staring across the river at the high escarpment, outlined in gold by the setting sun. She watched the muscles of his shoulders straining the cotton T-shirt and for a moment regretted that they had to be on different sides. She would have enjoyed looking at his elephants, hearing his plans for research. But that was wishful thinking. Their interests were poles apart.

'You won't be told, will you?' he said, coming back and throwing himself into the camp chair to the peril of the canvas seat. 'You're determined to stick your nose where it isn't wanted, whatever I say.'

'That's right. That's what I came to tell you. I'm not going to be scared, or browbeaten, or driven away by anything you do or say. Why are you so anxious to get rid of me?'

'Because I can't watch you every minute of every day!' he exclaimed with the familiar exasperation.

'I suppose I should be thankful for small mercies,' she said dryly. 'I don't want to be watched – either by you or Karel. What are you both afraid I'll do?'

'It's not what you'll do. It's what might be done to you.' She thought of the ram and shivered. 'Go back to nice, safe, civilised England and stay there. Don't you understand? You're in the way. I want to be able to do my job without worrying about you. I've enough on my conscience without that.'

'Your conscience?'

'Yes,' he said sombrely. 'After what happened to your husband I would have thought you'd know better than to meddle out here.'

'What do you know about that?'

'Only that he talked too much to the wrong people,' said Bay, and shut his own mouth with a snap.

'So you knew his death wasn't an accident,' she said slowly. 'You knew who I was before we met in Nairobi. You *were* waiting for me.'

He didn't deny it.

'And now you want to chase me away. To stop me asking any questions about Mark's death. Why? Don't you think I have a right to know why he was killed?'

'Leave it, Sally,' he said urgently. 'It won't do you any good to know. The big bad shark will swim away before you get anywhere near him: that is, if he doesn't take a bite out of you first.' He paused, looking her up and down with an intensity she found disconcerting. 'I'd be sorry if that happened. Very sorry.'

She stood up, clutching the blanket round her shoulders, annoyed to find that her breath was coming erratically, as i she'd run a long way. She wasn't afraid of him. The sun had vanished behind the escarpment and the clearing seemed a sinister gloomy place, the setting for violent death.

'You came alone?' he asked.

She nodded, adding quickly, 'Matt knows I'm here. I dropped in to see him as I came through town. I'm fetching him home tomorrow, and my sons will arrive the next day.' It seemed important to convince him that she was not a woman alone, an easy vulnerable prey, but part of a thriving family unit, buttressed by male protectors. Never mind that those male protectors were two small boys and an old man – the principle was right.

'Your sons? You're bringing them out here?'

'Any objections? No, don't tell me. I don't want to hear them and anyway, it's time I went. May I have my shirt? I can't drive home like this.'

'I'll lend you something.'

'I'd rather have my own.'

'Too bad. Anyway, you said it wasn't yours. Try this for size.'

The blue sweatshirt he handed her had ELEPHANT RESEARCH STATION boldly stamped across the chest. He turned his back with elaborate courtesy while she hauled it over her head. Though it hung off her shoulders and drooped almost to her knees, it was better than nothing.

She wondered if he would try to stop her departure, but all he said was, 'I saw your truck parked under the trees. Can you find your way back all right?'

'Of course.'

She felt chastened, dismissed. This wasn't how she'd envisaged leaving after delivering her warning against further interference at Redstone. She felt like a dog who had chased an intruder off his territory and unwittingly crossed the invisible line where his own courage diminished while his opponent's increased. She had rushed out barking, underestimating the enemy's strength; now she had to creep away with her tail between her legs. In no pleasant mood she started the engine and bumped away down the dusty track.

CHAPTER THIRTEEN

'I SUPPOSE YOU boys know how to handle a gun?' said Matt casually a bare two hours after Tim and Willy arrived.

'Gosh, no.' They goggled at their great-uncle, as surprised as if he'd asked if they could drive a steamroller.

Matt leaned back in his chair, drumming fingers on the polished table. The rest in the clinic had done him good. His complexion had lost its blue tinge and Sally thought he had put on a little weight. He was in high spirits: critical, inquisitive, abrasive – very much his old self. 'The twins could kill a duiker at eighty yards before they were nine years old,' he said. 'How old are you two?'

'Nine.'

'Nearly eleven.'

'High time you learned to shoot. Never know when you might need to.' Matt gave Sally a challenging glance. 'I kept the twins' guns. Nice little weapons. Ought to suit you two down to the ground. Like to look at them?'

'Oh, yes.' Hastily they rose, scraping back their chairs. Matt strode to the door with Tim and Willy glued to his heels like well-trained labradors.

It was a formation that became all too familiar to Sally over the next ten days, and she tried to stifle the feeling of being left out of things as she watched her sons spend all day, every day, in their great-uncle's company, leaving her to oversee the farm work.

'Where have you been today?' she asked Willy one evening as, with towel about his neck, he allowed her to trim his carroty curls. Tim was splashing in the bathroom next door, awaiting his turn for a haircut.

Willy's blue eyes in the mirror met hers rather anxiously. 'If I tell you, you won't stop us going there?'

'I shouldn't think so,' she smiled, snipping busily. 'If Matt thinks it's all right, why shouldn't I?'

He was reassured. 'Well, up in the hills there's a cave. It used to be a gangster hideout,' he said solemnly.

'Oh, I know that place. Your uncle took me there, too. It was the day he got ill and had to go to hospital. Goodness! It's a long way for you to walk. No wonder it takes all day.'

'I didn't know you'd been there. Did you – did you go right inside the cave?'

'Well, no. Actually we didn't quite get there because Matt had to rest. But I do know the place you mean.'

The splashing in the bathroom had stopped, replaced by a listening silence.

'Go on,' she urged. 'What's inside the cave?'

'I keep a few bits and pieces there . . .'

'There's nothing much in the cave, but if you go right to the back you find there's a sort of path. It goes through the hill.' He cast a quick look over his shoulder as the bathroom door-bolt rattled and said rapidly, 'If you follow the path, you come to Ivory Gorge. That's where –'

'*Shut up, Willy!*' Tim stood in the doorway, his face as red as his hair. 'You little beast, you promised you wouldn't tell anyone.'

'Mum doesn't count,' said Willy stoutly, though he looked abashed. He found it difficult to keep secrets. 'She's been there anyway with Uncle Matt, so there!'

'Liar!'

'Liar yourself!'

'Be quiet, both of you,' ordered Sally. 'And stop wriggling, William, unless you want me to take a chunk out of your ear. I don't want to hear your secrets.'

'But you asked!' he wailed.

'I only asked in case you were being a nuisance to your uncle,' she said, knowing that this unfair slur would unite them against her.

'Well, we're not,' said Willy perkily. 'We're having a fantastic time. Much better than at home.'

She knew she should be glad to hear it, but the feeling of isolation persisted.

'There's a stock sale down at Burnside tomorrow,' said van Ryn one morning when she rode down to collect the mail. He sat in his sports car beside the mailbox, unusually well-shaved and spruce in a green silk poloneck and the fringed suede jacket. She guessed he had been waiting for her and felt a pang of conscience for neglecting him.

'You might be able to buy a ram to replace that one you lost,' he added. 'Dee Mackenzie's got some good stock entered.'

'Are you going?'

'No, worse luck. I've got visitors.'

'Perhaps they'd enjoy the sale.'

'Some hope! Anyway, I thought I'd let you know in case you were interested.' He switched on the engine.

'Well, thanks. I'll certainly go over and see what they're selling.'

'Good hunting!' He waved, revved the engine, and scorched away.

Rather to Sally's disappointment, Matt had been unimpressed by her efforts to improve the look of the farm during his absence – in fact he had been a little scornful.

'Doesn't do to have the place looking too pretty,' he grunted. 'Thought I'd told you that. You'll only get a lot of trouble from squatters and the like. I suppose that new fencing was van Ryn's idea?'

'Actually it was mine.'

'Waste of time.' He was curiously uninterested in the state of the farm, and much preferred to spend the daylight hours entertaining Tim and Willy, leaving her to direct agricultural operations as she pleased. He wasn't even much concerned to hear of his best ram's death.

'Damned sheep – more trouble than they're worth. Always keeling over for some reason or another,' he said dismissingly. 'I knew a Border Leicester wouldn't do much good here. Too soft.'

Nevertheless, he raised no objection to her proposal to go to the sale and look for a replacement.

'You go and enjoy yourself, my dear; but don't ask me to come with you, that's all! Can't stand the gossiping bitches who spend their lives trailing round that sort of affair. Nothing else to do.'

'D'you think I should take the trailer?'

'Good lord, no. Don't want everyone to think you've money to burn! If you buy anything, we'll send young van Ryn over to fetch it later. He won't mind. He likes an excuse to come up here.'

'I'll take Tim and Willy –' she began.

'No, no,' said Matt at once. 'Leave them here. I'll keep them happy, don't you worry.'

'You're busy . . .'

She would have liked to have her sons' company for a change, but Matt wouldn't hear of it. He was going to give them target practise on the rifle range.

'Then we'll go down to the dam when it's cooler. They can swim, maybe catch a few trout for supper. They'd enjoy that.'

It was touching how he kept thinking of new ways to amuse them, and he was right, of course, thought Sally, trying not to feel abandoned. Undoubtedly they'd enjoy shooting and fishing more than a long bumpy drive with her. Particularly Tim, who was car-sick.

'All right? You don't feel I'm hogging their company? It's a treat for me to have youngsters about the place.' Matt looked suddenly anxious.

'Of course not!' She made her smile especially brilliant to hide the fact that he'd guessed her state of mind precisely. 'Don't let them run you off your feet, that's all. Boys of that age never know when to stop.'

'Oh, they'll stop when I tell 'em to!' he boasted, his eyes relaxed and confident again.

'All right, then – if you're sure they won't tire you.'

She told Karanja to fill the truck with diesel and be ready to start at ten the following morning.

Van Ryn heard the rattle of the truck as it crossed the cattle-grid and watched from concealment in the quarry from which the Redstone building materials had been extracted. The vehicle turned downhill; with satisfaction he recognised the back of Sally's head above the driver's seat. It would take her over an hour to reach Burnside, perhaps three hours more at the sale, and then the return journey. Plenty of time for what he had to do.

He had been watching the house since soon after dawn and knew that the houseboys had gone to their own shambas to doze away the heat of the day. Apart from Matt and the children, the place was deserted. He scrubbed a hand across his mouth and blinked as he took a long pull from the bottle in the glove compartment.

'All clear, Mac. Let's go.'

'What about the dogs?'

'They know me. They won't bark. Come on, man.'

They walked down the hill, keeping below the line of the fence, and crossed the quiet sunny yard. Passing the kennel, McKinnon trod cautiously, but Hansel and Gretel, stretched out in the shade of a tree in their run, merely waved lazy tails when Karel spoke softly to them. They mounted the wooden steps to the verandah and stood listening.

A murmur of boys' voices came from the middle bedroom. Karel jerked his head towards the window. 'There they are. Quick.' They pulled stocking masks over their faces and padded silently on rubber soles into the bedroom. Neither boy saw them. Willy was bending down, tying the laces of his track shoes, and Tim had his back to the window.

'Buck up,' he said. 'Uncle Matt will be –'

McKinnon seized him from behind and clapped a hand over his mouth before he could cry out.

'Half a tick, I've got to put on my shoes, haven't I?' Willy sensed movement behind him and looked up. 'Oh!' he squeaked, eyes widening in alarm at the stocking-flattened, featureless faces. 'Who are you? Let go of my brother!'

Like a copper-knobbed whirlwind he flew at McKinnon, feet and fists flailing, and got in several sharp kicks on his shins before van Ryn managed to collar him.

'Not so fast,' he growled, panting, twisting Willy's arm behind his back. It was like trying to hold an eel. The boy ducked and butted him hard in the stomach, stamping on his feet and shouting at the top of his voice.

'Quiet . . . you . . . little . . . swine!' Van Ryn yanked at the pinioned arm without much effect. 'Here, you! Tell him to shut up or I'll break his bloody arm.'

'Cut it out, Will.'

Reluctantly Willy stopped struggling.

Tim stared at the masked men, trying to pin down a memory. There had been something familiar in the voice: where had he heard those nasal vowels, those grating consonants?

'What d'you want?' he said.

'A few minutes of your valuable time, sonny,' said the man holding Willy, and immediately Tim knew who it was. Mr van Ryn who'd met them off the plane and driven them from the airport.

'Are you looking for my uncle, Mr van Ryn?'

Although his voice was calm, his eyes behind the heavy spectacles were afraid. He had been quick to sense the chained violence in Mr van Ryn as he drove through the rush-hour traffic in Nairobi muttering threats and insults at other drivers. Now Tim recognised the smell of alcohol hanging about him and realised that whatever these intruders had come for, it would be dangerous to thwart them.

Karel swore inwardly. The older boy looked a cissy but he was sharp. Well, he'd pay for his sharpness. It would never do to have little English tattle-tales telling what they'd seen and heard. Naming names.

'We'll talk to your uncle later, sonny,' he said. 'First we're going to take you to a safe place.'

They stared at him blankly. 'But why?' asked Tim at last.

Behind the mask the mouth stretched flatly. 'Call it a kind of insurance. So that your uncle will be glad to help us.'

'What sort of help?' Tim wanted to keep him talking. While he talked they were safe and any moment Uncle Matt might start to wonder why they had not turned up on the rifle range and come looking for them. They had never been late before. Or Charles might come back from his shamba. Or Mbugwa. Anyone would do. He didn't want to go anywhere with the alarming Mr van Ryn who smelt of drink and held Willy so tightly.

Willy said loudly and suddenly, 'Mummy won't know where we are. She'll worry.'

The stocking masks exchanged glances. Van Ryn said, 'If you boys do as you're told, you'll be back with your mother soon enough. Otherwise,' he paused and again his mouth stretched in the ugly grimace, 'otherwise Mummy won't see you again for a long, long time.'

While they digested this he nodded to McKinnon. 'Tie something over their mouths. We don't want any noise yet.'

'Right.' McKinnon opened drawers and ripped up Tim's best shirt to improvise gags. Willy had begun to shake with angry sobs, but Tim's mind raced coolly, thinking what he could do to attract attention. To let his mother know which way they'd gone.

He trickled a handful of pea-shooter ammunition down his leg and on to the floor, hoping the men wouldn't hear them fall. Then they were hustled out of the house and down the verandah steps, past the run where the dogs still dozed, and up the hill towards the quarry.

Sally stopped to check the tyres at the Indian-owned *duka* a few miles short of the turning for Burnside, and because she had time in hand before the sale began, she left Karanja sitting in the truck and went inside the cool, tree-shaded restaurant attached to the store.

It was early for lunch, and only two tables were occupied. At one sat a party of burly uniformed Africans with the unmistakable look of bodyguards. At the other was Bay Hamilton, deep in conversation with a short, thickset black man, wearing a well-cut pale-blue suit, a pink shirt with narrow stripes, and a dark blue tie decorated with small silver elephants. His broad, heavy-featured face seemed oddly familiar. As she hesitated in the doorway, trying to pinpoint where she'd seen him before, Bay turned and spotted her.

'Ah, come and join us, Sally,' he said, springing up and kissing her robustly on the cheek as if they were old friends. From his tone one might have supposed the meeting to be prearranged and eagerly awaited. What's he up to now? thought Sally, well remembering the chill of their last interview.

'There's someone here you must meet,' he said, herding her towards the table like a highly proficient sheepdog. His black companion had risen and was staring at her with an expression of shock which reminded her oddly of Matt's when he had stalked into the Norfolk bar and caught sight of her.

'I'd like to introduce Benjamin Kariuki, from the Ministry of Natural Resources,' said Bay. 'Benjamin, this is Sally Tregaron.'

Then, as Mr Kariuki continued to stare and say nothing, Bay covered the awkward pause with a laugh. 'What's up? You look as if you've seen a ghost.'

Kariuki made an inarticulate noise and passed a hand across his eyes as if to brush away a cobweb.

He looks ill – really ill, thought Sally.

'You must excuse me. I get these sudden migraines.' Kariuki's voice was deep and mellow. 'There – it has gone.' He drew a deep breath and held out his hand. 'Mrs Tregaron, I am most happy to meet you.'

'But it's not the first time, is it?' said Sally, smiling. She had remembered where she'd seen those heavy flattened features, the pale-blue suit. She guessed the recognition was mutual, and wondered if he would deny it.

He did. 'You are mistaken,' he said just a shade too quickly.

'I thought you'd recognised me, too.'

'No . . . Forgive me, I was surprised by your hair. A most unusual colour.'

'I think it's a beautiful colour,' said Bay, and she gave him a flashing glance which said *keep out of this*. Mr Kariuki's reaction interested her.

'It runs in the family,' she said. 'Are you sure you weren't in the blue Peugeot that nearly collided with Uncle Matt on the day I arrived at Redstone? I could have sworn it was you.'

'How can you ask such a question when your good uncle's antipathy to visitors is well known?' Kariuki slapped his palm on the table and laughed richly, but she thought his eyes were not amused. His voice had the smoothness of the born orator. Syllables flowed like thick dark treacle, soothing and persuading. 'We in Government tolerate his eccentricities because he is an old man and life has not treated him kindly. It is important to respect a man's privacy when he has suffered as Mr Matthews has. You are uniquely privileged to be invited to stay with him, Mrs Tregaron. It is a privilege denied to other mortals.'

'How very odd. I could have sworn it was you,' she persisted. 'You were wearing those silver sunglasses – the ones that reflect – and a blue suit like the one you've got on now.'

'I can understand your mistake,' he said earnestly. 'It is difficult for Europeans to distinguish at first between black faces, just as we find that all white faces look alike to begin with.'

Nevertheless, he seemed reluctant to look her in the eye.

'You're looking very lovely today,' said Bay quickly, as if to head her off the subject. 'Where are you off to?'

'The sheep sale at Burnside.'

'Oh, are you? Buying or selling?'

She said shortly, 'I need a replacement for Matt's best ram. It met an . . . an unfortunate end while he was in hospital.'

'Oh – bad luck.' He didn't ask for further details.

'Mr Matthews is in hospital?' asked Kariuki with keen interest.

'Yes – at least he was until a few days ago. He's home now.'

There was no mistaking Kariuki's disappointment. 'You did not inform me of this,' he said heavily to Bay, who raised his eyebrows in surprise.

'Should I have? Sorry. You were up country, so I kept messages to a minimum.'

For a moment Kariuki sat frowning and preoccupied, then he made an obvious effort to shake off his gloom.

'You must come and visit our Elephant Research Station, Mrs Tregaron. I have been there myself today, and it is progressing well. Soon it will be operational.' Again his voice assumed the oratorical swell. 'It will be the most up-to-date scientific institute devoted to research on elephants in the whole of Africa. We have substantial backing from our Government and also the World Wildlife Fund. We will spare neither effort nor expense in our pogramme to preserve the unique wildlife of our country. Nothing shall stand in our way.'

When Sally was silent, he gave her a sharp, calculating

look. 'I hope that Bay has managed to convince you of the importance of our work?'

She felt a sudden urge to shake that smooth self-righteousness; to show him there were other points of view to take into account.

'Bay's methods of persuasion are certainly forceful; I can't say that I find them particularly convincing, though. The fact is, Mr Kariuki, it would take more than forceful persuasion to convince me that it's necessary to turn my uncle's whole farm into a *keddah*. Nor can I see why an elephant fitted with a radio collar should be less likely to fall victim to a poacher than an elephant without one. This talk about research is all very fine, but aren't poachers really the main threat to elephant survival? Couldn't you do just as much good by stepping up the anti-poaching patrols and leaving the research alone?'

They exchanged a glance.

'It is disappointing to find you show no enthusiasm for our project,' said Kariuki sombrely. 'I hoped for your cooperation. We will endeavour to find a means of making you change your mind.'

Genuine regret, or a veiled threat? She could not be sure.

'I must go,' she said. 'Thank you for the beer, Mr Kariuki. It has been interesting to talk to you, but I must warn you I'm not likely to change my mind. Goodbye, Bay.'

She walked to the door, very conscious of their eyes following her, but neither made a move to detain her.

Towards the end of the sale she outbid three farmers for a handsome two-year-old Cheviot ram, and the buzz of interest that broke out when she gave name and address to the auctioneer brought home to her the degree of isolation Matt had succeeded in imposing on himself.

'Excuse me, ma'am – did you say *Redstone* Farm?'

bellowed the auctioneer's clerk across the straw ring.

'That's right.' He shrugged, consulted his companion, and turned back to her. 'And the name, please?'

'Matthews.'

Eyes swivelled and mouths moved avidly, just as they had at the inquest. Abruptly she left her seat and went to make closer acquaintance with her purchase, thankful that he, at least, regarded her as a normally tiresome human being and not some strange apparition from another planet. It was easy to see why Matt had avoided coming.

The vendor, a wizened, ginger-haired Scotsman, readily agreed to keep the young ram until she could send a man to collect him, and Sally set off home, feeling that the whole expedition had been worthwhile.

As she passed the turning to the Dante Tea Estate, a sudden impulse made her swing the wheel over and drive up the well-kept avenue between tall stands of blue gums. Karel would be interested to hear about the sale, and she would be interested to meet his visitors.

Towards the top of the winding red track that ran between slopes closely planted with tea bushes as level and brilliant green as a billiard table, she came to a triple fork. *Manager's House* to the right, *Staff* straight ahead, and *Factory* to the left. After only a moment's hesitation she chose the left-hand branch.

Everything looked well-maintained and orderly: she remembered that Karel's father had apparently been fanatical about the appearance of this property, and thought that something of this obsession must have rubbed off on his younger son. It brought to mind Serena Logie's remark that the Dante lost money hand over fist. This wasn't good tea-growing country. All Fergcon's other estates in the area had been sold off or turned over to stock. Only the Dante struggled on, with Martin Essex's backing, although the other Fergcon directors would have liked to be rid of such a financial liability. Yet judging by the fresh paint and edged lawns, the Dante's manager still gave window-dressing a high priority. She thought that Mark, with his keen eye for economies, would have found such an attitude hard to swallow.

The afternoon sun struck hot on the truck's roof. For Karanja's comfort she ran it deep into the shade of an evergreen oak, whose sweeping branches practically hid the whole vehicle.

'I won't be long,' she told him, and he grinned and curled up to sleep in the passenger seat as contentedly as an old gundog. He was, she reflected, the ideal travelling companion: silent until directly addressed, always ready to leap out and open gates, change wheels, or tinker with engines; never in a hurry for the journey to end.

Walking softly in the shade of the trees, Sally approached the large hangar-like factory building, curious to see Karel at work – or at least the place he worked. Recently he had complained that production was at a standstill until enough rain fell for the bushes to shoot again. The long drought was exhausting them, and many of his close-planted hedges were covered with bracken to conserve moisture.

The building was very quiet, but not far away she could hear the click of a typewriter and guessed it came from the secretary's office. She went towards the sound, up a flight of steps, and through a sliding door that stood half open.

Coming in from bright sunlight, it seemed very dark inside the factory. The heavy damp smell of drying tea-leaves hung in the air, but all the machinery was idle. Fascinated, Sally walked along the rows of shallow trays where leaf was wilted, and past a line of heavy-doored safes with impressive padlocks and cryptic abbreviations stencilled on them. *E. Jul. '73. Ldy. DARW.* She couldn't guess what they meant.

She had entered the building at first-floor level. Peering over the gallery rail at the belts and chutes, elevators and fans below, she could see through the half-glass partition of an office on the ground floor where a girl was busily typing.

Her back was turned: all that was visible were slim shoulders in a pistachio-green sleeveless dress and a fall of sleek black hair. As Sally watched, wondering whether to go down and ask if she knew the whereabouts of Mr van Ryn, she heard hasty footsteps crossing the factory floor. Instinctively she moved back from the rail until she could see who had entered. She had no wish to be discovered snooping round the factory by Karel's unattractive assistant manager.

The girl in the office had heard the footsteps too. With swift movements suggestive of fear, she wrenched her work from the typewriter, folded it, and thrust it into a drawer. She scooped up the sheaf of documents she had been copying and slammed them into a filing cabinet. Quickly she inserted a fresh sheet of quarto on which she typed a few lines.

The man reached the door of the office and paused with his hand on the doorknob, listening to the quick chatter of typewriter keys. Sally had a bird's-eye view of thick dark hair, powerful shoulders, a lean muscular back tensed for sudden action. Her heart skipped a beat. It wasn't Karel's assistant, or anyone else with legitimate business in the empty factory.

'I guessed I'd catch you here.' With a swift movement he flung open the door. The girl turned in her chair with a little cry of alarm. For the first time Sally saw her face and got another shock: it was Elaine Chan.

'Bay! What are you doing here?'

While the door was open their voices were plainly audible to the watcher in the gallery.

'I came to find van Ryn, but since he's not about I'll pass on the message to you.'

'Message? Do you treat me as your errand-boy?'

Elaine's tone was provocative. The smile she flashed up at him showed she had regained her composure – might even be pleased to see him.

Bay shut the door and moved to stand very close to her.

Sally could still see them like actors in a silent film, mouthing and grimacing, advancing and retreating in the cramped little office. Only the sound-track was missing.

He bent to examine the sheet in the typewriter, and spoke emphatically for some time. Elaine went on smiling, glancing up from under her lashes, her expression demurely mocking. He spoke again.

She shrugged and lit a cigarette.

If only I could hear thought Sally.

Elaine moved round the desk until she was between him and the filing cabinet. Her body moved sinuously, pressing against him like a cat that begs to be stroked. Impatiently he opened the door and again the soundtrack switched on.

'. . . that's what would happen,' said Elaine, 'if you did anything foolish. I'm not joking, you know.'

'Leave her out of this,' said Bay abruptly.

'Oh, I'd like to. I really would. *I* don't like to see people hurt. I didn't want poor Mark to get hurt. I tried so hard to make him see sense. Silly Mark . . . he wouldn't listen. You're more sensible than he was, darling.' Her small hand with its pointed scarlet-tipped fingers caressed his arm, sliding sensuously over the skin. 'You're a big strong sexy sonofabitch, darling, but you're not in the same league as the boss. You've got to realise that.'

Roughly he shook off her hand. 'Tell van Ryn to lay off or he's for the high jump. That old bastard has wiped out most of the family units in the area, and unless Kariuki stops dithering and pulls his finger out, the rest will go the same way. I've got him where I want him now, but van Ryn needn't think that gives him carte blanche to move in.'

'Don't be so serious, darling.' Elaine's laughing face was turned up provocatively; her tongue flicked across her painted lips. 'Being serious doesn't suit you. You're a rough wild jungle man and you don't understand the little subtleties of business. Never mind. You understand what girls like and that's far more important. Has the little shepherdess succumbed to your fatal charm yet?'

'As far as she's concerned, I haven't any,' said Bay shortly.

'Don't tell me she hasn't slept with you yet?' She laughed shrilly. 'She will, darling. She will. But until she does, why not have some fun with little me? You used to like that.'

He looked at her dispassionately as if considering whether or not to accept the offer. Then he said, 'I can hardly believe it. Sorry, Elaine. You'll have to make do with van Ryn.'

He turned on his heel and walked away.

She watched him go a few steps then called: I'm seeing Marianna next week, darling. How she'll laugh when I tell her the Great White Stud has lost his balls. Or perhaps she knows already. Perhaps she quit just in time.'

The factory door slammed behind him. Sally waited until the angry rattle of typewriter keys began again, then slipped softly out.

CHAPTER FOURTEEN

THE LIGHT WAS fading when she turned up the Redstone drive, and as the truck tackled the final slope a sudden deluge of rain clattered against its roof. Even with the wipers working double speed it was hard to see through the streaming windscreen. Before they reached the cattle-grid, small torrents were racing them down the hillside, washing away the hard-packed surface and turning the road to liquid chocolate.

The rains, she thought with a mixture of excitement and apprehension. So eagerly awaited, so potentially damaging in their violence. The ditches were clear, the irrigation channels dug out, thanks to the concentrated work of the past month. All the ravages of the last deluges had been made good. Now they needed the right amount of rain, for the right length of time. No more, no less. Too much would wash away roads and bridges, uproot trees and drown livestock. Too little, and any shallow-rooted plants would not survive the dry season. To anyone accustomed to England's hesitant seasons and gentle weather, the Kenyan climate's exotic extremes were bewildering, even frightening.

Hollywood rain, she thought, running across the yard to the porch, getting soaked within three strides, hair plastered to her head. As she slammed the front door, the drumming downpour ceased as abruptly as a turned-off tap.

'I'm back!' she called into the sudden silence. 'Anyone at home?'

There was no answer. Puzzled, she kicked off her sodden

shoes and padded into the living-room, expecting to hear the slap of playing-cards or the click of chessmen. The room was empty: cushions plumped, curtains drawn, a bright fire burning.

Odd, she thought. A frisson of anxiety touched her.

'Matt? Willy? Tim?'

The shuffle of feet and Charles appeared to take her wet jacket. His shiny lined face was worried.

'Where is the bwana, Charles?'

He shook his head. 'I do not know, memsaab.'

Perhaps they're still at the dam, fishing, she thought. Perhaps they've taken shelter from the rain. But it's eight o'clock! It's dark. You can't fish down there in the dark.

Charles said, 'The bwana said to Mbugwa that he will bring fish for Mbugwa to cook, but he has brought none. What shall he cook now?'

Sally said slowly, frowning, 'Did they go fishing? Did you see them?'

'No, memsaab. The rods are waiting. The bwana would not go fishing without the rods.' He called them 'roddas', which normally would have made her smile, but now she was too anxious to be amused.

'What can have happened?'

When she saw he had no explanations to offer she felt a stab of real fear. Her two sons missing, in the dark, in a strange country where wild animals abounded, in the charge of an eccentric old man who had recently suffered a heart attack. How could she have left them with him?

She said, stifling panic, 'We must go and look for them at once. Tell Karanja I want the truck again. I'll drive round to the dam and see what has happened. You'd better come with me and bring a rope, and blankets and torches.' A picture had arisen in her mind's eye: the two boys struggling to raise an unconscious Matt from the water . . .

'Are the dogs here? Bring them as well,' she said and went quickly to put on another jacket. Moments later

Karanja brought the truck to the door and they all piled in, with the dogs whining excitedly in the back of the pickup.

Shining black and turgid as treacle, the still, secretive surface of the reservoir, broken only by artificial croys, seemed to mock them as they shouted and shone torches around the banks, encouraging Hansel and Gretel to hunt through the undergrowth for any indication that their master was about. Startled night animals rustled and pattered in flight. A buck barked and frogs plopped and croaked, but of humans there was no sign.

'They are not here,' pronounced Charles at last.

Sally looked up at the towering cliff above, with its white-plumed waterfall. It was a relief to know that her sons had not drowned in these still black waters or plummeted over the vertiginous drop, but the question remained: where were they?

'*Someone* must have seen them,' she said. 'They can't just vanish into thin air.'

'I am asking in the shambas,' said Charles, and she dropped him at the cluster of tin-roofed huts near the cattle-grid.

The house was still as quiet as they had left it. Sally tried to drink the bowl of soup pressed on her by Mbugwa, but her throat felt too tight to swallow. Both her sons, *lost* . . . Waiting for Charles' return, she wandered restlessly from room to room, searching for some clue as to where they'd gone, while all the time her conviction of what had happened to them grew stronger. In her mind's eye she saw Matt slumped across a rock; darkness closing in, the eerie screams and giggles of night-hunting hyenas. It had happened once: it could happen again.

Tim's room first. As she'd expected, his squirrelling instincts had been allowed full rein. Every surface was cluttered with treasures. Expended cartridges, targets shot full of holes, trout flies, teeth, bones, feathers. Stones and shells which had caught his fancy; an empty tubular beehive as used by Kikuyu, cassette cases, letters, half-written postcards. Sketches of birds and animals. Poster paints, brushes, a paint-rag.

No – it wasn't a paint-rag at all, she realised, examining it with some indignation. It was Tim's very best shirt – a dashing affair of broad stripes and buttoned pockets – smarter and more sophisticated than any previous shirt he'd owned. Also a good deal more expensive. In what moment of madness had he torn both sleeves asunder and cast it on the floor of his room? Dried peas crunched underfoot. That wretched pea-shooter, she thought, pushing at them ineffectually. Every time Tim took out his handkerchief a shower of dried peas came with it.

She heard Charles calling and hurried back to the living-room, but he had no news. After talking with Koinange and looking at a mysterious blight which had struck the pyrethrum, the bwana had apparently vanished off the farm, and no one had seen him go.

'Are any of the vehicles missing? A tractor, for instance?'

He had considered this possibility and checked. 'Nothing is missing, memsaab.'

'The bwana wouldn't go into the forest on foot, would he?'

Charles said emphatically that this was unthinkable. For one thing it was too far; for another there were many *kali* animals – fierce wild animals – in the forest. The bwana never walked there without a gun.

'He hasn't taken a gun?'

Again he shook his head. 'All guns are in their places.' After a moment's pause he added, 'In the office there is a letter for the memsaab, but it is not from the bwana.'

'A letter? Why didn't you say so before? How d'you know it isn't from him?'

'The letter is written with the machine, memsaab. The bwana cannot write with this machine.'

She knew this was true. She had wondered why Matt kept the high, old-fashioned Imperial gathering dust in his office. Presumably he felt a sentimental attachment to it since it had belonged to Janet. 'Bring me the letter.'

The square white envelope had her name on it. Brushing aside a superstitious shiver she ripped it open. Charles was wrong: it was from Matt.

> *'Sally –*
> *'Counting on you to hold the fort till we get back. Say nothing to anyone.*
> *'Matt'*

The lines seemed to dance before her eyes. Oh God! she thought. He's gone poaching again and taken the boys with him. She looked up and met Charles' curious stare.

'Is there news, memsaab?'

'No,' she said slowly. 'No, there's no news.' She crumpled the sheet of paper and dropped it in the waste-basket. As she did so, the telephone on the desk began to ring.

'Redstone Farm. Hello?'

'How did you get on at the sale?' asked Bay's voice. 'Did you get what you wanted?'

For heaven's sake! she thought with a silent scream. You never rang me at this hour to ask *that*! She forced her voice to say calmly, neutrally, 'Yes, thanks.'

'Glad to hear it. Well I didn't really ring up about that –'

Here it comes, she thought. She must have made some sound because he said sharply, 'Are you still there?'

'Yes. Yes, I'm here. What is it?'

'I'd like a word with your uncle.'

'That's . . . that's impossible,' she blurted, her brain seizing up, unable to think of excuses.

'Impossible?' His voice was gently mocking. 'Weren't you ever taught there's no such word? Go and fetch him, there's a good girl. It's important.'

'I can't. He's – he's asleep.'

'Then wake him up.'

'I'll give him a message.'

'Sorry, this is confidential. Strictly person to person. Go

on, wake him up and tell him the Ministry for Natural Resources is on the line. That ought to fetch him.'

'I can't,' she said desperately. 'It'll have to wait.'

'It won't wait.'

Impasse. Silence dragged out on the line. Then Bay said briskly. 'Very well, then. If you won't wake him up I'll come and do it myself.'

'No! Please don't.' She couldn't hide her anxiety.

'He *is* there with you?' said Bay in an entirely different voice. 'You're sure of that? He hasn't gone wandering off in the hills again, by any chance. Leaving you to cover his tracks?'

'Of course not.'

'You're a rotten liar, Sally,' he said with a strange kind of weariness. 'All right, we'll leave it until the morning, but I warn you that if Matthews isn't there when I arrive, and ready to talk to me, I'll have the anti-poaching boys on his tracks so fast he'll never know what hit him.'

He hung up before she could answer.

She called Charles back to the office, knowing now what she must do.

'That was Mr van Ryn,' she told him and ignored his look of surprised disbelief. 'He says the bwana will spend the night with him. He took the boys to see the tea factory. There's no need to worry. You and Mbugwa can go home and get some sleep. Thank you for helping me.'

He looked still more doubtful, thrusting out his lower lip. It was unheard-of for the bwana to go visiting.

'Go on,' she said sharply. 'Do as I tell you.'

'*N'dio*, memsaab.'

He padded out of the room and she heard him chattering excitedly to Mbugwa. A few minutes later the back door clicked and she was alone. She would have to hurry. Bay suspected where Matt had gone. He wouldn't waste time getting on his track. She had at most a five-hour start.

*

Apart from the feeble glow of candles, there was no light in the cave to show that it was brilliant morning outside. The two boys, chilled and stiff after a night on the floor, shivered miserably like abandoned puppies as they watched their uncle prepare to leave them. Ever since quitting the farm he had argued and pleaded with Mr van Ryn to let them go, and protested that he had no hidden cache of ivory. He'd never been a trophy-hunter. Everyone knew that.

'You've shot elephant for years and no one's ever had a sniff of the tusks, that's true enough,' said van Ryn dourly. 'But you're going to show me where they are and no messing – otherwise those boys will get hurt. It's up to you.'

Matt cursed the fact that he'd sent Sally off to the sheep sale alone. She would come back and find them gone, and then what would she do? Too much to hope she remembered the way up here; and even if she did what could she do against van Ryn and his thug of a manager?

'I tell you there's no ivory. You're wasting your time,' he said wearily.

Van Ryn ignored him. He turned to McKinnon. 'You stay here. If those boys give any trouble, shoot the pair of them. And if I'm not back before noon, put a bullet through their heads anyway.'

'Very good,' said McKinnon, as flatly as if he'd been told to give them a meal.

'You can't do that!' roared Matt. 'You can't murder children.'

'Like to bet?' Van Ryn slapped his shoulder. 'Get moving, Matt and show me your hoard if you want to see them alive again.'

At the far end of the cave, a yawning crack stretched across the path that elephants had trodden for countless generations. Years ago, Matt had blown out a section of rock, effectively cutting the trail. Now he uncoiled a rope which he had attached high up on the opposite wall, took a short run and swung across the artificial chasm with the ease of long practice.

He hesitated an instant before flinging back the rope. As clearly as if he could read his mind, Tim knew he was tempted to leave Mr van Ryn stranded. *But he can't*, because of us, he thought bleakly. After that tiny hesitation, Matt coiled the rope and sent it hissing back so that van Ryn could follow.

A moment later the beam of the torch faded, and the boys were left alone with McKinnon.

'Sit there where I can see you,' he ordered, pushing them into the little circle of light cast by the primus. They obeyed instantly. Anything to avoid being shoved and prodded and stroked by those thick, inquisitive fingers.

'I expect you're hungry. Want your breakfast, eh? Well, you can watch me have mine first.'

He busied himself with saucepan and tin opener, heating baked beans on the primus and shovelling them down with a wooden spoon while the boys watched in silence. They were very hungry.

'Greggeedeggy peggig,' murmured Tim out of the corner of his mouth, hoping to cheer Willy up. To his dismay McKinnon set down the saucepan with a crash and stalked across to stand menacingly over them, his thumbs hooked in his belt.

'What did you say?'

'He didn't say anything,' piped Willy quickly. 'He's always coughing and people think he's talking.'

Tim gave him a silencing nudge, but too late.

'Then I'd better move you away from one another. I don't want you both coughing your heads off. No, I don't think I would care for that. You – what's your name? Tim – you stay where you are, and little Willy can come over and sit beside me.'

'I'm all right here,' said Willy.

'Ah, but if you're good and do as I say, I'll let you finish the beans. How about that?'

'I'd rather stay with Tim.'

'What brotherly love!' mocked McKinnon. He hitched at the front of his trousers and belched loudly. 'Come on, Willy – move! You turn round and face the wall, Tim.'

'Why?'

'Because I say so! I don't want you staring at me like an owl.' Without warning his hand shot out and grabbed Tim's spectacles, wrenching the hooked ends from behind his ears. He flung them across the cave and they shattered against a rock. Tim gave a sob of fury and dismay. Without his spectacles the dimly-lit cave became foggy and blurred. He could barely distinguish McKinnon's features, though the man stood only a yard away.

'That'll teach you not to ask so many damned questions. Move!'

Reluctantly Tim pivoted until he faced the wall. All he could see of his brother and McKinnon were faint moving shadows silhouetted against the light.

There was some low muttering and scuffling noises, then a sudden snarl from McKinnon.

'You bloody pup! By God, you'll pay for that. Off with your trousers and bend over. I'm going to thrash the living daylights out of you.'

'No. Please, *no*!'

Tim sat frozen, waiting for the sound of a blow. Without his spectacles he was helpless and could only guess at what was going on behind him. Then he heard an odd little choking chuckle from Willy: the kind of half-ashamed laugh of a ticklish person trying to remain unmoved by tickling.

'There, you like that, don't you?' The hoarse whisper made Tim's skin crawl.

'I – I don't!' But Willy laughed again.

'Then why are you laughing?'

'I can't help it . . . Ow! Stop it. That hurts! *Tim*!' he yelled frantically, 'He's hurting me.'

'Keep still and it won't hurt,' whispered McKinnon.

Suddenly Tim could bear it no longer. He blundered to his feet, hands outstretched in front of him, and knocked one candle after another on to the floor. With a kick he sent the primus stove flying. The cave was plunged into blackness.

The scuffle in the corner intensified as Willy saw his chance to escape. Under cover of the noise Tim felt his way across the cave, trying to keep his bearings and horribly aware of the danger of getting too near the fissure. In the thick blackness it was hard to remember just how far the crack extended.

When he was near the struggling figures he tripped over the saucepan that had contained baked beans, and it clattered underfoot.

McKinnon froze, then lunged in Tim's direction and Willy broke free. 'Where are you?' he hissed.

'Here.' By a lucky reflex, Tim managed to grab his brother's hand and they tiptoed away across the cave. McKinnon was silent and they sensed he was listening, guessing where they must have gone.

There was nowhere to hide. Tim prayed that the man had no matches with which to relight the candles. After what seemed an age, they heard his cautious footsteps moving towards the waterfall entrance. Then his voice boomed, unnervingly close.

'Come here, you boys, unless you want to get hurt. I know where you are. Come out and stand where I can see you.'

Not bloody likely, thought Tim. He's bluffing. He can't see us, and I don't think he'd dare to fire a shot in case it ricocheted. He held tightly to Willy's hand, edging slowly away in front of McKinnon as he felt his way along the wall. The darkness was intense, and Tim was conscious that he had lost his bearings. The crack ran diagonally across the floor of the cave, and at some point met the wall. Any minute now his foot might hover over empty space. He inched forward, keeping his weight on the back foot until he could be sure the other was firmly planted; but Willy kept pressing him on, desperate to put as much distance as possible between them and McKinnon, whose breathing sounded very close.

Although he'd been expecting it, the moment when Tim found nothing solid beneath his questing front foot gave him a sickening lurch of the stomach. Hastily he stepped back from the brink, bumping into Willy who gave an involuntary moan.

Like a hunting animal, they heard McKinnon's indrawn breath and rapid movement towards his prey.

Tim dropped to his knees, pulling Willy down with him, and began to crawl at right angles to the fissure, feeling the edge to guide himself.

McKinnon heard the faint rustle of their clothes and gave a bark of triumph: 'Got you!' He lunged forward to grab at where the boys must be, tripped over Willy's legs and sprawled headlong. His arms went out to save himself and clawed at empty air.

Desperately he tried to fling his weight backwards, but the momentum of his lunge had carried him too far. He gave a wordless bellow as he felt himself slipping. Jack-knifing sideways, he caught a small projection of rock, but it came away in his hand.

'Help!' he groaned. 'I'm falling.'

A few feet away the boys crouched motionless, frozen with fear. They dared not move in case they, too, tumbled into the abyss; nor could they go backward where McKinnon's flailing arms might grip them. Through their hands and knees they could feel the floor of the cave trembling, and Tim had a dreadful fear that the whole lip of rock was about to collapse under them.

'Help me!' grunted McKinnon. 'Can't hold on . . .'

Did he really expect them to try to save him? Neither boy stirred. The next moment there was a wild, long-drawn-out shriek that echoed eerily round the cave and died into silence. They strained their ears for a splash, but there was nothing.

'He's . . . gone.' Tim felt in his pockets for a match, but when he tried to strike one his hands shook so much that he dropped the box.

Willy picked it up and struck a light. The weak flame transformed the cave, which had seemed huge and terrifying in the dark, into their old familiar hideout, but of McKinnon there was no sign. They avoided looking at the place where he had vanished.

'What shall we do now?' asked Willy in a voice that wobbled.

'Better get your clothes on.' Tim was shocked to observe that his brother wore nothing but a shirt and shoes. While Willy hunted for the rest of his belongings, Tim considered their next move. The choice lay between going back to the farm or following Uncle Matt.

'Mummy will be awfully worried,' said Willy.

'I know.' Tim frowned, wishing he wasn't the eldest. It was all very well for Willy; when it came to the crunch it was the eldest who had to make the decisions. Without his spectacles his mental processes seemed as blurred as his vision. He wandered across to pick up the shattered remains, but they were useless and he laid them down again.

'What shall we do?' asked Willy again. 'We can't stay here.'

'Do shut up. I'm trying to think.'

'Well, tell me what you're thinking.' Willy dug in his pocket and produced a fluff-covered roll of peppermints. 'Have a couple.'

'Thanks.' As Tim chewed the decision seemed to take itself without further effort on his part. There was really, he thought, no choice.

'We'll go on,' he said.

'I thought you'd say that,' agreed Willy, and ran to unloop the rope from the wall.

*

Matt felt the warning pains prickle in his chest and knew he was near the end of his endurance. A bitter sense of failure engulfed him. He had hoped to give van Ryn the slip and double back to rescue the boys, but the Dutchman had stuck to him like a burr and there had been no help for it but to lead him into the secret valley.

The steep-sided gorge behind the waterfall opened out at the bottom into a smooth bowl cut by the lazy loops of a wide shallow river. Five miles away, at the other end of the valley, Benjamin Kariuki's bulldozers were tearing down the walls of rock that had kept the gorge inviolate so long; but here above the waterfall the animals lived cut off from the rest of the world by the rockfall which Matt had engineered.

Already the pressure of population was destroying the valley's trees. Its dense vegetation had changed dramatically in the years Matt had known it. Directly in front of him now, beneath the feathery fronds of winter thorns, the ground was trampled as flat as a ballroom floor, and a grove of barked and dying baobabs pointed splintered branches skyward like accusing fingers crying to heaven to witness the destructive power of elephants.

They're too crowded, thought Matt. Give elephants all they need: safety, food, water, shelter – and what happens? Population explosion. Standing room only. If General Tembo saw the place now, he'd hardly recognise it.

Van Ryn had recovered his breath. He shaded his eyes, staring at the skeleton trees. 'Where's the ivory?'

Matt didn't answer. His eyes roamed over the valley which had been his private kingdom. His trap for Tembo.

Monkeys swung chattering from branch to branch of the marula trees and a long-tailed, yellow-rumped whydah flew like a streak of sunlight across the clearing. He noted fresh puddles beneath the trees and the shape of a lappet-faced vulture hunched on a rock beside the river. The twin-bumped brows of many hippos showed above the dark, still waters of the nearest pool. There were probably twenty of the great blubbery creatures submerged in that small area, delicately tiptoeing on the sandy bottom, passing the hours of daylight in waterlogged idleness.

A shadow moved in the shade of the thorns, and his gaze became riveted. A reddish-grey shape with a curved back and trunk that reached straight up twenty feet to twine round and shake a branch. The rattle of falling pods must be beating a tattoo on hard-packed earth, because more elephants were gliding into view, trunks snaking along the ground like industrious vacuum cleaners as they sucked up the fallen pods and blew them into their mouths.

Matt counted them. Fifteen in this group led by Old Buddha, the cow with drooping tusks like a mandarin's moustache. There was Willy's favourite, the Nought Elephant: this year's baby, his small trunk waggling like a piece of garden hose, his fat little body tucked beneath his mother's belly.

Matt sighed. He'd confined the elephants to this valley, gambling that they were a bait Tembo could not resist. But the terrorist had not come to his trap. Years of watching, years of dreaming of revenge had crumbled into dry dust. It was too late. Tembo wouldn't come now.

Van Ryn stared at the herd with an expression of baffled rage.

'You bloody bastard! You cheating swine!' he said thickly.

'You wouldn't listen,' said Matt wearily. 'I told you, but you wouldn't listen.'

Van Ryn's eyes bulged. He grabbed the old man by the collar and shook him. The violence in him was frightening. A red mist swam before his eyes and he knew nothing but the urge to shake the life out of that bony contemptuous face, to smash the man who had lied to him, sneered at him, despised him as a coward and now was cheating him of his ivory.

Slowly the madness died out of him. 'Those three bulls down by the river,' he said harshly. 'They'll do me.'

'What about them?' Matt touched his throat gingerly where van Ryn had nearly throttled him.

'Shoot 'em. Drop 'em where they stand.'

'You do your own dirty work,' said Matt.

Van Ryn made a show of consulting his watch. The hands stood at ten thirty-five.

'Took us an hour to get here, didn't it?' he asked. 'Bit over an hour, by my reckoning. That gives you thirty minutes in which to drop those bulls, or your precious nephews get a bullet between the eyes. How about it?'

Silence stretched out between them.

'Give me the gun,' said Matt at last. 'And the bullets.'

When he had loaded it, he turned silently and they filed down the dusty red path towards the little cove where the group of bulls van Ryn had marked for slaughter stood rocking and dozing: three sagacious old clubmen tranquilly soaking up infra-red rays, with their eyes half veiled by sweeping lashes as they snoozed away the morning, unaware of the two-legged menace that moved stealthily towards them through the dry grass.

CHAPTER FIFTEEN

THERE WAS A dented green truck parked brazenly in full view at the top of the forest track. So that's how they got up here, thought Sally, and wondered where Matt had been hiding the vehicle. She had never seen it about the farm.

Dawn had broken, but here in the forest the mist was thick among the trees, muffling sounds and distorting shapes. She reversed her own vehicle carefully over the leafmould until she had it well concealed behind vines. She filled in time until the light improved by brushing out the wheelmarks with a bunch of twigs.

When she had come here with Matt she had felt reluctant to leave the safety of the truck. Now she was alone she could hardly face the prospect at all. She prowled round the alien green truck, testing locked doors, telling herself it was hopeless to look for Matt's cave until she had better light.

Half an hour passed. The mist was definitely thinner and she could put off the evil moment no longer. She bent to examine a little cluster of berries at her feet and found they weren't berries at all, but dried peas. This evidence of Tim's recent presence encouraged her, but hardly had she taken a dozen steps into the forest than her straining ears caught the sound of an engine. Yet another vehicle was climbing the forest track. She hid herself and waited.

A few minutes later a white Range Rover came slipping and sliding over the damp ground. Bay was at the wheel and beside him sat Benjamin Kariuki. Her heart sank. The start she had counted on was wiped out, and with it her chance to warn Matt. The two men jumped out with the eagerness of dogs on a scent and briefly examined the green truck.

'He is here,' declared Kariuki. 'Follow me.' The urbane, sophisticated veneer had split like a snake's cast-off skin, revealing the wild jungle-dweller beneath. Both he and Bay wore belted kammo smocks and olive denims above calf-length boots: she saw that Kariuki had a holster strapped to his belt.

'Where's Sally, though? They said she drove in this direction.'

Kariuki shrugged. 'She is not important. Come, we must hurry.'

He slid into the undergrowth without waiting for an answer, and after a second's hesitation Bay followed.

She had to keep them in sight. So keen was Sally's fear of losing them that she hardly noticed her aching, shaking legs and the sweat that coursed down her body as she toiled up and down slopes and crossed streams in their wake, constantly alert for a sudden stop that might bring her to their notice. But Kariuki's attention was focused ahead: he picked his way with the concentration of an animal returning to some dimly-remembered lair. She wondered how he knew so exactly where to go.

Her puzzlement increased when they reached the spot where Matt had been taken ill. The twin black circles of her bonfires still scarred the ground. Above them rose the frowning cliff, honeycombed with caves. Without hesitation Kariuki headed for a crevice between two rocks and disappeared.

Warily she followed, and found herself in a cleft that was open to the sky and wider than it had appeared from outside. The men had vanished, but she could see the faint glimmer of a torch in the black mouth of a cavern ahead. She hurried to catch up.

The torchbeam stopped moving suddenly. Sally froze in a niche of the wall as it started to flicker in a circle, picking out rough shelves, boxes, an overturned primus.

'Somebody left here in a hurry.' Bay's voice echoed in the gloom. She heard the scrunch of glass and he exclaimed sharply. His huge shadow danced on the rock wall as he bent to examine something.

'Spectacles. Broken.' They tinkled as he dropped them again.

Tim's glasses, she thought with a lurch of the heart.

Ahead in the darkness there was a hiss of alarm and Bay shouted: 'Look out!'

The torchbeam zigzagged wildly. She had the impression of a brief, violent struggle and then Kariuki gasped, 'Aiee! The old fox has cut the trail. One step more . . .' He sounded very much shaken.

There was a moment's silence, then Bay said, 'You didn't expect that?'

'Would I throw myself in an abyss? It is many years since I came in this place.'

'There's a rope. We can get across.' The torch flickered busily about the rock wall. She saw Kariuki step back holding a long rope that seemed to be suspended from some point above him. He ran forward and swung into the darkness.

Bay followed.

Silence swept back into the cave – silence broken only by the slow drip of water. They had gone.

Sally went cautiously forward and shone her own torch into the chasm that had so nearly swallowed Benjamin Kariuki. Her head swam as she stared into its dark depths, but she forced herself to grasp the rope. *If they can cross that, so can I.* A moment later she stood safely on the far side, looking at a pinprick of daylight in the distance.

The boys lay on their stomachs, elbows propped to support binoculars. After a moment Tim gave an exclamation of disgust.

'It's hopeless. Everything's wuzzy. You'll have to tell me what you can see.'

Willy was torn between pleasure at being shot into the

hot seat and fear of making an ass of himself. He wiped the binocular lenses and fiddled with the focus until he was sure he could see as sharply as possible, then said slowly, 'There are a lot of hippos in the top pool. They're making massive waves just below that big sausage-tree. Two of them are fighting.'

'Oh, they're always scrapping,' said Tim impatiently. 'That doesn't matter. Are there any elephants about?'

'No. Oh, yes! There are three under that overhanging rock by the river, at least I think it's only three. There might be another just behind them in the grass. Oh!' he exclaimed, and fell silent, concentrating furiously on what he saw.

'What's up?' demanded Tim.

'Wait a bit. I've lost it. I thought . . . It looked as if . . . Yes, there they are again.'

'There what is? Stop gibbering and tell me what you can see.'

'I think I can see Uncle Matt and that foul brute Whatsisname.'

'Where?'

'Down at the bottom of the game trail, practically in the river. They're crawling over the stones – I bet Uncle Matt's knees are giving him hell. I say, Tim – they're getting awfully close to those three elephants. D'you think they don't know they're there?'

'How can I tell?' said Tim savagely. 'I can't even see the elephants. Oh, damn that bloody man for breaking my specs!'

'They've stopped. They're looking through binoculars. They *must* know the elephants are there. Oh Tim,' he said with a note of anguish in his voice, 'they do know they're there. I think Uncle Matt's going to shoot one.'

'Don't be an idiot. Matt wouldn't shoot an elephant,' said Tim scornfully.

'What if Mr van Ryn's making him do it? You know how he kept nagging on about ivory?'

Without his specs, Tim's eyes looked nakedly defenceless. He turned a horrified gaze on his brother. 'We must stop him. I know, we'll scare them off. Make a racket and drive them into the trees. Come on!'

They sprang up and pelted down the game trail, worn by animals' feet into a shiny winding ribbon through the thick bush, yelling and whooping like Indian braves. Before they had gone more than a couple of hundred yards, the heavy crash of a rifle sent shockwaves through the path and halted them in their tracks.

'What's happened?' cried Tim, peering into the blurred distance in an agony of helplessness.

Willy put the binoculars to his eyes, but found he could see better without them because his hands were shaking so much. 'One of them's going round and round in circles.'

The sunken-eyed leader of the three bulls had staggered and swerved as the heavy .470 bullet took him just behind the shoulder, and his screech of rage and pain sent his companions charging blindly out of the peaceful suntrap, which had become a death-trap. They vanished into the head-high dry grass that fringed the river.

The injured bull tried to follow, but the bullet had smashed his elbow-joint and he could only stagger in ever-decreasing circles until the leg gave way under him and he pitched forward on his head with a deep moan, tusks driven into the sand, hindquarters strained upright as if he was trying to somersault.

'Finish him off!' hissed van Ryn at Matt's elbow. 'Go on, quick!' Elephant fever had gripped him. His body shook with convulsive spasms and his eyes glittered glassily.

Matt levered himself up stiffly from his firing position and reloaded. He walked cautiously towards the dying animal, keeping out of its line of sight, ready to put another bullet into the back of its skull.

As he reached the twitching hulk, there was a snort and flurry of movement in the long grass where the other bulls had vanished, and a red-caked monster with a single huge tusk charged squealing like a runaway express. His tattered ears flapped open and his trunk curled tightly against his chest.

Matt had no chance to run. He dropped to his knees, flinging his body under that of the stricken elephant, and the rifle went off with a tremendous double blast. The snaking trunk whipped round his body and tossed him high in the air, cartwheeling over and over before he hit the ground with a bone-shattering thump. Karel van Ryn turned and fled blindly, unreasoningly, over the rocks towards the river.

The sun struck Sally with hammer force as she emerged from the hillside tunnel, and for a second her head swam. She had been moving at full stretch since dawn, after a sleepless night: suddenly she realised with alarm how near she was to collapse.

Bay and Kariuki had vanished. She thought she was unlikely to catch up with them now. Her best plan was to rest for a while and recover her strength while watching and listening for some clue to the whereabouts of Matt and the boys. She had no doubt that this hidden valley was Willy's Ivory Gorge. The thought that she might unwittingly stumble into the middle of Matt's stalk and find herself between hunter and hunted brought her out in a cold sweat.

She sat down in the shade and pulled from her pocket the hunk of bread and cheese she had stuffed there just before leaving Redstone. Her mouth was painfully dry and she ate slowly, wishing she'd brought a waterbottle. And lots of other things. Apart from the food and a Swiss Army knife she was woefully ill-equipped for a day in the bush.

Matt and the boys could not be far away. From this perch on the hillside she could see clear across the valley which was no more than a mile wide at its broadest point. Once it must have been heavily wooded, but now around the river clumps of trees had been stripped bare, their bark hanging in tatters from whitened dying trunks. Elephant damage, she thought with a little shiver. So this was where Matt still found tusks to poach: the place that young van Ryn would give a bit to see.

She stood up stiffly. The short rest had done more harm than good; she would have done better to keep moving. Her muscles had begun to ache and what had been a slight thirst was now a burning torment which drove her towards the river, heedless of danger which might lie in her path.

The water drew her like a magnet. Meandering in lazy coils like a silver snake, it promised a cool refuge from the stunning heat. Stumbling over the rough ground, tripping on vines, she went towards it on legs which hardly seemed to belong to her. Fear of the bush, fear of her own vulnerability, even fear of what had become of her sons had vanished before her need for a drink.

The clarity of the air made distances deceptive. By the time she reached the outcrops of rock that bordered the river her thirst was so acute that she flung caution to the winds and ran the last few steps to the shallows. She flung herself on her knees and gulped greedily. Compared to dehydration the risk of bilharzia seemed a trifling hazard, hardly worth worrying about.

She drank until she could hold no more, then splashed water over her head and neck and felt it trickle cool and delicious down her spine and between her breasts. She would have plunged in fully clothed, but a sound behind her made her turn sharply.

'*Jan!*'

She raised her dripping head and stared at the blue shadow cast by the cliff. Had she imagined that low, urgent croak? She rose uncertainly and walked a few steps towards the cliff.

'Help . . . me . . .'

Sally ran forward with a cry. Matt lay on his stomach, just as the elephant's trunk had flung him, his olive-drab clothes blending perfectly with the long sere grass. She must have run past within feet of him without seeing him. His face was turned towards her, caked with dust, stubbled with beard, grey and twisted with pain.

'Elephant . . . got me,' he gasped.

The shock of finding him alone made her cold with dread. It was a moment before she could say, 'Matt – what happened? Where are the boys?'

'Tell you . . . in a minute. First shoot the elephant.'

Perplexed, she stared at him; then she looked up and understood. What she had taken at first glance for a stony outcrop some fifty yards further up the slope was, in fact, an elephant.

It was stretched flat on its side on a little ridge, the stubby soles of its feet towards her, ears hanging in folds, and the mound of its belly rose like a smooth rock outlined against the sky. One shining tusk was buried in loose soil, but the other curved upward to make identification certain though the trunk and most of the flung-back head were out of sight from this angle. She was appalled by the sheer size of it: still more appalled when she saw the tip of the trunk rise above its back, feebly waving to and fro. A moment later the whole stricken hulk emitted a deep moan. Matt had bungled the shot: the elephant was still alive.

'Take . . . the gun. Finish him off.' His bloodshot eyes pleaded with her.

'I can't!' she said, aghast.

'Put him out . . . of his misery. Poor devil's suffered . . . long enough.'

'I tell you I can't.' She was suddenly angry. Whose fault was it that the elephant was suffering? Why had he shot it in the first place? Matt, she thought. Damn all men who kill for the sake of killing.

'Thought you had more guts.' The whisper was weakly contemptuous.

'It's not a question of guts,' she snapped, goaded. 'I can't shoot a thing that size. I don't know *where*, for one thing.'

Again the trunk waved pitifully. The great grey head

moved until one beautiful dark eye became visible, full of intelligence, waiting for the end.

'Size makes no odds. Put a bullet behind his ear. Don't think about it . . . just do it. May be hours . . . before he pegs out.'

'Oh, God!'

She gritted her teeth and picked up the rifle. 'Bullets?'

'In my pocket.'

She extracted the flat leather case, dark and shiny with age, with no time to wonder at the R. v R. deeply embossed on its front. With shaking fingers she loaded both chambers.

'Good . . . girl.' He made a ghastly attempt to grin.

'I haven't done it yet,' she said tightly, hating him for making her do this. Her heart hammered until it seemed likely to choke her as she approached the prostrate grey hulk. The enormity of what she was about to do threatened to paralyse her will. The skin was like wrinkled armour, immensely thick, powdered between the cracks with grey-red mud. The dark eye regarded her steadily, and she saw with dismay that tears were rolling down the sunken cheeks.

I can't do it, she thought, and halted. I can't just murder him.

The problem was practical as well as emotional. In order to put the rifle's muzzle close enough to the enormous ear to be sure of hitting the right spot, she would have to get above the elephant and lean across his back, putting herself within reach of the feebly questing trunk. She waited until the trunk lay flat on the ground, apparently lifeless, then cautiously manoeuvred until she had the muzzle in the right place. At once the trunk rose waveringly, the fingered tip trying to feel what was touching it. Sally's nerve broke and she snatched the gun away. Again the elephant groaned cavernously.

It was no good waiting: every minute that passed made her task worse. With the kind of resolution that comes with despair, Sally jammed the muzzle once more into the hollow behind the elephant's ear, thumbed it off Safe, and squeezed the trigger. There was a double pressure on the trigger, and for a moment she thought it wasn't going to fire. Then came a shattering crash and recoil that sent her staggering backward, her ears ringing and her collarbone on fire.

The elephant shuddered convulsively, and his trunk flopped into the dust with a kind of finality. Long minutes crawled by as she stood tensely gripping the gun, ready to fire the second barrel; then she sighed and lowered it. He was dead. Reaction set in. Shaking all over she stumbled down the hill to Matt.

'Now . . . do the same for me,' he muttered.

'Don't be absurd.'

'Mean it. Nothing . . . left to live for. Tembo won't come back now. Wanted to trap the murdering swine. Wanted –' His voice died away.

The sun beat down on her head and she wondered vaguely if she was going to faint or be sick. She felt very peculiar. Then she heard the quick beat of running feet. Before she had time to put down the incriminating weapon or even unload it, Bay Hamilton and Kariuki, followed by her two sons, burst out of the long grass beside the river.

CHAPTER SIXTEEN

THE TWO MEN STOPPED, breathing hard, staring from her to the dead elephant and back again as if unable to believe what they saw. Then Kariuki thundered: 'Who has done this? Who has killed the elephant?'

'I did,' said Sally quietly.

'That is impossible.' He looked past her at the still figure of Matthews, crumpled on the red earth, and said with less certainty, 'Impossible.'

Tears poured down Willy's filthy face. 'It's Mzee,' he sobbed. 'Why did you shoot him?'

'He was dying, Willy. There was nothing else I could do. Uncle Matt's been hurt.'

Willy gave way to noisy grief and she tried to put her arms round him to comfort him, but he pushed her roughly away. 'He was almost my favourite. He was the cleverest elephant of all.'

Out of the corner of her eye she saw that Bay had gone straight over to where Matt lay, but Kariuki, head bowed, stood close to the dead elephant.

Tim's face was as white as his brother's was red. He stood apart from her, silent and tight-lipped, looking suddenly much older. 'Leave Mum alone, Willy,' he said in a cold little voice that cut her to the quick. 'She doesn't know what she's done.'

She felt like a leper. 'What have I done? What do you mean?'

Tim said in the same tight hard voice, 'You've ruined everything. Tembo will never come back now. You've killed his father's spirit. Uncle Matt's waited for years for him to come and find his elephant again, but now you've killed him.'

'You're talking nonsense.' Relief at finding them unharmed rapidly gave way to anger. 'Why did you go off without telling me? I've been worried sick, imagining all sorts of things.'

The boys exchanged a quick glance. 'Well, you see, Mum,' began Tim but he was interrupted by a call from Bay.

'Here, Sally –'

He was bending over Matt. 'He's pretty bad,' he said in a low voice as she joined him. 'We're going to have a job to get him home. We'll need drugs, a stretcher . . . The crazy old fool!'

He slung the rucksack off his back and rummaged for a flask.

'Drink this,' he ordered, forcing it between Matt's teeth. He gulped and spluttered and some of the liquid ran down his chin, but a moment later he opened his eyes.

'Did you get him?' he whispered.

She supposed he meant the elephant, and nodded.

'*You got him*! Good show, Sar'nt.' His hoarse voice became clipped, military. 'Bring him over. Let's take a look at the bastard.'

'But, Matt –'

Bay put a restraining hand on her arm. 'Benjamin!' he called. 'Will you come over here a minute?'

Kariuki approached, she thought reluctantly, and stood looking down at Matt, his heavy face furrowed, lower lip jutting.

For a long moment Matt stared at him in silence, then he gave a queer little satisfied sigh.

'General Tembo,' he said. 'I knew you couldn't stay away for ever. I knew you'd come back one day.'

'I am Benjamin Kariuki,' said the deep mellow voice. 'I do not know this man you speak of.'

Matt's lips drew back from his teeth and his eyes glittered

in the way Sally dreaded. If he said something unforgivable now, she would never manage to talk Kariuki round. She tugged at his arm, trying to get him away. 'He's delirious,' she whispered. 'He doesn't know what he's saying.'

'I know damn well what I'm saying,' grated Matt. Anger gave him a spurt of vitality. He heaved up on his elbows, and his mad blue eyes glared at Kariuki. Saliva flecked his chin as his words spewed out. 'I know you're Tembo, whatever damn name you call yourself now. You can't fool me. For twenty years I've waited, you murderous bastard, and now you'll get a taste of your own medicine. Sar'nt!' he shouted to an invisible NCO, 'peg this black swine out in the sun and let him fry. Cut off his balls and stuff them in his lying mouth. Let the ants pick him clean . . .'

His voice broke. He sagged like a broken puppet.

Kariuki lowered his head and glowered; abruptly he turned and stalked away.

Sally followed him. 'I'm sorry,' she said, conscious of the word's inadequacy, 'you must forgive him. He's living in the past.'

'He should not say such things to me.'

'He didn't mean it. He – mistook you for someone. Someone he knew long ago.'

Kariuki turned a sombre, searching gaze on her. 'You seek to make excuses, but I tell you this: we have been patient too long with bwana Matthews and how does he respond to our patience? He breaks the law and shoots elephants. He calls me wicked names and drags my reputation in the mud. He will pay for all this. I, Benjamin Kariuki, declare it.'

'Give him another chance,' she pleaded. 'You know he's had a lot of trouble. His wife and children –'

'That *shauri* is ended,' he said with finality, and she knew that nothing further she said would make him change his mind.

Bay had been talking quietly to the boys. Now he left them and came over to where Sally and Kariuki stood.

'We're going to need help to get Matthews home,' he said. 'Would you go back to the truck, Benjamin, and call up your boys? Take the children with you. They've had a rough time by the sound of it and they're out on their feet. I'll come as far as the cave and pick up anything useful I find there. The old boy seems to have used it as a base for this kind of sortie. Tim says there are blankets and tinned food.' He raised a questioning eyebrow at Sally. 'How does that sound to you?'

It was strange how he had taken command. She said, 'What about Matt?'

'We can't move him without a stretcher. I haven't seen all the damage yet, but it looks –' he hesitated – 'pretty serious. An elephant gave him one hell of a thump. Serve him bloody well right.'

'Don't say that!'

'I'll say what I like. If you'd alerted me the moment you knew he'd gone bush, none of this would have happened. That elephant would still be alive.'

That's all he cares about, she thought. She said, before he could suggest it, 'I'm staying here. Someone will have to look after Matt.'

He nodded. 'Good. Don't worry. I'll be as quick as I can.'

'I'm not worried,' she said coldly, knowing it was a lie. She hated the thought of being left alone with Matt in this shadowed valley.

'That's settled, then. We'll be off. Come on, boys. You know the way better than I do.'

'Isn't Mum coming?' Tim sounded anxious.

She smiled to reassure him. 'I'm staying with Uncle Matt until Mr Kariuki's men bring a stretcher. Go on, darling. Don't argue.'

He opened his mouth to protest, then shut it again as Bay's hand caught him and propelled him forward. 'Come on, Tim, don't hang about. We haven't got all night.'

In silence Sally watched the little procession file away

towards the hills. Kariuki in front, the two boys shuffling like zombies a little behind him, Bay bringing up the rear. Just before they passed out of sight he turned to wave, but she didn't respond. The heavy silence pressed down on her. She had never felt more alone.

When Karel van Ryn discovered that McKinnon had deserted his post he cursed with the range and fluency that was the lasting relic of his five years in South Africa's armed forces, but beneath the surface anger he was uneasy. McKinnon might be bone from the neck up, but he was utterly reliable. He had always carried out orders to the letter. Although it was much later than the proposed time of rendezvous, van Ryn had confidently expected to find his assistant waiting in the cave with dog-like patience, having disposed of the Tregaron boys just as he'd been told to. Without his assistance it would be difficult if not impossible to recover the big bull's tusks and so salvage a few thousand dollars' worth of ivory in place of the priceless hoard he'd counted on Matt to lead him to.

Damn Matt. Damn McKinnon. Most of all, damn that interfering red-haired bitch who had put his whole future in jeopardy. Nothing had gone right since she came to live at Redstone Farm and upset his careful plans for stepping into Matt's shoes. She had made it plain enough that she intended to stay: plain too that she wouldn't even consider marrying him. She had that amused, assessing way of looking at a man as if she was secretly laughing at all his weaknesses, and her refusal to throw a fit of hysterics over mutilated sheep and strangled cats was positively unfeminine. Losing both sons, he thought vindictively, might be another matter. That ought to send her scurrying home with her tail between her legs . . . unless, like Matt, she was prepared to sit there at Redstone for twenty years in the hope of revenge. You could never tell with women. Least of all with a cockteasing gold-digger like Sally Tregaron.

Again he wondered how the hell he was to get those tusks back to the Dante. He depended heavily on the money Essex sent whenever a false-bottomed tea-chest neatly packed with rhino horn or sections of tusk arrived in the Fergcon warehouse. Without it the Dante could not pay its way – had never paid its way – and certainly couldn't support his own lavish life-style. It might be best to cut out the tusks and bury them until he could return with more carrying-power. There were a couple of Kamba boys working at the Reserve who would do the job for a bottle of whisky apiece and no questions asked. But first he must recover his father's rifle.

Deep in thought, he made his way back to the spot where the dead elephant lay. Shadow had crept across the valley floor in the past hour and the great upcurving tusks gleamed rosily in the sun's red rays. He approached the massive grey hulk cautiously, scanning the ground for the missing gun, and froze as a low mutter of voices caught his ear.

Very slowly he pushed aside the long grass around the elephant's head and peered out at the little clearing. Matt lay where he had fallen, but he was not alone. Kneeling beside him, her hair catching fire from the setting sun, was Sally Tregaron.

How the hell did she get here? he wondered; then remembered the earlier occasion when Matt had taken her into the hills. The lying bitch! She pretended she'd forgotten the way – played the helpless hopeless female with no sense of direction – and he'd fallen for it.

His mind began to run here and there like a questing ferret, seeking how to exploit the situation. Obviously she had no idea of his presence: what was less clear was whether or not she'd come alone. Wait and see, he thought. Excitement bubbled up in his veins. Suppose – just suppose – the stupid cow had come alone! She must have read the typed note he'd left for her, signed with Matt's name. He guessed that she would have kept her mouth shut about where she was going, but it was essential to be sure she'd brought no one with her. He didn't want to stick a simi between her ribs then find Karanja, or Mbugwa, or any other blabbermouth Kikuyu watching him.

It was Matt's low feverish muttering that had alerted him. From time to time Sally would answer, but to van Ryn it seemed that her responses were automatic, as one would try to quiet a fretful child. Matt's mind was wandering far from the time and place in which his body lay dying, and from the phrases van Ryn managed to catch, he was back in the days of the Emergency, hunting Mau Mau terrorists.

'*Shenzis* caught him at dawn . . . strung him up by the heels. Took him three days to die. Blew the women to bits in their huts . . . Blood and brains all over . . . never caught Tembo . . .'

Tembo. The word recurred over and over again.

'Don't talk about it,' said Sally, but the hectic muttering continued.

Van Ryn wormed closer through the long grass, his hand on his knife. She must be alone. If anyone else was with her, he'd have seen them by now. Cautiously he stood up, but the simi clinked against a rock.

Sally whirled round like a nervous filly at the starting-gate.

'Bay? Is that you?'

The low sun was full in her eyes, as van Ryn had intended. She cupped a hand to shade them, straining her ears to catch the sound again. Metal striking stone: no animal made a noise like that.

The silence was profound. Even Matt's murmurs had ceased. *Now*! thought van Ryn, and rose from behind his rock like a springing panther. The knife glinted in his hand.

'*Bay*!' screamed Sally on a note like a power-drill.

At once there was a faint answering shout. 'Hang on. I'm coming.'

So quickly that Sally couldn't be sure whether she had actually seen a man about to knife her or imagined the whole thing, van Ryn melted back into the shadows. She blinked and stared at the place where he'd been, but there was nothing.

With the crash of a charging rhino, Bay burst through the thorn bushes and instinctively she ran towards him. He dropped his load and his arms closed round her, hugging her to the rocklike comfort of his chest. She could feel his ribs heaving from the dash through the bush to her rescue. 'What happened? What made you scream?'

'I thought . . . I saw . . .' She struggled to control her voice.

'What was it?' He pushed back the hair that had fallen across her face and for a moment she had a crazy feeling that he was going to kiss her. Quickly she disengaged herself, ashamed of her panic.

'I'm sorry. I thought I saw a man, creeping up on me. All right – I know it doesn't seem very likely –'

'Hm. The light plays some funny tricks. How's Matthews?'

When they bent over him Sally realised why she had felt so utterly alone in that intense silence.

'He's dead.' Bay withdrew the hand that had felt in vain for a heartbeat. Some of the tenseness seemed to leave him. He drew a deep breath and added quietly, 'I'm sorry.'

'Are you?' Without waiting for an answer she said jerkily, 'What shall we do now? We can't just – just leave him here.' She rubbed her stinging eyes, shivered and yawned uncontrollably.

He watched her with narrowed gaze. 'Cry if you want to. It's no good bottling it up for later. Better still, take a walk around and get your blood moving. You've been sitting here for hours. I'll deal with this.'

'But how?'

'I found a spade . . .'

'You knew he was going to die?'

'Come on. It was always on the cards. When a man

collides with an elephant, he usually comes off second best. Buzz off and leave this to me. Give me about half an hour. Oh, and Sally –'

'Yes?'

'Stay within shouting distance – OK?'

As she walked numbly away she heard the steady clunk-clunk of a spade striking earth and knew that tonight, at least, Matt would rest beyond the reach of hyenas. When she rejoined Bay after washing in the river she felt a great deal better, though the sensation of being watched would not quite leave her. Imagination, she told herself, and said nothing. He was collecting chunks of rock to weight down the long mound of newly turned earth.

'Good timing,' he said. 'I've found a better place to camp. We'll carry our stuff up there right away. I don't know about you, but I'm ravenous.'

'Why don't we start to walk back? There'll be a moon.'

'Frankly, I'm not sure of finding the way in the dark. I think we'll stay put and wait for Kariuki and his boys. Haven't you done enough walking for one day?'

The enforced intimacy of a shared camp was not to her taste, but it seemed she had no choice. In silence she helped collect the equipment he had brought from the cave, and with a last glance at the long quiet mound, she followed him a little way up the hill.

Only when they had built a fire and the singing of the blackened kettle had begun to give the scene an air of normality did she ask: 'Did Tim and Willy tell you why Matt brought them here? I still can't understand it.'

'No, they didn't have much to say on the subject. In fact they were pretty uncommunicative altogether.'

'Poor darlings, they must have been really tired. Usually hind legs on donkeys aren't safe.'

'I don't think it was tiredness . . . I think Matthews must have put the fear of God into them. The poor little devils were too frightened to talk.'

'That's absolute nonsense,' she said quickly. 'They

weren't a bit frightened of Matt. He treated them like his own children.'

He gave her a curious, searching look. 'I don't mean they were scared of *him*. But he'd fed them so many horror stories about General Tembo that they weren't exactly happy to find themselves in his company,' he said matter-of-factly, reaching for the kettle. 'Here, this thing's boiling. How about some tea?'

'*General Tembo*?' She stared at him in undisguised horror. 'You don't mean –? You can't mean –'

'That Kariuki was once General Tembo? Well, that's what your uncle told us, wasn't it?' His tone was utterly reasonable, frighteningly reasonable. 'I'd have thought he'd have known, if anyone did.'

'He was delirious! He had Tembo on the brain. He was obsessed with the idea of meeting him again and just lashed out at the first black face he saw. He didn't know what he was saying.' A horrible suspicion that he might be right formed in her mind as she struggled to suppress it.

'On the contrary, I think he knew exactly, and so did Kariuki. I've suspected for some time that was the reason he would never actually confront your uncle. He needed his land for the Research Station. He had endless provocation over the poaching business. Time and again I told him the work of the Research Station would be crippled while Matthews was free to shoot all the elephants he pleased right in the heart of it, yet I couldn't persuade him to meet Matthews and thrash it out face to face. Why? Because deep down he still feared that your uncle would recognise him.'

'My God,' she breathed.

'You saw Kariuki's face when he first met you,' he went on inexorably. 'He looked as if he'd seen a ghost – right? And how did he know the way into this valley if he hadn't hidden here in his terrorist days?'

'Stop . . . Stop, I don't want to hear any more.' She remembered how Kariuki's warm confident greeting had faltered; how he'd brushed a hand across his eyes as he looked at her. He *had* seen a ghost. The living breathing ghost of Janet Matthews, whom he had butchered all those years ago.

Sally jumped to her feet, upsetting the kettle, her eyes wild. 'You knew! You knew who he was and you left Tim and Willy with him! Where's the torch? I'm going after him . . .'

'Sit down!' The hand that caught her shoulder was anything but gentle. She struggled in an iron grip.

'Let me go!' She struck his face with her free hand, jabbing at his eyes.

'Stop it.' The stinging slap he gave her rattled the teeth in her head. Her mouth opened soundlessly and she stared at him with wide, shocked eyes.

'Sorry,' he said more calmly. 'I didn't mean to hurt you but I couldn't have you blundering off into the bush in the dark. Listen: your sons are perfectly safe. There's no need to go off the deep end because Kariuki belonged to the Mau Mau. Tim and Willy are just as safe with him as they'd be with Mbugwa or Charles. Probably safer.'

'How can you say that when you know he's a murderer? He killed my cousins and my aunt.'

'If he did, I should guess that he's regretted it ever since. Not from remorse – I doubt if he'd suffer from that any more than a hunting lion would – but because that ill-advised bit of youthful score-settling must have taken a lot of living down. It's given his enemies a stick to beat him with, even if he's managed to keep most of the gory details under wraps. Your uncle wasn't the only man who'd like to see Benjamin Kariuki thrown out of office. The Kikuyus still haven't got used to the fact that they're not the only tribe to take an interest in politics nowadays, and the men like Kariuki often find themselves fighting on more than one front – inside the tribe and outside it. As for him being a murderer – what makes you so sure that Charles, for instance, and Karanja and Mbugwa didn't behave in just the same way during the Emergency? They're all over fifty – and they're all Kikuyu.'

'Matt wouldn't have kept them on unless he knew they were loyal, of course.'

'That's where you're wrong. You probably don't realise that at the height of the Emergency, ninety per cent of the Kikuyu people had taken some kind of Mau Mau oath. Nine out of every ten. It was as much as their lives were worth to refuse it, poor devils. Can you really be sure that all your uncle's house-servants belonged to the remaining ten per cent?'

He was upsetting all the reassuring theories with which she had tried to stifle the instinctive fear of Africans – fear that originated in her childhood memories; showing her that treachery and violence might still lurk behind those smiling black faces.

'One of Matt's houseboys was killed trying to defend Aunt Janet.'

'Yet he may have let the terrorists into the house.'

'That's right. General Tembo and his gang. Your friend Benjamin Kariuki in his former incarnation,' she said bitterly. 'What makes you so sure he's changed?'

'You heard what he said: "That *shauri* is ended." Tembo and all he stood for ended when Kariuki realised that Mau Mau was never going to give him what he wanted. When he came out of the forest. Don't forget, if he hadn't spent those years in the forest, he'd never have developed such an interest in his country's wildlife.'

'So every cloud has a silver lining.'

He ignored the jibe. 'That's where his admiration and affection for elephants stems from.'

'Whence your own admiration and affection for him, I suppose.'

He thought it over, then said seriously, 'Affection – no. Admiration – certainly. You have to admire the old rogue. He started from less than scratch – those terrorists caught by the Security Forces after years in the forest had become genuinely sub-human – and look at him now. The complete political animal. Suits from Savile Row; in line for a Ministry next time round; mopping up awards from the World Wildlife Fund; speaking at City banquets. He pulled himself there by his own boot-straps.'

'And everyone except Matt has conveniently forgotten that he ever had anything to do with the Mau Mau. Well, Matt's dead, but I'm not going to forget.'

'Don't be a fool,' he said harshly. 'That *shauri* is ended. If you're going to live out here, Sally, you'll have to come to terms with reality. Stop living in a dream world.'

'Who said I was going to live here?'

He shrugged. 'Call it a guess. A hope, maybe.'

'What d'you mean?'

Before she realised what he meant to do, he took her in his arms with an easy confidence that caught her unaware. His face was very close to hers: the strong planes of chin and cheekbone, lit from beneath by the fire's glow, had a reckless, daredevil look. The dark-rimmed pewter eyes held her in a gaze that was both mocking and curiously intent.

'Work it out,' he said.

It was largely her own physical response to the kiss which made Sally so furious. She wrenched free, prickles raised like an embattled hedgehog. Elaine's shrill laughter seemed to ring in her ears.

'Don't waste your *fatal charm* on me. You won't get your grubby hands on Redstone that way,' she said bitingly. 'Save it for women who appreciate it more – women who like big strong sexy jungle men! Perhaps I should make it clear that Miss Chan's cast-off admirers really aren't my cup of tea.'

His arms dropped to his sides: he stood very still. 'Where were you?' he said. 'How much did you hear?'

'Enough. Too much.'

'What were you doing prowling about that place, spying

on me? Don't you realise what a damnfool dangerous thing that was to do?'

'I had a perfectly good reason to be there, which is more than you can say, I imagine,' she flashed. 'I had some business to discuss with Karel van Ryn, and I happened to find you and Elaine enjoying a little heart-to-heart. It didn't seem quite the moment to disturb you,' she added dryly.

With elaborate concern she bent down and began to poke small sticks into the fire, stirring up the blaze. 'So let's keep the party polite, shall we? You sleep your side of the fire and I'll sleep mine, and we'll pretend that the last few minutes didn't happen – right?'

'If that's what you want.' He arranged himself comfortably on the opposite side of the fire, back against a rock, long legs elegantly sprawled, no more ruffled than the cat which misses its pounce, then retires to wash itself and wait for a better opportunity.

Alert and watchful, the grey eyes followed her movements as she opened tins and stirred tea. 'You're quite wrong, you know,' he said after a suitable interval.

Sally said nothing.

'Your husband may have been one of Miss Chan's admirers, but I'm certainly not. Never have been. If you'd done your eavesdropping more thoroughly you'd have discovered that, at least.'

'I tell you I wasn't eavesdropping.' His insensitivity in referring to Mark's relationship with Elaine provoked her into speech.

He grinned. 'Sorry – a slip of the tongue. I mean my conversation with Elaine which you accidentally happened to overhear. You obviously didn't hear the message I gave her, though.'

'Would it have interested me?'

'I think so. You see, I've been going over the same line of research as your husband, but beginning from the other end. He knew that Martin Essex was involved in a smuggling racket, but he couldn't be sure where the ivory came from. He suspected someone at the Dante Tea Estate was involved, but he had no proof. I, on the other hand, knew that ivory was leaving this area, but I couldn't be sure where it was going. Miss Chan provided the link.'

She stared at him, thinking it out. 'So what was your message?'

Bay said deliberately, 'I told her the game was up. If van Ryn wanted to stay clear of Nyeri gaol, he would stop sending ivory to London.'

'And if he refused?'

'I'd put the facts before Benjamin Kariuki. That would be the end of the Dante Tea Estate, and the end of van Ryn's career as well.'

'Why don't you tell him anyway? What makes you think Karel will take any notice of what you say?'

'Because he's only the middleman. The person I really want to see behind bars is the man who shoots the ivory. The poacher.'

'Uncle Matt?'

He nodded. 'That's how I persuaded Kariuki to come with me today. To see if we could catch the poacher red-handed.'

'So that was why you were sorry he died. How very disappointing for you! Never mind, your worries are over now, Uncle Matt dead and Karel warned off. Your elephants should be safe as houses – until another poacher comes along. By then I expect you'll have the whole Reserve surrounded by barbed wire entanglement and electronic eyes, and every elephant fitted with a radio collar and half a dozen thermometers to monitor its feeding and breeding and God knows what else, and Redstone Farm will look like Passchendaele . . .' She challenged him with bright, angry eyes. 'It won't seem like Africa at all, will it? Forward in the name of science!'

'Sally's vision of the future,' he murmured, and leaned forward to touch her arm. 'I think I prefer this one.'

'Oh . . . !' She caught her breath.

Swaying with the stately grace of galleons under canvas, a file of elephants – cows and calves – was approaching the river in perfect silence, a black frieze beneath the silver moon. One minute they weren't there: the next they had appeared as if by magic. They rolled over the sandy ground with the smooth deliberation of a wave; untamed, majestic, serene.

Only when they reached the spot where the dead elephant lay did their orderly progress falter. The lead cow, an imposing matriarch with long slender tusks that drooped almost vertically, like the moustaches of a mandarin, reached out her trunk to touch his back, and quickly the others gathered round in a tight group, snaking out exploratory trunks to finger their fallen comrade. Some attempted to lift him on their tusks. A small cow seated herself on the dead elephant's head; when she finally rose again several others began to push and strain until the corpse had been moved several yards towards the river.

For what seemed a long time they milled about aimlessly, returning again and again to stand near the dead bull. When their efforts to rouse him met with no response, most of them drew back with loud growls and belly-rumblings, but still the old matriarch and two others persevered, pushing their tusks beneath the dead bull's body from opposite sides, apparently trying to raise him to his feet. They talked to him with little grunts and squeals, as if refusing to believe that he was really dead.

Even when her companions moved off to the water, the lead cow remained, a tragic grieving figure, swaying from foot to foot and occasionally reaching out to slide the tip of her trunk over the dead bull's head. Sally was glad when a cloud covered the moon and blotted out the sad little tableau.

"'*Any man's death diminishes me*,'" said Bay quietly. 'I'd take it further and say any creature's death diminishes me, because I am involved in creation. We all are.'

Sally gave him a quick, surprised look and said nothing. Instead she smothered a yawn, and found that once she'd begun, she couldn't stop.

'You're all in,' said Bay. 'I'll sit up and keep the fire going while you get some sleep.' He grinned. 'Don't worry. I'll stay on my own side.'

She looked at her watch. It was only half-past eight although it felt like midnight. 'Let's share the watches,' she said. 'Wake me up about one, and I'll do the second stint.'

'Fine.'

They shared out the bedding and he insisted she took the quilted mountaineer's sleeping-bag with its thick down filling. He rolled himself in blankets and propped his back against a rock on the other side of the fire.

'Sleep well,' he said.

He wished he had a gun, but there was no point in saying so. Then he wondered what had happened to the rifle Matthews had used to shoot the elephant. It was probably still where Sally had put it down when they burst into the clearing. No use looking for it now, but as soon as it was light he would have a proper hunt for it.

CHAPTER SEVENTEEN

SALLY SLEPT THE deep sleep of exhaustion. In her dreams she heard Bay moving about the clearing, stoking the fire, but she could not swim up to the surface of consciousness and only stirred and went back to sleep. Vaguely she was aware of hands rearranging the hood of her sleeping-bag, drawing it closer round her neck.

'Thanks,' she murmured. 'Better . . .' She snuggled into the delicious cocoon of warmth.

A man laughed softly and footsteps crackled on twigs. Then silence returned.

When she woke at last it was full sunlight and she realised with a jolt that Bay had allowed her to sleep the night through instead of rousing her for the second watch. Without moving, she looked round the little clearing. Last night's camp fire was a circle of grey ash with a perimeter of unburnt sticks. It had not been stoked for some hours.

Her mouth was dry and gritty and she felt far too hot. She tried to push down the smothering sleeping-bag and found that the drawstring was knotted so closely round her neck that she could not get her hands free. She was imprisoned as if in a straitjacket.

Alarm at this discovery set her pulses racing. Something was definitely wrong. For several minutes she struggled to undo the cord but it was impossible to get at the knot. Equally impossible to break it or kick a hole in the material.

Sweat began to stream down her face and she had no means of wiping it away. She felt suffocated, as if in a steam bath. She forced herself to lie still: to think. Where was

Bay? Why had he left her like this? If a predator came near she would be helpless.

Now her vague memory of the hands pulling up the sleeping-bag took on a new and sinister meaning. He hadn't been tucking her in against the night's chill. He had been making sure she was immobilised, unable to run away. Unable to follow him.

Again she fought to loosen the neck of the sleeping-bag, and this time succeeded in locating the knot, which was firmly tied behind her neck. Although she could not manoeuvre it within reach of either hand, she managed to duck her head low enough to catch a section of material in her teeth. Grimly she began to chew, spitting out shreds of nylon and feather which threatened to choke her. At last she felt the material rip: she had made a hole just big enough to poke a finger through. Another five minutes of concentrated effort enlarged the hole to allow her hand to escape. She wriggled across to the rock on which she had stacked the remains of last night's supper, and grabbed their only knife. It was the picnic variety, small and blunt, but armed with it she sawed and slashed her way out of the nylon prison. Like a snake sloughing its skin, she struggled free of it and emerged hot and dishevelled, with the taste of fear in her mouth.

In the clearing nothing stirred. But from the direction of the river she heard the steady thump of axe on bone and knew with sickening certainty what it must mean.

Not Bay, too, she thought. I can't bear it. A sense of utter desolation overwhelmed her. She felt as if she'd stumbled into a quagmire and each time she succeeded in freeing a foot the other sank in deeper. She might regard Bay as an adversary who'd stick at nothing to acquire Redstone's land; but in a strange way the very fact that he'd made his intentions so plain had led her to trust him. She'd believed in his concern for the future of Kenya's elephants, even if she didn't share it. Worst of all, in some secret, unacknowledged part of her mind she'd been pleased to know he found her desirable; even enjoyed his rough handling. As a contrast to Mark's romantic, kid-glove approach, she found it exciting. No doubt sharing a cage with a partly-tamed tiger would provide a somewhat similar thrill. She didn't want to know that he was just a common poacher.

He fooled me, she thought bitterly; and anger crept in to replace the sense of loss. He fooled me properly, but he'll regret it. I've still got one trick up my sleeve.

Guided by the sound of the axe, she crept through the long grass towards the clearing where the elephant lay. Matt's rifle was still where she had propped it, in the fork of a thorn tree, and the leather bullet-case beneath it. With hands that shook only slighly she loaded both barrels and put on the safety catch. Slinging it over her shoulder, with one hand supporting the stock to prevent it bumping on the ground, she crawled slowly uphill.

A horrible smell of putrefaction assailed her nose and a worse sight her eyes. Vultures were wheeling overhead, and it was plain that they had already feasted on the enormous carcase.

Stripped to the waist, glistening with sweat and liberally smeared with blood, Bay was engaged in cutting one of the tusks free from the spongey, porous bone of the dead bull's skull. A greeny-sheeny blanket of flies covered the raw flesh where the skin had been stripped away. They rose in buzzing clouds whenever he touched them and instantly settled again.

He worked slowly and with great care, slashing back the tough skin of the lip to expose the gleaming ivory, and cutting round the pulpy central nerve with a surgeon's precision. Watching him closely, equally absorbed in the grisly task, was Karel van Ryn.

Van Ryn and I are not on the best of terms . . . Was every single thing he'd told her a lie? Here they were, the poaching brothers-in-law – brothers-outside-the-law – extracting the ivory which would later be despatched in Dante tea-chests addressed to Martin Essex.

She lay and watched them, wondering how Bay would explain his absence when he returned to their camp. She must not let him know what she'd seen. The removal of the second tusk took a long time. Bay continued his slow careful work while van Ryn fidgeted and cast sweeping glances round the horizon. He must be anxious to get the job finished before Kariuki and his party appeared.

When at last Bay drew the long shining tusk clear of the skull and plugged the hollow end with grass, she was surprised to see him shoulder it alone. It was evidently heavy, and an awkward burden that dipped back and forth like a coolie's carrying-pole, yet Karel followed him, unencumbered by anything except the spade.

Slipping stealthily from rock to rock, keeping them in sight, she followed. They halted in a little gully and Karel gestured. This'll do. Bury it here. She took careful bearings to be sure of finding the spot again. Bay picked up the spade and began to dig while Karel looked on.

When the first tusk was buried, the whole performance was repeated. Then with shocking suddenness the pattern changed. While Bay filled in the second hole, Karel turned away so that he faced the spot where Sally lay. She saw him draw a hand-gun from under his jacket. Holding it out of Bay's sight, he said something and pointed with his left hand. As Bay turned to look in that direction, van Ryn brought up the gun and placed it at the back of his head.

Sally screamed.

The effect on both men was electric. Van Ryn's head turned sharply, and Bay exploded into action. He dived sideways, swinging the spade in a low arc. It caught van Ryn behind the knees. They rolled over in a cloud of dust, grappling with deadly intensity. Then there were two shots in rapid succession. The mêlée broke apart.

One man lay huddled on the ground. The other struggled to his feet, stooping to retrieve his gun. As van Ryn aimed once more at the helpless man lying at his feet, Sally thumbed off the safety-catch and fired.

Afterwards there was no doubt in her mind that she had meant to blast him into oblivion. Indeed she often thought it would have been easier to live with her memories had she done so. But again the recoil of the heavy .470 took her by surprise. The barrel bucked in her hands, the butt thumped against her already bruised shoulder muscle with a kick like an infuriated cart-horse, and the bullet went wide. Before the echoes had died away van Ryn was running, leaping like an impala over rocks and scrub, heading for the river.

She swivelled to follow the line of his flight, aimed and fired the second barrel, scarcely feeling the pain in her shoulder, but he went on running. A moment later she saw him dive into the river in a flat shallow arc, and the splash as he hit the water.

Instantly, like a conjuring trick, the calm shining surface began to heave and whiten as if a mirror had been sprayed with polystyrene foam. A hideous cacophony of primeval noises, grunts and groans and roars rent the air. Blinking, she peered through the telescopic sight. A dozen grotesque heads swam into focus, wide-muzzled, wider-jawed, their little ears flat and huge scarred bodies like inflated rubber tyres churning the water where van Ryn had dived in.

For a moment she could never erase from memory she saw him standing neck deep in the water, his arms outstretched as he tried frenziedly to wade back to the bank. It was like running in a nightmare. Though he splashed and strained he made no headway, and when his legs were jerked from under him he fell forward on the water, dragged like a long olive torpedo into mid stream, where abruptly he vanished and the polystyrene foam turned brownish pink between the bobbing heads of the hippo herd.

Sally dropped the rifle and scrambled up. Beyond the gully Bay lay ominously still, while the heat haze danced and shimmered around him. Slipping and slithering over the bank, into the gully and up the other side, she ran towards him, her steps slowing as she got nearer and he didn't move. She flung herself on her knees beside him.

'Oh, darling!' The word came from her heart before her brain had a chance to censor it.

Bay opened his eyes. 'Never thought I'd hear you say that,' he said weakly, and grinned.

She took his hand and gripped it hard. 'I thought he'd killed you.'

'Would you have minded?'

'*Idiot* . . .!' She helped him to stand. Beneath the tan his face looked grey, and he winced as he moved his left arm. Leaning heavily on her he limped across to the shade of the nearest tree and sat whistling slightly between his teeth as she used his pocket-knife to cut away his torn and bloodstained shirt. His left shoulder looked a mess. One of the bullets had smashed into it just below the collarbone and she guessed it had lodged beneath the shoulderblade.

'What happened to van Ryn? Did you miss him?'

She swallowed. The memory of that desperate wading figure was horribly clear. 'The hippos got him. They – they pulled him under. He didn't have a chance.'

He was silent for a moment. Then he muttered, 'Poor bloody bastard. He never had a chance.'

'Why did you help him? Why did you leave me tied up like that? I thought you'd left me there to die.'

He grunted. 'I couldn't do much else with a gun pointed at my head. He'd have shot you too if I hadn't told him you were drunk and dead to the world.'

She had recovered from her shock enough to feel indignant at such a slur. 'You mean he believed you?'

'He said he always reckoned that Tregaron bitch had a drink problem . . . Having one himself, I suppose he thought he knew the signs. Listen: in that rucksack of mine there's a first-aid kit. I could do with a shot of morphine. This damned arm.'

She was off before he had finished speaking, and when

she returned with the rucksack she found him gingerly exploring the wound with his good hand. 'It hurts like hell but I don't think it's too serious provided Kariuki gets a shift on. Can you give me a jab?'

She broke open the tiny ampoule and administered the injection automatically as she tried to sort out the events of the last hours.

'That's better,' he said a moment later. 'I'm afraid I owe your uncle an apology. Too late to give it to him, of course, but I don't suppose he'd care. He never cared much what people thought of him, anyway. The fact is, he didn't come here to shoot elephant. Far from it.'

'Then why did he bring the boys here?'

'That was Karel's doing. He grabbed your two boys as hostages to force Matthews to show him his famous cache. It's a well-known local myth: I've heard it myself. For years people round here have been telling one another that the old bwana must have buried all the tusks he'd shot, and they were hidden in these hills. Van Ryn, poor sod, believed it.'

He paused, then went on reflectively, 'I knew he needed money, but I never dreamed he would turn . . . dangerous. Always preferred the stab in the back technique. I should have known he was desperate when he killed Nelson Kamau. That was his jacket you were wearing when you came to my camp. He must have dumped it at Redstone and you happened to pick it; I could see it was too small for Matthews . . .'

'Why did he kill Nelson?'

'It was Sam Kamau, Nelson's brother, who'd been supplying van Ryn with poached ivory, and when he got killed Nelson tried a spot of blackmail. I don't suppose he thought van Ryn was dangerous, either. He's always been a fall guy – a bit of a joke. No nerve for hunting big game, you see. Even Janni used to laugh at him, until one day they went after a leopard together and Janni didn't come back.'

He sighed. 'The only person he worshipped was Marianna. She was his little sister – the one who thought he was wonderful. I expect that's where a lot of his money went – trying to keep pace with Marianna's extravagance.' His mouth twisted. 'Taking over my responsibility when I copped out.'

'But she deserted you!'

'He thought I treated her badly. Left her in the lurch. D'you know what he said as he shot me? "That's for what you did to Marianna."'

He leaned his head against her shoulder.

'You're talking too much,' said Sally.

'I feel like talking,' he protested but his voice was drowsy. 'Wonderful stuff, morphine. Makes you happy and dozy and without a care in the world. Tell me one thing before I pass out completely. Will you marry me?'

She shook her head. She felt suddenly very happy too. 'You're out of your mind. I can't take advantage of your weakness.'

'Balls. My mind is crystal clear and I've never felt stronger,' he said deliberately. Like a wireless needing a new battery his words came slower and slower. 'Will you or won't you?'

'What about one of those temporary arrangements you're so fond of? A gentlemen's agreement?'

His hand gripped hers painfully. 'Because you're no gentleman, darling. I insist on a proper contract, legal and binding. If not, the deal's off.'

'It'll have to be subject to review,' she said rather breathlessly. 'Notice to be given on both sides . . .'

'Done!'

He leaned forward and kissed her. We're both mad, thought Sally, but the happiness persisted. Bay shifted carefully until his good arm was round her waist and his head pillowed on her shoulder.

'Darling?' she said experimentally, trying out how it sounded, but he didn't stir.

She looked at the river and saw the elephants. They were

rolling across the sandbanks, line abreast, and when they reached the shallow water they waded in with happy squeals, like children arriving at a swimming-pool. They sucked up water and sprayed it into their mouths and over their backs. They dug industriously with feet and trunk combined, scooping out sloppy gobs of mud and slapping it on their foreheads like custard pies, creating private wells into which clear water could seep. They strolled up and down the shallows, greeting acquaintances with trunks touched to brow or mouth.

Today, she recognised individuals. She saw the stately cow with vertical tusks who had grieved over the dead bull, and the smallest calf of all, who clung tightly to its mother as if still attached by an invisible cord, its small trunk flopping like half-cooked spaghetti. Some affectionately twined trunks, some sprayed themselves with dust or ponderously scraped their haunches against handy termite hills. Others stood contemplatively rocking, enjoying the sun.

For half an hour she watched them: charming anachronistic giants, gentle and loving, destructive and terrible, and began to understand Bay's attitude to them. The world would be a poor place without elephants.

Suddenly a ripple of alarm passed through the scattered herd. The elephants bunched nervously and began to move away, leaving only the noble straight-tusked matriarch like a royal champion guarding her family's retreat. She flapped her ears until they stood out like tattered sails and scraped dust with a forefoot. Her hooded eyes were alert above the curled, segmented trunk; her cheeks sucked in, every muscle tense. She was the epitome of raw courage squealing defiance at the future.

What was that future? Sally followed the line of her challenge and nudged Bay awake. 'Here comes Kariuki.'

'Tell him to go away,' he said drowsily. 'I like it here. Just you and me in the Garden of Eden. It'll never be the same again.'

The approaching file of pin-men grew larger. The matriarch shifted feet as if contemplating a charge, then wheeled to follow the others.

He's right, thought Sally, surprised by her own regret. The serpent has appeared in Eden. The elephants will survive – but at a price. Soon this valley will be scarred by roads, dotted with tourist buses, craft-shops, a hotel.

Bay smiled at her. 'There are other Edens, you know. If you stick around I'll show you where to find them.'

She bent and kissed him. 'I'll stick around,' she said.